Before turning to crime, **A.M. CASTLE** had a long career as a feature writer on national newspapers including the *Daily Express*, *The Times* and *The Daily Telegraph*. She grew up in south London and, after a stint in Brussels, she is back where she belongs. As well as writing psychological thrillers, she also writes cosy mysteries as Alice Castle. She is married with two children, two stepchildren and two cats.

The Perfect Widow

A.M. CASTLE

ONE PLACE. MANY STORIES

HQ
An imprint of HarperCollins*Publishers* Ltd
1 London Bridge Street
London SE1 9GF

First published by HQ Digital 2019

This edition published in Great Britain by
HQ, an imprint of HarperCollins*Publishers* Ltd 2020

ISBN: 9780008364724

MIX
Paper from
responsible sources

FSC
www.fsc.org   **FSC** C007454

This book is produced from independently certified FSC™ paper
to ensure responsible forest management.

For more information visit: www.harpercollins.co.uk/green

Printed and bound by CPI Group (UK) Ltd, Croydon, CR0 4YY

To William, Ella and Connie, with love

Prologue

Louise

I thought nothing of it, the first time the doorbell rang.

Parcel delivery guy – bound to be. It was that time of the evening. School run done, supper running late. They just want to catch you at home, don't they? Don't care if the timing's terrible, up to your elbows in kids and cooking. Not their problem.

I did a quick mental scan through my recent purchases. Hmm. A few. Well, I had to keep up appearances. And it was hard to get it right just now. A strange September, sweltering by day, then plunging straight to frost when night fell. I wanted to get everyone twittering in the playground when I appeared in something shiny and new. For a second, I was excited. Was it that red handbag? Bit pricey, but I hadn't been able to resist. But no, it was bound to be those boots I'd ordered last week on sale. Helping Giles was more important.

I looked over at him. Dark head down over the exercise book. Bless. That maths. I could see the line of jagged numbers. He was snagged, like a lamb on a barbed wire fence. But would he ask for help? Ha. I stayed put. Boys. If I didn't nurse him through it, he'd go off the boil, drift. I'd lose him to that new game, the one he'd been hankering after. He'd be skulking in his bedroom for hours. That would be that. So I called to Emmy – well, yelled. It's a big house.

'Love? Can you get that?'

I cocked an ear. No reply, no movement. I sighed inwardly. Girls were no easier. Emmy was 11 going on 17 when it came to attitude. Especially towards her mother. The more love and encouragement I lavished on her, the more elaborate the eye-rolls at everything I said or did. I envied her the freedom to rebel. Did I begrudge it? Most days, no. Today, I was feeling a bit antsy already. I couldn't face more shouting. That last yell up the stairs had done my head in. It had been a busy day. *Very* busy.

I was about to give in and get up, but then Giles turned to me. 'Don't go, Mum. I can't do this.' The voice was all over the place, now he was 13 – Barry White one minute, Sam Smith the next. That pushed-out bottom lip, though, was the same as when he'd been 4, trying to ride his new bike without any help from us, and coming a cropper. I smiled, love filling me like light pouring through a window. Who could resist?

The bell shrilled again. I couldn't break off, not now Giles was finally concentrating, but I certainly didn't want to be schlepping to the post office tomorrow to pick up those boots. Outside, the guy would be scribbling the usual hieroglyphs on his card, ready to drop and run. I was torn. But, just in time, there was Emmy, scampering down the stairs, two at a time. Miracle. Bless her. That was the only little-girl thing about her, the bouncy gait.

She never did it again, after that afternoon.

I turned back to Giles. 'Now, you take this number . . .' But I still had half an ear out for Em. Heavy click as the door opened. Murmurs. The sharp slap of cold air. Distant street sounds. More talking. Too much.

I thought for a beat, then two. Why would she chat to the delivery guy? And was that *two* adult voices I could hear? A man and a woman?

2

Something was off. But it couldn't be . . . could it? Not yet. Surely not.

Then her stifled gasp.

I breathed in, hard. But I was still reluctant to leave Giles, the books and pens at the table. If I didn't move, everything would stay the same. The cluttered table, the peaceful room, the pristine house. My house, that I'd fought so hard for. I was paralysed.

'Mum!'

Now there was no mistaking the bleat of fear in Emmy's voice. But I sang out, 'No need to yell, love,' as though she was just being a pain as per usual. I pushed myself up, felt a twinge. It had been a long day, my muscles ached. That morning pilates class. And the rest. I even remembered to give the spag bol a quick stir as I passed the stove.

'*Mum!*' came the shout again, desperate now.

'Coming.'

But as soon as I got out into the hall, there was no more escaping it. The door was flung wide open. Cold air, gusting in, knifing us after the sizzling day. Normally, I would have told Emmy off, letting the heat out, letting too many curious neighbours peer in, but my eyes flew straight past her to the two figures in the doorway, silhouettes bulky against the cold blue lights pulsing from their car.

Police.

This was real. It was actually happening. I felt sick, but my voice stayed steady.

'Patrick,' I said, looking from one granite face to the other, automatically reaching for Emmy. She burrowed her head into my side. I heard the maths book thud heavily from Giles's hand, his chair scrape back. He ran out into the hall. And then we were three.

3

Chapter 1

Now

Louise

Looking back on that night, I see the whole thing playing out like one of those jerky black-and-white newsreels. Some bits speeded up, some in slow motion. That policewoman moving towards me, breezing down my hall as though she owned the place – this part was fast, much too fast. Then, when we'd all reached the kitchen, time got stuck, snagging on her brutal words. Patrick. Dead.

Then my mouth was open in a big, round O. Was that right? I didn't know what to do, how to be. Where to put myself, even in my own home. There I was, backed up against a unit, the handle pressing into me. And wearing Lycra, of all things. I was suddenly horrified. I should have been in black, a proper widow's weeds, but instead, I stood there in my least favourite yoga pants, with the waistband going and the colours clashing.

The kids had no such qualms, they just did what came naturally, both running to me. Giles slamming into my side so that the bruise was visible the next day, Em trying to crawl almost up into my arms like the baby she'd so recently been. They knew what to do, what was necessary, without being told. The three of us, then, clinging together as though we were on a raft and too much motion would pitch us off into the deepest, darkest sea. A little clump of sorrow. That felt right at least.

Even if you are ready for the news – if someone's being dying of cancer for years, say – there is still no preparing you for the actual moment when you hear. The gulf between your acceptance of the way things must soon be, and the bald fact itself, is as big as the divide between the living and the dead. That last goodbye, the final slam of the door. Patrick gone, already?

Now time was moving like treacle, as I tried to compute it all, get my head round it. Patrick was beyond explanations, apologies, reproaches. All the opportunities I'd had over the years to sort things out, call a truce, make things better, or even just to enjoy life with him, were just ashes now.

Of course I asked, I had to. I forced the mask that was now my face to frame the question. Whispered it over their heads. 'What happened?' I didn't want the kids to hear, but I knew it had to be done.

'A fire. At the office.'

The heads that had been buried into my side lifted at that, both of them. 'Dad hates fires,' said Giles. We were the only house that didn't have a big shiny barbecue in the garden. No scented candles. And the fireplace by the sofas was gas, flicking on and off with a remote control.

I couldn't quite see Giles's face from the angle he had found, but I could imagine it crumpling, like all the times he'd cried as a small child. The mouth suddenly shifting sideways, the rest of his face creasing over it as though to hide the shame of giving in to tears. Em cried differently, so much more openly. Her face now was as wet as though she'd been under the shower. She held it up to me, my beautiful broken-hearted girl. I pressed a kiss onto the top of her hair, with its summer holiday scent, the coconut shampoo she loved. Which I would now forever associate with this moment. I wrapped my arms tighter round the two of them.

'There were smoke alarms . . .'

'Yeah. Didn't work, did they?' This was the stocky little police-woman, her head on one side as she looked up at me, face as

5

shuttered as an off-licence after closing time. 'Or no one heard. Inhalation.'

Did she want a reaction of some sort? I could do nothing but stare back at her, feeling these two smaller hearts beating against mine. It made me think of all those months when I'd carried them inside me, long ago. I didn't have time to appease her, too. Things were going fast again.

'Do I need to . . .?' I tailed off. Swallowed. I couldn't bring myself to say it. Someone had to identify him, didn't they? Go to the mortuary, give that nod so they'd pull back the sheet. I felt nauseous at the thought.

'No, that's being taken care of.' The policewoman looked at her notebook briefly. 'His mother.' There was a stab of pity for my mother-in-law, but also a wave of relief. The building?' She looked back at me. Her eyes, dark as currants, were narrowed, expectant. Had there been a question?

'Sorry?'

'The building.' She tapped the notebook with her pencil. 'It would have been insured?' she persisted. This time she was shushed by her colleague. A big, kindly man. Now he apologised, put a hand very briefly on my arm. His knees creaked slightly as he bent forward, almost like a toy policeman. He had the kind of pale skin that mottles with the sun, hair that would have been ginger once but was now the colour of a British beach. His eyes were a watery blue. Patrick had had a polo shirt that exact shade. My sight blurred suddenly. At last. 'So sorry for your loss. Anyone we can call?'

I shook off all offers of help, even their suggestion that they make me tea or coffee, though later I realised that had no doubt come over as churlish. The widow should accept things gratefully, graciously, after all. Pity is her lot. And the woman officer was probably dying for a cuppa, not to mention a biscuit or three. Never mind. I had very little faith in the ability of that great cure-all, hot sweet tea, to improve this mess. I just wanted these two

6

out, away, gone, with their platitudes and darting eyes. I wanted the doors shut, I wanted to sit and comfort my babies. To push all this horror far away. As far away as my dead husband now was.

So the three of us could start living again.

Chapter 2

Now

Becca

PC Becca Holt turned to leave Louise Bridges' house, whacking her hip painfully against the doorjamb. She still wasn't used to the extra inches her stab vest put on her, together with all the paraphernalia of radios, cuffs, pocketbook . . . the list went on. Ironic, really, when you thought about the hours – who was she kidding, *years* – she'd put into dieting. In this little lot, you couldn't see if she weighed eight stone or fifteen.

She remembered her mum's face. Wanting to be proud of her daughter, longing to cheer her on after all that training. Then, seeing her in the full kit, she hadn't been able to hide her disappointment, rushing forward to try and yank Becca's stab vest down over her bust. But there was nothing even the most determined mother could do to make this rig look attractive. So much for all that stuff about uniforms being sexy. 'Well, the hat's nice, anyway, love,' her mum had finally managed, turning from her with a sigh at the grandchildren she'd never have.

Becca felt it all the more sharply, ambling out of Louise Bridges' place. There was something about the woman's freshly ironed blonde hair, even the way she stood there, pushing the wooden spoon into the spaghetti Bolognese once she'd finally allowed them over the threshold, her work-out gear (*athleisure,* Becca sniffed) gliding over yards of leg. On Becca, those leggings would have been creased like an accordion, cratered like asphalt after snow. But Mrs Bridges' thighs were as smooth as an airport runway, and as long. Cellulite? How very dare you.

All that shouldn't matter. It was irrelevant, absolutely. And so was the fact that the house – what a house! – was like something you'd get in a sitcom about perfect family life. Though Becca had a suspicion that there weren't many laughs around the place, even at the best of times.

It was all very serious. Seriously stylish. The huge, open-plan kitchen-cum-living room, with high-gloss units that looked like they were polished on the hour, every hour. The whisper-grey velvety sofas in an L-shape, arranged around a plasma telly on the wall, just an inch short of out-and-out vulgarity. The large room, lined floor to ceiling in books, that they'd passed in the passageway. Even that kitchen table, casually strewn with the homework that had been abandoned and sheaves of papers that Louise had rapidly gathered up and tried to shove in a cupboard. A mess that wasn't really messy. It gave Becca a pang. It was a symbol of family life, something that, according to Becca's mother's ill-concealed fears, she was unlikely ever to achieve, going on the way she did.

Becca was acutely conscious that she and her partner, PC Tom Burke, had lumbered into this show home like creatures from a sub-standard zombie movie, where things went wrong and life got tangled.

Was she crazy, envying a woman who'd just had the news they'd broken? It was surely the worst thing that could ever befall a wife, a family. How could Becca even be thinking this way?

It was the woman's behaviour. Yes, she'd clasped her children to her, yes, she'd asked all the obvious questions. So far, so normal. But had she really been shocked? As shocked as you should be if you got the news, out of the blue, that your husband had just died a horrible death? Becca really didn't think so. It had been more like the kind of reaction you'd have when a nasty rumour about a nextdoor neighbour is confirmed. It's unpleasant, it's upsetting for the kids – but it's something you're half-expecting.

No, there was something out of kilter with this Louise Bridges woman. She'd been too watchful, too guarded. And, crucially, she was not nearly sad enough, in Becca's view.

It was a cliché, a woman breaking down, sobbing, turning pale, tearing out her hair. Expressing some genuine emotion. But clichés existed because, well, they fitted the bill.

Maybe it was because Becca herself cried if she ran out of teabags. She might be built like a tank, yes – and now like a tank festooned with novelty items, like cuffs and sticks – but she was a marsh-mallow inside, welling up whenever she saw an anxious child or a dog waiting for its owner outside a shop. She felt for others. But not for this Louise Bridges woman, it seemed. Becca had looked on for once, a disinterested observer. She hadn't had to restrain herself from coming over all unprofessional, hugging and crying too.

The fact that Becca's not-insubstantial sympathy gland wasn't working, at this of all times, said something. Surely?

As she buckled up in the car, she turned to Burke. 'What'd you make of her, then?'

Burke was silent for a moment, his face hard to read in the gloom. The drive at the Bridges' place was long, and the street-lights were a way off. Becca waited.

'Totty, obviously.'

She swatted his arm and he laughed. 'Well, come on, I'm only human. Yeah, she's a bit chilly, if that's what you're getting at. But seriously, Becca, what are you expecting, news like that? She's not going to welcome us like long-lost members of the family.'

'No. But don't you think something was odd? The way she kept stirring that bloody stew?'

Burke faced the front for a moment, hand on the ignition. 'Bolognese, you heard her. They've got to eat. She's got to feed the kids, whatever's happened.'

'But—'

'Becca. Not everything is more complicated than it looks.' He sighed, his hand dropping from the car key, resigned. She knew he found her attitude tiring at the best of times. 'Poor woman, give her a chance. You're expecting her to be on the floor. She can't do that with the little 'uns. She's got to be strong, hold it together.'

'What about when she saw us at the door? The first thing she said was "Patrick!" She *knew*. She knew what was up. That means – that means she must have had something to do with it.'

There was a silence. Becca could almost hear the cogs turning. Finally Burke spoke. 'You're right, that was a bit funny maybe. But you're making a huge leap. She makes a wild guess, so she's a killer. Nah, I don't think so. Look at it the other way, who else would we be coming about? The rest of the family was already sitting there. It was obvious, wasn't it?'

'Yes but . . . she didn't know we were coming with bad news, did she? Could have been anything. Neighbour's cat missing, whatever.'

'People always know, Becca. There's an instinct.'

Becca hated it when Burke adopted that lofty 'seen it all before' tone. She tried again. 'Yes, but when we asked her if she wanted someone with her? If she wanted us to ring her mum, for example.'

Burke gave her a look. She could just about interpret it as exasperation in the gathering dusk. 'I can't think of anything worse than having my mum around in a situation like that.'

'But what about your kids? Wouldn't it be good to have their gran there?'

'You're making a lot of assumptions. Not every family works like yours. Mine aren't crazy about their nan, she's pretty strict. Maybe Mrs Bridges, or whatever, is the same? Maybe they just don't get on?'

'OK, so not her mum – but why not another friend? Is she seriously going to sit there all night on her own with those kids? After what we've just told her?'

'Why not? Maybe she wants to get her head around it first. Maybe she doesn't actually have any friends. Basically, Becca, that's not a crime.'

'I'm not saying it is, but—'

'You've got to stop expecting everyone to be the same as you. When you've been doing the knock for as long as I have, you'll realise people take it all ways. Forget the textbook, forget what you think you'd do.'

A cold drizzle started to fall. The windscreen wipers were soon beating a soothing tempo, as English as a nursery rhyme.

'Truth is, you won't know till you're there. Where she's sitting now. Just pray you never are,' Burke said, turning the key at last, putting the car into gear with his usual heavy deliberation and signalling to pull out.

Perhaps he was right. He had years of experience, in the end. All she had was instinct, and they were always being told to make that secondary to the rule book.

'Amen to that.' Becca shrugged, accepting defeat. For now.

Chapter 3

Now

Louise

All I want to do today, the day of the funeral, is make sure Giles and Em get through it, that we all do, as best we can. It's not going to be easy. There was the delay, due to the . . . circumstances. You'd think that would make things less painful. It should be less raw. But it's like pulling the plaster off bit by bit. They've had time to get used to the pitch of their grief, we've pared down our lives to fit around it. Now we have to open ourselves up again, parade in front of strangers.

Still, if we can keep putting one foot in front of the other, get to the end of this long and dreadful day, then it's one major ordeal over. I'm not saying we can then move seamlessly on with our lives. I know now that recovery will be slow. But still, it will be one less thing hanging over us.

Em is in a dark-purple dress, one that Patrick liked. Better than black, for a girl of her age. We've scrambled together a dark suit for Giles. Boys can look wrong, dressed up in men's clothes. Vulnerable necks, shiny jackets. But Giles looks good. Pale as his shirt, of course, and so sad, so brave. But smart, well turned out. Just like his dad.

I'd taken one of Patrick's suits to the undertakers. His best. They'd asked me if I wanted to see him then. I refused, of course.

13

Unwisely, I mentioned it to the kids and then, of course, they felt obliged to see him. So I had to do it after all. Back to the funeral parlour, the careful obsequiousness of the staff, the décor that was so inoffensive it managed somehow to be revolting. We waited with another red-eyed family, offering each other stunted little smiles. Then we were led into the ghastly viewing room. Real flowers, at least. A pale pink carpet, suspiciously clean. I loathed it all. I looked at anything except the dazzling high shine of the coffin we'd picked, and the snowy white satin around his head. We were a tight little clump again. I could feel their fear and dread, the horror the living have of the dead, but I could feel their determination too. They are the best part of me, that's for sure.

I shuffled them forward, tried to make things easier, all the while averting my own eyes as much as I could. I couldn't avoid a glimpse. And the worst thing was that he somehow looked so untouched, after all that he – we – had been through. That dressmaker's dummy was not my husband. But he was still my children's father.

Chapter 4

Now

Becca

Becca Holt stumped into the station building and dropped the results of her shopping trip on her desk. It was cluttered already with clumps of empty Costa cups and plastic bags as shrivelled as autumn leaves. Tutting audibly so her colleagues wouldn't think it was all her rubbish, she shoved the lot into the nearest bin, hesitating only briefly over whether it should go into 'recycling' or 'general waste'. Even throwing stuff away was complicated nowadays.

Once the decks were cleared to her satisfaction, she snuffled in the pristine white paper bag she'd brought in. Just inhaling the doughnuts calmed her, the reassuring, wholesome smell of vanilla undercut with the hidden raspberry jam. She breathed in a bit too hard and had to splutter, finding a sudden unwilling sympathy for the coke addicts they were constantly moving on from under the arches down near the station.

She darted a quick glance around. At most of the desks, her fellow PCs were sprawled flat or had their noses pressed up against screens. Opposite, Burke was knocking a biro against his teeth in a rhythm that was doing his dental work no favours and would soon be messing with her head. She'd bought the doughnuts to share. She knew she should be tearing open the bag, leaving it on the side of her desk, making a general announcement of her largesse. Getting them all to love her. But bugger that. She wanted them all to herself.

She carefully edged a doughnut up a tad in the bag, ducked her head down, bit and sighed. It was good. So good it was bad. A bead of jam oozed down the side of her mouth and she licked and rubbed ferociously. Didn't want to look like Dracula, did she? Or be caught snacking, either. She could do without being teased. As she'd discovered, the banter here wasn't imaginative. Give them a stick, and they'd be beating you with it until you collected your pension.

She chewed carefully and swallowed, the movement making her waistband dig in that little bit more. She felt a prickle of shame. It suddenly made her think of that woman's thighs. Her first and only knock, and as such seared on her memory. But she didn't think she'd have forgotten it anyway, even if she'd called on as many of the recently bereaved as the Co-op Funeral Service.

Louise Bridges. That had been her name.

There'd been something about her, for sure. She couldn't say it had been eating away at her. She was the one who had been eating away, and not at that case, but at mounds of stuff she shouldn't even be looking at. She knew that. But this was a tough job, physical. She could walk it off. In theory. Unfortunately, her beat didn't cover Land's End to John O'Groats. As often as not, she was welded to the seat of her patrol car, and even that was stationary in traffic.

The truth was, it was the kind of work that you wanted to compensate yourself for doing. Demanding, sometimes demeaning. Requiring a lot of patience. Being polite, however absurd the calls on her time. Stepping in to defuse rows between grown men that would have shamed toddlers. Picking drunks up out of the gutter, and still treating them with respect, even when they hurled all over her clodhopping shoes. She needed a treat after a long day – and sometimes in the middle of a long day.

And occasionally, like now, right at the beginning of what was, after all, bound to be a long day.

Unbidden, that woman's legs unfurled in her mind again. How did you even get legs like that? Genetics, that's how. Her own tree trunks would always be just that, even if she ate nothing but tofu and quinoa from this day forth. She knew that to be the truth. Yet there were steps she could take, to make sure the rest of her didn't run the same way as her legs. She didn't need *Mrs Bridges* rubbing it in.

But that wasn't really why the woman had stuck in her mind. Or wasn't the only reason, at any rate. Something didn't stack up. Whatever her partner said, Becca hated a loose end even more than she hated an untidy doughnut. She lowered her head to the bag again, and nibbled the corner until it was flattened off. Perfect. But was that another bit poking up? She sighed. And nibbled again.

Even the hit of sweetness wasn't enough to keep her mind off Louise Bridges for long. With a powder-white thumb she prodded her terminal into life. Burke would kill her, but he didn't have to know. Thanks to her IT degree, she could just sneak a quick peek, set her mind at rest. Then enjoy her snack for as long as the job would let her. She licked her fingers, pressed a couple of keys, realised they were getting sticky and shrugged. This wouldn't take a sec. Then she could give the whole keyboard a good wipe down. She fumbled in her drawer, found a piece of paper, studied the letterhead and tapped in the name.

A few strokes later and she was in. The doughnut, jam haemorrhaging away quietly inside the bag, was forgotten.

Chapter 5

Then

The first time I ever laid eyes on Patrick was at work. He just sauntered right past me. He didn't need to tangle with me and Jen, the beautiful bookends sitting on reception. He was already in, shoulders swinging in his sharp suit, security pass wafted at the guard. Not that the fat, middle-aged geezer they'd hired to protect us all would have been able to stop anything other than a rampaging doughnut. Patrick knew where he was going, walked as if he hadn't a care in the world. He owned everything. The job. The building. And now, suddenly, me.

That confidence. That sense of blithe entitlement. It wasn't arrogance, he wasn't really flash. He was just sure, steady, unshakeable. He was in the right place, at the right time. Everything was within his grasp, his for the taking. That definitely included me. Patrick was a living, breathing symbol of everything I'd wanted, my whole life.

I was attracted, an iron filing to a magnet. Stuck forever, just like that.

He gave Jen the ghost of a wink as he passed, shirt like a washing powder ad, glimmer of a smile, then clocked me and something changed in his expression. Too soon, he'd passed us and was at the lifts. On a better day, I might have mustered the boldness to get up, sashay past him, pretend I was on my way to the ladies'. But as it was, I just felt as though I'd been socked in the stomach.

That's all it takes, sometimes. A look, and your life is sealed.

It was my first day in the job. God, I loved that place, the office building. Looking back on it, it was very 'new millennium', as they now say with a sneer. At the time, the shiny glass, chrome and marble seemed breathtaking. A palace to commerce, to possibilities, to a bright, clean future. Smart. Glitzy. Everything I badly wanted to have – and be.

So many things to remember, that morning. Who was who, where everything should go. It was crucial I shouldn't look as though I was out of my depth. I'd blagged my way onto the temp agency's books. The middle-aged woman at the dingy office had been deeply sceptical, but – surprise, surprise – the manager, puffing out of his shirt, was dead keen to have me on his books. Probably in all ways, but I just didn't want to go there, even in my imagination.

This was my second temping gig. The first had been fine; boring. A solicitor's office. Sitting there, I'd soon felt there was more dust settling on me than on the files they guarded so jealously. I hadn't expected much from this next booking, as a result. But as soon as I approached the building, I got butterflies. Even the door handles looked like they had more class than I did. Long, chrome rods, running the length of the sheet glass doors. I was reluctant to grasp one, get my smutty prints all over it. But that only lasted a second. They had people who spent their days buffing this stuff. I took a deep breath and strutted in like I wasn't dirt, like I didn't come from nothing – as if, contrary to everything I knew in my heart of hearts, I had some sort of a right to try my hand at a better life.

It must have been an Oscar-winning performance, as Jen, the permanent girl, barely raised an eyebrow. They'd taken me on to cover her colleague's two-week summer break, the idea being

19

that Jen would bring me up to speed, though if I couldn't hack it, it wouldn't much matter, as she had everything under control. I couldn't believe my luck. From the moment I sank into that leather-and-chrome swivel chair, rich and squishy as chocolate mousse, I was determined they'd never drag me out of it. It was beyond me why anyone would want time off from a job like this.

It's hard work, pretending everything's fine when it's not, pretending you know what you're doing when you really, really don't. But I'd had practice. Sucking in every possible clue you can glean from your surroundings, your companions, can make the difference between passing unnoticed and getting into, well, let's just say, a sticky situation. 'Where are you from?' Jen's eyebrows were elegantly arched, but geography wasn't on her mind. Her eyes travelled up and down as I gave out the mixture of truth and lies I practised every morning. She smiled and returned to her keyboard, shoulders relaxing slightly. She was somewhat reassured. My answers had passed muster. But I'd clocked that my outfit was a catastrophe which needed immediate attention.

As soon as I could, I ran to the loo. This little get-up had cost all the money I had. But it was wrong, wrong, wrong. I looked at myself in the mirror. Shame and disgust blurred my vision and when it cleared, I saw my fancy sheer blouse for what it was. So pretty, when I'd popped it on this morning and slid my feet into my towering scarlet heels. So tarty, now I looked at it coldly, while the shoes would have been better on a street corner. The tiny pucker between Jen's eyebrows had shown me the terrible error of my ways. Highly polished invisibility was what we were after, as though we'd grown out of our marble reception desk like Greek goddesses.

I was devastated. Humiliated, yet again. A less determined girl might have thrown her hands up at that point, called the agency, asked for something . . . more suited. But I swallowed hard. Got to work. The desk would shield the shortness of my skirt. I couldn't do much about the silly shirt, except fasten every single button, right up to the neck. I felt as though I was being strangled, but instantly the look was less . . . available. Anything else I could do? I scrutinised myself, tried to be dispassionate. The bling. I took off a bangle, then two, and stashed them in my bag. The fewer personal touches, the better. Instead of refreshing my make-up, I scrubbed half of it off, brushed my hair with furious vigour until my scalp burned. I did my best to glide back to my seat with a detached smile, just like Jen's.

Every morning after that, I pared myself down, shedding hoops and necklaces, dumping outfits I'd saved up for, sloughing off the vibrant shades I'd loved. Working out that they shouted so much that I wanted unsaid. In the space of days, I became a monochrome, sober version of myself. The only ray of light left was my curtain of hair. It hung like the sun in the sky during that long, hot summer. Something told me that blonde would always be the one colour that went with everything.

Sometimes I'd see a hand on my keyboard and wonder who on earth it belonged to. Those tasteful taupe nails, just long enough to show they were high-maintenance, could they be mine? Fire-engine-red had been my favourite since I left school, except when I went for blue or a green or a shrieking neon. But soon I was swiping through my bathroom shelf at home, chucking my little rainbow straight into the bin. That was now definitely in my past. And the mound of jewellery on my bedside table, so beguiling when it was bought? It oxidised almost overnight, showing me who was right. *All that glitters is not gold.* Lucky I was a quick learner.

Chapter 6

Now

Louise

Standing in front of my mirror, today of all days, I know that, ironically, I've finally found a look I can definitely pull off. Well, who doesn't suit a little black dress? Patrick's wedding ring round my neck on a simple chain. And lilies – the other perfect accessory.

The rest of it isn't so great. My eyes seem to have shrunk from crying, while the lids are as puffy as the vol-au-vents which are already standing in serried ranks downstairs in the kitchen for the wake. Well, reception. Or aftermath? Whatever you want to call the ghastly gathering after the funeral, where we will all chat awkwardly until the alcohol kicks in. Then the laughter will suddenly ring out too loudly and we'll be embarrassed again.

Meanwhile, my children are in pieces and my mother-in-law has barely spoken since it happened. Because of the delay, you'd think things would be less awful. They're absolutely not. By the time we get to the crematorium, I feel as though I'm floating about a foot above the scene, or six feet below it.

Jill's arm is round my shoulders, mine round hers, as we progress slowly up the aisle. The children sleepwalk in front of us. It's like a negative of my wedding photos, all that white tulle and hope swapped for black and nasty pine veneer.

Patrick is already here, as arranged. We meet at the top of the aisle, just like we did before. But this time I slide into my pew, leaving him in lonely splendour on his dais. The shiny coffin nailed down hard over his smart suit. Goodbye, my love.

I planned the service down to the last word but after it's over I couldn't tell you a thing that was said, done or sung. I know the pieces complemented him, and our life together, and celebrated our children, our finest achievement by far – and I know they did the trick because I could hear the sniffs behind me from the congregation. Giles and Em too, they snuffle on either side of me, tiny soft creatures again, needing all the protection I can give them. Jill is on the end of the pew, back ramrod straight, knuckles white on the shivering service sheet.

It feels right to be here, instead of in a church. We've only ever been fair-weather members of any congregation, only there for the jolly bits, not slogging it out every Sunday. The kids aren't at church schools so, to put it bluntly, there's been no need. The last time we were in one was probably Em's christening, at Jill's urging. She was too shattered to insist that we hold the funeral there. I'd feel bad about this awful municipal solution to Patrick's death, but I really don't have that much emotion to spare. I'm sure God, and Jill, have worse things to worry about.

As far as I know, Patrick had never given a thought to all this – death and the rigorous tidying away it requires. But he would have enjoyed being centre stage, all eyes on him. People often say that, and I've thought how discordant it sounds, yet today it's true. The full rows of friends, neighbours, distant relatives and vague acquaintances who have turned out for him. And quite a number of attractive women sobbing. That would have tickled him. He loved to cause a stir. If he'd been here, he'd have been so busy, up and down the aisle, a handshake there, a kiss, a look, a word. And turning, now and then, to give me that wink.

I think about him as the recorded organ music starts up. It was loud and rousing during the hymns, filling out the gaps where we all blundered, after the first couple of familiar lines. I muttered along for form's sake, while Giles and Em were hardly audible. What do you expect? They don't do proper hymns anymore at school, even the posh places like theirs. If they sing, it's all about dolphins, not *Dear Lord and Father* and *forgive our foolish ways*. Jill's voice was husky, catching on cigarettes and grief.

Now, the organ sound dribbles away, mild and meandering, ushering us out of the crematorium and onwards, to the rest of our lives. We shuffle obligingly to our feet when the celebrant, whose eulogy for Patrick gave new meaning to the word bland, gestures for us to go first. Once again, it's a wedding march, except now Patrick is being left behind forever.

On the way back down the aisle, where once I grinned from ear to ear, my veil thrown back, ring gleaming on my third finger, my prize the wonderful man on my arm, now I walk uncertainly with Giles and Em, glancing quickly at the friends and colleagues who don't know whether to smile or not. There's Patrick's university friend, they shared a flat back in the day, after graduation. A group from our old firm – it all seems so long ago now. A few more recent clients – I dread the chats to come. The miscellaneous blondes – my gaze skates over them and they busy themselves with bags and tissues, darting out of my view like a shoal of silvery fish. And there's Jen, kind and lovely Jen. Still gorgeous. Still with that idiot Tim. She gives me such a lovely smile. Ah, Stacy Johnson, my best friend, right in the middle of a row. She's in bits. Of course she is. I try not to catch her eye. I really can't afford to set myself off again. I need to hold it together.

Then, in the last pew, I do a double take. The little police-woman. Not in uniform, but I recognise those bold, beady eyes, running over my face. She's wearing a hoody and jeans. Not even black. Is nothing sacred? What is she doing here? It was bad enough that evening, her stare. But at my husband's funeral? I hope the children haven't seen or recognised her. I press them closer to me. Her gaze follows me as I pass. I do a mental tut. *Here? Really?*

And I swish on out, the flawless skirt of my black crepe dress flowing around my legs.

Chapter 7

Then

By my second day, I'd found a skirt that was within shouting distance of my knees, and I listened like an over-eager schoolgirl, lapping up everything Jen told me. Not that I needed much help to work out how the great bank of phones worked. Yes, it looked like something Lieutenant Uhura would have sat in front of in *Star Trek*, but I had mastered it in minutes. At least it wasn't the olden days, when you had to plug in little wires and make a cat's cradle, physically joining one call to another. That might have given me pause. Now it was just the flick of a switch.

Reception was all about smiling, really. The name said it all. Receiving people, welcoming them, looking them right in the eye. And pacing yourself so you didn't feel as though your face was going to split after the first half-hour.

Where had I got the training for this? Ushering friends into our home? Ha. Don't make me laugh. It had all been about keeping people out. 'The busies,' my mother called them. Not just the police. Social workers, top of the list. Then all the other undesirables. Relatives, not that they bothered much. Mum had successfully alienated all of them. Various complex grudges that I never really got the hang of, though I suppose everything boiled down to money and sex in the end. Women friends were the same.

Sometimes she'd shout about it all, depending how far down the bottle she was. I learned to block out the noise. Then there were the more obvious no-nos – ex-boyfriends, retribution on their minds. Money lenders, occasionally. And, more than once, the bailiffs. Hard to stop them, though, after they'd stoved in the door. All of the above could fit more than one category, a Venn diagram with more circles than hell.

So my instincts were to curl up, protect myself, hide from the light. But I was desperate for this to work. So I learned. And soon, I blossomed. Not in a showy way. Concealing my feelings was one of the very few transferrable skills my upbringing had given me. But I could pin on a smile brighter than the chrome of my fancy office chair when I had to. And I felt so much more at home at that desk, than I ever had anywhere else before. Including my actual home.

Partly, that was because of Patrick.

I couldn't have told you what it was about him that clicked with every bit of my DNA. But it was as though a key had been turned, somewhere. Like a Chinese puzzle, my shrivelled heart was now open, ready to be trashed. I distrusted the feeling. Protected myself as best I could. But it was no good. I didn't know his name, which floor he worked on, or anything else about him. Yet I was already his.

As it turned out, the more I found out, the more I loved the idea of him. Or just loved *him*. I asked Jen, all casual, as soon as the lift had swished closed on him that morning, but of course she was no fool. Immediately, she warned me off.

'He's a bit of a player, Louise. You need to be a bit careful there. I'd think again, if I were you.'

Whether it was genuine concern for me or not, I neither knew nor cared. All it did was make me keener. If that were even possible. Though those words of hers would come back to haunt me.

27

Chapter 8

Now

Louise

As I glide around town, going about my business, I'm used to feeling eyes on me, tracking me. As often as not, I look up at some man and shake him off with the force of my indifference. I'm a widow. I'm in black. Are they sick?

But sometimes it's a woman and then I wonder. Was she one of *them*?

I wonder about Patrick and about how many there were, before there was one too many.

Because Jen was right, he was a player.

I sometimes wondered if she knew this from the outside in, or whether she had once been one of his, shall we say, *playthings* herself. I never asked her, and she never admitted as much. But the strength of my love for him made me preternaturally aware. I used to think I'd be able to spot a woman who wanted him at thirty paces, and certainly sniff one out if I was sitting next to her.

But whatever might or might not have been between them was history by the time I arrived and slid behind the marble desk. If I'd been Jen, I wouldn't have liked it, the way he started to flirt with me. Even if they had never really been an item, it was asking her to play gooseberry in an outrageous way. And if they once had been together, well, then it was insensitive in the extreme. But what can I say? That was Patrick.

The girls I see now are Patrick's type: self-contained and sleek. They look sophisticated, aloof. They are basically just like me, but annoyingly they are ten to twenty years younger. Of course, I have no proof. And it's so much better, so much more dignified, to turn a blind eye.

I got very used to doing that, so keeping going is no stretch. Carving out a new role for myself as a widow is much more difficult. I no longer fit into anyone's dinner party plan. I'm an extra even for drinks, and there's always the possibility that I might bring down the atmosphere, be sad. Weep, even. Good gracious. Or, worse still, I won't be sad enough, won't live up to everyone's image of what grief should look like, how long it should last, how deep it should go. Everyone has a view about how a woman like me does things.

As usual, I'm playing a part and it's tiring. But I don't really care, at this stage my life has had more costume changes than Madonna. What I do care about is my kids.

People ask me why we don't move. 'A change of scene, that's what you all need, it'll be good for Giles and Em.' To me, that seems ridiculous. Patrick will still be with us, wherever we go. He's an inescapable fact of our lives. The centre of everything, even if he's no longer there. So I'd rather stay here, in the home we built together.

I've written letters to the school, I've got the kids sessions with a counsellor, I've put photos in their rooms of their dad looking his best, and I've put a big one of Patrick in the kitchen, looming over us, even though I love my clear surfaces.

It won't bring him back, nothing can or will. But it means that the children feel that, unlike Elvis, Patrick hasn't quite left the building.

Chapter 9

Then

There's no accounting for taste, is there? I wouldn't have swapped my shiny marble desk for a thousand beach bars and all the sun in the sky, but the dozy girl I was replacing decided to stay on in Malaga or Portugal or wherever. I was overjoyed when they made my job permanent.

That left me and Jen, smiling serenely through our days. We were like the figureheads on a ship in full sail. Then the wind suddenly dropped. The company was in the doldrums and there were whispers in corners about economy measures. The talk was of a cull, of people being 'let go' from all departments. It terrified me, that expression. I would be in free fall if I had to leave, I knew that. This place was my only solid ground. I dreaded getting the tap on the shoulder.

Jen had been with the firm for two years and didn't want to move on either. But by now, we had an even flashier phone system, one which was a nightmare to operate. Jen, who'd taught me so much at the beginning, struggled with the nuances of the new rig. Well, we both did. At first, anyway. It didn't help that the instruction booklet was nowhere to be found. In those days, you couldn't just download another from the internet. So it was me trying to give her pointers. It was a reversal of our normal roles and it felt odd for her. Jen had once held all the cards, played them with the effortless élan of a major-league poker champ. Now she kept fumbling.

I was lucky – I'd just happened to pop to the loo when a crucial call had been booked in for the managing director. Funding. From the States. Jen accidentally cut him off in his prime, the source of revenue went south and no one was amused. I told her we'd just talk our way out of it, blame the machine, mechanical error. But the more we blathered, the stormier the faces grew. The chop. I looked on, gutted, but the chaps upstairs had the excuse they'd needed. Just her, though, not me.

I owed Jen so much. From my perfect beige nails to my immaculate blouse (now real silk) to my accent, which had been gradually morphing into hers. The desk wouldn't be the same without her. I hated crying, couldn't ever afford to start in case I never stopped, but my eyes were stinging the day she left. I felt so sorry for her, exiled from the firm. She had been its serene public face. Now she was gone. For a while, I felt as though everyone who came through that door was searching for her, disappointed that there was only me. I tried to beam more brightly to compensate.

Chapter 10

Now

Louise

Just when I think we're beginning to make progress, something comes along to upset all our apple carts, throw a pall over our lives again.

We managed to stagger our way through Christmas. It was hideous. We spent it with Jill, mourning her son but doing her best to celebrate what she still had – her grandchildren. They'd become all the more important to her. To us.

We'd had our differences, in the past. In fact, I'd blamed some of Patrick's wandering ways on his mother turning a blind eye way back. There wasn't a woman alive, it seemed, who didn't let Patrick off the hook. And fair's fair, it was his father who'd done the dirty, upping and leaving Jill for a younger version, begetting another bunch of kids. It didn't take a genius to work out this displacement was the reason Patrick constantly sought reassurance, acceptance, attention.

But now Patrick was gone, taking all his faults away with him. We were left with the man smiling from the photos, who was perfect, of course. I much preferred to pretend this was the man I'd lived with and known, and as far as Jill was concerned, it was gospel. Meanwhile, Giles and Em took comfort from seeing him around.

I was glad once the last cracker was pulled and the dried-up

Christmas pudding could be decently ditched. Only Patrick had ever liked it. This year, Giles had solemnly swallowed down a symbolic mouthful and the rest had mouldered until I could bear the sight no longer.

Chucking all that wrapping paper into the recycling was more liberating. It seemed to promise some sort of renewal, the end of yet another test, like the funeral. But I hadn't realised, then, that every single day would go on being an ordeal of a sort.

This time it's Em, coming home from school with that ominous cried-out look. What's happened? I instantly want to know, but I resist asking straight out.

'Nice day?' Sometimes the oblique question nets the answer. Not this time.

'Fine.' She storms off to her room. I turn pointedly to Giles. He slings his bag on the counter, shrugs his shoulders. I realise, suddenly, that he's grown again. One day soon he'll be his father's height. Every day he looks more like him. I have to be careful, on the landing in the dark. More than once, he's nearly given me a heart attack, coming out of his bathroom all of a sudden, dumping his towel on the floor just like his dad used to.

'Well, *something* happened,' I say.

'What's for tea?'

'*Supper*. Pasta bake.' This is in honour of Em's new status as a vegan. I'm hoping she won't notice the cheese; that the whole phase will, in fact, be over as quickly as possible. Giles's wince at the prospect doesn't help my temper. 'Do you know what happened? Going to tell me?'

He cracks under pressure. 'School project. Family tree. Someone teased her.'

'What about?' I immediately square up to fight. How dare they? And our tree, thanks to my marrying into Patrick's lot, is perfectly respectable.

'Oh, some cow. Said there were so few people on Em's, it was more like a stick.'

I close my mouth. Whoever it was, she had a point. With my parents MIA, her dad now dead, little contact with his half-siblings, and me an only child, our family tree is indeed a slender branch rather than a mighty oak. But Em doesn't need it rubbing in.

I march up to her room. I don't wait to be asked in. Don't want to be standing there until the Day of Judgement, do I? She is bunched up on her bed, sad as dirty laundry. I ignore her token resistance, give her the biggest hug I have and tell her straight. She has a family to be proud of, a mum who will always love her, a doting gran and a big brother who really isn't that bad.

And a dad whose memory she should always treasure. And never once let go of.

Chapter 11

Now

Becca

Becca sat in her car, slowly and carefully peeling the wrapper off a Twix. Not really her favourite, but her dad had loved them. She wasn't quite sure why she still bought them. No, that was a lie. It was something that brought him closer. She remembered him opening the packet, handing one stick to her, eating the other himself. They'd chomp together in harmony, while her mum was out.

That stuff will kill you. Her mum had a point. Maybe her father wouldn't have died so young if he'd reined in on the chops and chips and chocs. But it wasn't as though Mum was into health food herself, was it? She battled the scales, same as Becca did. She just denied it, got ratty on her chickenfeed diet, and had a go at her daughter instead.

Becca sighed, looked out of the window. Her breath was steaming it up, giving a dreamy edge to the view. Suburbia stretched on mistily, trees bare and black now on the edges of still-perfect lawns. It was like the place she'd grown up in, just that bit bigger and better, as though everything had been inflated by some sort of celestial bicycle pump. Even the streetlights seemed taller. They'd flick on soon, twilight was falling. An SUV purred up the road, swung in to park outside a nearby garage, crunching over the gravel drive. Not the Bridges lot. Children and a dog burst out. Before anyone could pop a head up over the privet to complain about the sudden din, they were engulfed by their huge house. The silence settled over Becca again.

Leaving the car heater on meant her Twix had melted into a lump. She held it up to the light, strangely deformed, the bars fused together. She thought again of Louise Bridges' legs in that get-up. Bloody woman. She snapped the biscuit crossly, munched for a while. Then, when she was feeling soothed, she started licking the residue off her fingers. You could say one thing for chocolate, it always tasted delicious, no matter what shape it was.

The daylight was leaching away now, greens fading to browns, browns to velvet black, and still she sat on. She knew none of Louise Bridges' neighbours would complain about the car. There'd been so much to-ing and fro-ing lately. The police, then the papers. Attracted like flies by death, the fire, the inquest. People were inured to it now. And she'd sat here often enough. Just watching. Waiting. Plain clothes, they'd assume. If anyone knocked on her window, she was always ready with a story. *Just keeping an eye on the place.* They'd wander off nodding, happy as Larry. But no one would knock. That was the joy of the suburbs. All that rabid curiosity, but contained by its own net curtains, as though they were made of steel. Nobody would confront you. Write an anonymous note, yes. Ring the station to complain, possibly. But that hadn't happened yet.

She could stay on here for hours, waiting, watching, and all these little householders would actually feel safer for having her around. She smiled and dealt with the last blob of chocolate. She was willing to bet the neighbours were in her camp. Suspicious, but unable to voice the dark thoughts in their heads. Yet. They didn't know as much as she did, but they were all waiting, just the same. Just like her.

Then Louise's door cracked open. Yellow light shone behind her, highlighting that hair. She wasn't in the yoga gear this time, she was in flowing black trousers. Becca couldn't see the detail, except for the way the fabric fell, caressing as nothing ever had on her own body. Pricey. Of course. A sweater, equally black. Soft, understated. Was it a bit fluffy? A boat neck, they called that. Ordinary clothes, on anyone else. On Louise, they developed a special sort of grace and elegance, her collar bones rising up, carved like a dancer's. Becca wished she hadn't finished that Twix. Then wished she had another to crunch to oblivion. Then she thought about the calories and felt sick. The usual backwash of guilt.

Louise strode out, oblivious. Though Becca was sitting there large as life – *well, larger*, as her mother would have said with a sigh – Louise never seemed to see her. Was she invisible to the woman? Or just so insignificant that Louise didn't give a toss? It would make things harder if Louise did know she was here, and Becca wouldn't be able to watch her like this. But sometimes, like tonight, she was tempted to lean on the horn, make the bitch look up, acknowledge her existence, at least.

But Becca stopped herself and Louise moved fluidly on, eyes never once flicking to the parked car. She went round to the side, unlatched the little hutch that cocooned her wheelie bins. Not for her the vulgarity of an exposed rubbish bin, oh no. That sort of thing had to be tidied away, hidden, so she could pretend that she and her brood didn't generate used teabags, carrot tops, coffee grounds, tissues, rotten fruit, sanitary pads . . . the usual detritus of human life. Now she was pushing the bins out onto the street, one at a time, putting her back into it. Becca watched with a smirk. *That's a proper work-out for you, isn't it, love? None of this pointless stretching and bending that you pay through the nose for.*

When all three bins were finally out there, beyond the garden wall, Louise smoothed her hair back from her forehead and went back inside. *Ha. Don't like the donkey work, do you? Not such a clever idea to get rid of the hubby after all, was it?* Once the door clicked shut and the outside light went off, Becca decided reluctantly that it was time to move on. The show was over. For tonight. She turned the key in the ignition and flipped on the headlights at last.

She drove back through the dark streets to her empty flat, a silent promise running through her head. *I'll be back, Louise, don't you worry.*

I've got my eye on you.

Chapter 12

Then

Jen and I kept in touch. The idea of losing her made me feel dizzy. What would I do? How would I know if I was getting it right? So we got into a habit of having drinks after work and bitching about our bosses, though my heart wasn't in the whingeing. I loved the company almost as much as I loved my desk – and Patrick.

We became even better friends once she'd left the company. From the outside, I liked to think we were now peas in a pod, but keeping tabs on her felt like touching wood, keeping myself grounded, checking I was really where I needed to be. So much of what I now was, I owed to her template. And having a friend like her was proof of how far I'd come. The girls at school would have collapsed in amazement if they could have seen me, swanking about in wine bars, with gorgeous, poised Jen. She would definitely have been one of the popular gang back in the day, the ones in giggling gaggles, while the likes of me slunk past, friendless and invisible.

So I was surprised, one night, to see her in stacked heels with chunky ankle straps, far from the pure lines and vertiginous height of the stilettos she normally favoured. Perhaps I wasn't the only chameleon in town.

I'd worried about her, once she'd got the sack, but of course she'd found a job within seconds of leaving. Who wouldn't snap her up? She was with an ad agency now, and her clothes seemed to be edging out to match. Nothing crazy, just a zing of colour, a bag by a bad-boy designer. It disconcerted me. I understood why it was imperative that I reinvent myself, but Jen? She'd been perfect as she was. I'd seen her as the fixed star in my firmament, an ideal to aspire to, a goal I was – sometimes – close to reaching. But if Jen herself had to change, what did that mean for less perfect mortals like me? Was there nothing but constant messing and fixing ahead? Would I never really know what I was aiming for, let alone attain it?

It turned out, of course, that she'd fallen for one of the account directors, all flash car and expense account lunches. Perfection wasn't enough; now she had to be trendy with it. We were all just lumps of clay when it came to getting our man. My mother had been the same, bending over backwards for whatever lowlife had had her that week.

I didn't know it then, but the germ of a resolve was forming, as I sat at the bar with Jen, sluicing my week away with white wine spritzers. I'd always have more work to do than anyone else to fit in, make the grade. That I accepted. It was my fault, the price I'd be paying in perpetuity for being my mother's daughter, and for daring to try to escape that life sentence. And though I was willing to tweak the externals as far as they needed to go, I now promised myself that, inside, I'd be true to myself. Whoever that was.

I came to love those evenings, chucking Chardonnay on my own troubles, sighing along with Jen's non-existent worries, pretending to take them seriously. She dithered endlessly about which dishes to cook for her dinner parties, stressed about the nuances of who'd said what to whom at the agency. I knew that these things didn't matter, they were tiny glitches in an otherwise perfect life.

Sometimes it amused me to enter into them with Jen, pretend

that I cared whether she served watercress soup or rhubarb fool. But part of me was always leaning back from the table, chair tilted on two legs in the way people used to warn me about at school, as if toppling was the thing I had to fear. I couldn't help but be angry that I was forever shut out of feeling such mundane concerns. How could I care about gravadlax, when I knew that I was worthless? And how could Jen be hanging on for my opinion? If she cared what I thought, that meant she was worthless too. It was a spiral of nihilism that no one wanted to know about or go down, least of all me. So I'd push it away, lean forward, and debate liver pâté versus smoked duck starters as though my life depended on it.

Jen knew, of course, about my passion for Patrick. How could she not? Twice a day, more often if he went out for lunch, I'd been transformed right in front of her eyes from the reasonably together, elegant young woman I'd fashioned in her likeness, into a tongue-tied, beetroot-blushing idiot. She didn't need to be Hercule Poirot to realise something was afoot.

'Made your move yet?' she'd josh me every time we met, knowing the answer would be a mumbled negative. 'Come on, Lou. You'll be old and grey by this rate. Or he'll get snared by someone else.'

This was my dread. That, during the many hours of the day when Patrick wasn't under what I thought of as my roof, he'd wander into the clutches of another. I couldn't bear the thought.

Jen was patient, talking through strategies with me, week after week. We were like chess grandmasters, trying to outwit Deep Blue. Would that scenario work, or was this the way forward? It was much more time-consuming than our actual jobs.

I was the one who came up with the idea. I'd move off the desk, into Patrick's department. It was a measure of how desperate I was at this point. The desk was, without a doubt, the best part of my life – apart from these sessions with Jen – and I wanted to hang on to it like a wino clutching their last can of Special Brew. On the other hand, I was getting nowhere with Patrick; if I was more colleague than underling, and in his own space instead of marooned out in reception, surely something would give?

Jen was unconvinced. Did this reflect doubt in my abilities to hold my own in the inner office? I'd like to think not. But then, she'd never dared try it herself. As we both knew, she was less flexible than me. I seriously doubted she'd ever have been as much of a whizz with our current comms package as I now was, even if that manual hadn't gone walkabout. And she had that very ordinary failing, of believing that if she couldn't do something, no one else could. Least of all her erstwhile junior.

Sometimes I thought she might still have a soft spot for Patrick herself. She'd sat up straighter when he was around. But then, of course I could see why. Her own boyfriends – she always had one on the go – were generally so wet, I felt like handing them a towel. Nothing wrong with them, they just didn't measure up to Patrick. Then along came Tim from the ad agency, the one she'd become trendy for.

On paper, Tim was great. Tall, solvent. An account director. He was, she whispered, 'so artistic'. I assumed that meant he did strange stuff in bed. He certainly looked a bit more edgy than her previous numbers. Enough to get her reconsidering her wardrobe, at least. But at my age, I felt I was looking for a lot more than he could offer. Even Jen, after the initial thrill wore off, started treated him like a mildly disappointing pet she'd somehow got lumbered with, at least in our chats. I couldn't understand it. She was only five years older than me. Surely she should be living a little, before she settled?

But it cut me to the quick when she turned up to All Bar One with an extra glow about her. I was just wondering what it was, and how I could get it – new moisturiser, special eye shadow? – when she flashed her left hand at me. There it was, a rock of a ring. I'd thought she was wasting her time with Tim, and hoped I was the one getting it right, wanting more. But the sight of Jen's diamond cluster made me realise I wanted one too.

Obviously I didn't want Tim. And I didn't envy Jen at all, being stuck with him for life. But I did immediately buy into all that wedding stuff. Well, it's inevitable, isn't it? Every little girl is brought up on a solid pink diet of handsome princes, ballgowns, fairy godmothers and, crowning it all, the massive fuck-off wedding at the end. I hadn't had a lot, growing up, but my mother had always been willing to stick a DVD on, keep me occupied while she got up to . . . whatever. I'd more or less taught myself to read, freeze-framing the credits of *Cinderella*.

Part of me knew the whole idea was seriously flawed. Relationships didn't last. I only needed to look at my mother to see that writ large. But the fact that her own romantic quest had been never-ending, despite the pitiful results, showed me how hard-wired the desire for a happy-ever-after was. As a young girl, I'd sneaked books of fairy tales out of the school library and read them under the covers at night, *Matilda*-style. And I still loved a bit of chick lit. Who doesn't? From Sophie Kinsella all the way back to Jane Eyre, the idea was the same. Man equals happiness. Once you've got rid of the madwoman in the attic.

I would have questioned it more if every cell in my body weren't crying out for Patrick. If I had him, oh, if I did, my troubles would be over. I *knew* that, and no one could tell me any different. I'd seen the kindness behind his confidence, you see. He had the most beautiful manners, the way he always held the big glass doors open for colleagues. He had charm, at ease with everyone from the chairman of the company to the security guard. And he was fun. He told the best jokes, he set the tone.

And, on the rare occasions when he was alone, he changed the energy in the building as soon as he set foot in the door. I knew, before looking up, when he'd arrived in the mornings. Something changed in the very air of the place. There was a new feeling of urgency, full of promise. He usually stayed much later than I did – he was hard-working as well! – but if he ever left before me, the life went out of the building the moment the door swung closed on his sharp suit.

There were other men around who were confident, some who were good-looking too. But there was no one who combined it all like Patrick. It made him irresistible to me. He was so different from anyone I'd met before, so open in what he wanted. He seemed so honest and free, unafraid to aim for the top, unabashed about looking at me. He wasn't, like my mother's men, giving me sneaky little glances, opportunistic, speculative. He had no reason to hide, nothing to feel guilty about. He made me feel clean, instead of dirty. He was the chance of a new life, the hero who would, finally, save me from the fiery dragon.

So when I saw the ring sparkling as hard as it could on Jen's freshly manicured hand, I suddenly saw my own future in those glittering facets. This would be me! Me and Patrick. I mouthed all the right things, oohed and ahed at the proposal (actually not bad – Tim had got down on one knee at an up-and-coming Soho club, managing to fuse the arty and the traditional in a way that couldn't fail to melt Jen's heart) and pledged to help her arrange the wedding. After all, it would be good practice for my own.

Jen's success, again, had shown me the path. I could get what she had. And I would. All I needed was a strategy to follow. I'd been idling away until now, not realising how serious the game was, not conscious that everything, including me, had an expiry date. But Jen's ring had shown me the prize I should be aiming for, and had also reminded me that I needed to get on with it. Things changed. Look at Jen. She'd left the desk, and yes, she'd still thrived and found Tim. But if *I* left, would I ever see Patrick again?

I had him near me, five days a week, yet I was relying on

chance, fate, kismet, something other than myself, to organise things for me. Everything about my life so far should have told me that wasn't the way to go. If I wanted something, I had to go out and get it done myself.

Chapter 13

Now

Becca

Becca threw her biro down onto her cluttered desk. It ricocheted off yesterday's sandwich wrapper and rolled onto the floor. She grimaced as she rooted for it, but a decision had been made all the same. She needed to sort this out. There was no other way. She'd been worrying at this puzzle for what seemed like forever, after what she'd found online. She'd been going through the motions here, doing her job to the best of her abilities, but her mind was always . . . elsewhere. All right, on Louise. Checking up on the woman was becoming a habit. Too much of one, people would say. But she *knew* there was something there. It wasn't imagination. Nor obsession. Not this time.

She still didn't have quite enough at her fingertips to dare to confide in anyone else, though. She stared away from her screen, accidentally catching Burke's eye. His sandy hair was plastered down today, his usually mild blue eyes giving her a shrewd glance. She bobbed her head back. She could just imagine what he'd say if he knew what she was spending her time doing.

She yawned and drooped back over the latest report, struggling to fill it in. Registering all this stuff had never seemed so pointless, when she knew that, not more than ten minutes' drive away, sat a woman who was literally getting away with murder.

Becca knew Louise Bridges was a bad 'un, she could smell it on her. There was no doubt in her mind that there was more to the whole business than it seemed. So what if the coroner had taken one look at the grieving widow and rubber-stamped everything? So what if no one else seemed to bat an eyelid at the way *Mrs Bridges* was carrying on with her life as though nothing had happened?

As usual, the thought of Louise filled her vision and she stood up abruptly. At the desk opposite, a colleague stopped scratching behind her ear with a pen and ran their eyes up and down her, then turned away. Becca felt more conscious than ever of the soft rolls straining against her uniform trousers. Across the way, Burke tutted, then went back to his in-tray. He'd be happy doing paperwork forever. Routine, structure, block capitals on the dotted line. This wasn't what she'd joined the police for.

Why had she joined? It was partly something that her mother couldn't reproach her for. She was never going to get a job doing anything her mother really rated. The sort of glamorous career celebrities dabbled in, between interviews with *Hello!* The police, though, that was solid, respectable. Her mother could see the point of it. It seemed to cancel out that one brief wobble Becca had had, the depression. She'd been ill, but she was better.

Unfortunately, it turned out that she didn't want to do the bits of the job that Mum thought would keep her nicely out of trouble. She wanted to do the tricky stuff. Search out the hidden. Make deductions. And, above all, make sure people didn't cheat justice.

One person in particular.

It was going to be a slog, she could see that. So far, no one had ever seen her potential – apart from poor old Dad. She'd have to claw her way up alone. But this Louise Bridges business could help her. Becca would just have to prove them all wrong about the woman, simple as that. Shatter some illusions.

And no, it wasn't going to be like last time. She was perfectly fine now.

She was just a person who liked to *focus*.

Chapter 14

Then

I blush to admit it, but at this point I hadn't really got as far as saying two whole consecutive sentences to Patrick, unless you count stammering and stuttering as conversation.

At first, Patrick seemed determined to keep a constant distance of three metres from my orbit. Perhaps he sensed that if he got any closer, he'd be sucked into my gravity like a hapless meteorite. I mooned over him twice a day, more often if he was getting a sandwich. I had failed to move up to his floor, though the big bosses hadn't quite told me no. It was just *not yet*. I wondered if they were stringing me along. I should have wondered the exact same thing about Patrick, but I was too much in love.

Because all of a sudden, he was sauntering over. He'd always had a bit of a chat with Jen, and sometimes winked at me. But now he was coming over just for me. *Me*.

The first time, I felt like a flower singled out by a bee, every cell of me was alive and producing nectar at a prodigious rate. From a single word, 'OK?' we were soon up to a sentence, 'How's it going?' Then, one day, he smiled properly, right at me, and we actually had a real conversation. It was a red-letter day.

All right, he was only asking if a courier had left a package for him. They hadn't. If they had, I would have been on the phone to him like a shot. I didn't say this, of course. I just stammered and blushed like a stupid idiot, shaking my head as though I had some sort of neurological misfortune, while he looked at me, amused blue eyes running over every inch of my overheated face and body. It was a wonder I didn't spontaneously combust.

After this, the wink and a little 'hello' became our regular thing. I spent hours, at home and in the ladies' at work, practising responses, acting cool, trying desperately to develop some vestige of nonchalance.

Then, for no reason that I could divine, things went backwards again overnight. He started passing me by. The whispers and winks dried up. Days and weeks passed and I was in the desert. He still walked by, regular as clockwork, sometimes with his little coterie of admiring colleagues, sometimes on his own with that brisk, purposeful stride I loved, but he didn't glance over anymore. I was distraught. Had I done something to put him off? Smiled too widely, given myself away somehow?

I tried everything to lure him back. New perfume. Undoing another button on my blouse, then rapidly doing it up again when I attracted the others instead. I straightened my hair, then plaited it, then put it in a bun. Finally I left it hanging down, as dejected as I was, though I carried on smiling my merry smile.

But just when I wasn't expecting it, just when I was resigned, there he was again one fine morning, leaning towards me. I almost swooned into his eyes, they were so blue up close. Even the pores in his skin were beautiful. I was concentrating so hard on not hyperventilating that I forgot to listen.

'Sorry, what?' I was flustered.

'Just asked if anything had been dropped off here for me? It was supposed to be in the post, but it hasn't come.'

The mail was sorted elsewhere and delivered by various spotty youths with red trolleys. I did my best not to be aware of their presence in the building, just as Jen had shown me. Now it seemed as if Patrick, for all his years in the firm, was equally ignorant of the workings of the post room.

'Um.' I looked frantically under my desk, and then wondered why I was doing it. There was nothing there, except my box of tampons, and though I might be discombobulated by his presence, the scent of his clean shirt and the slight citrus waft of his aftershave, I wasn't far gone enough to get those out. 'I'm so sorry, no,' I said, my eyes pleading. Had I let him down in some way? Was it my fault? I felt as though the world might easily come to an end.

'Don't upset yourself, darling,' he said with a wink. 'I'll get them on the phone. Bang a few heads.'

My eyes opened wider and now I knew I wasn't imagining it. A current ran between us for an electric moment. I loved his voice. His gaze. I basked in the way he looked at me, as though we were equals, as though we were seeing each other for the first time. As though I was really worth the time of day. But then he was off again, and that was that. He sauntered away with me watching every step, wishing I could call him back but with not a thing to say for myself. Then I subsided, a tulip deprived of water.

God, I was hopeless. I cursed myself. Other girls would have known what to do, would have quipped back at him, would have stretched that moment like bubble gum. They would have had him snapping back to their desks time and time again. But no, not me.

I kept up my façade but underneath, depression rolled over me like a sea fog.

If I hadn't filled my non-working hours with my quest to get on (I was now taking evening classes in French), my life would have been totally empty. The continuing squeeze on the business meant a freeze on promotions, or so they'd told me. So I was still stuck at my desk, likely to take root in the marble.

It was clear, now, that Patrick would never make a move of his own accord. He knew who I was, vaguely, but didn't care nearly enough. Yes, he gave me that twice-daily twinkle, when it suited him, but what was that worth? He'd done the same to Jen, until she'd left. Then he'd moved his twinkling on to me. It was just a reflex – the kind of low-level acknowledgement that a cocksure man with everything on his side felt he owed to subordinate but attractive women. 'Hi, I'm busy and successful, you're lowly and unimportant, but if we had world enough and time, I'd probably give you one.'

I'd thought about it, of course I had, in the long lonely hours of my empty nights, and had come up with every possible answer as to why he'd started speaking to me, only to stop again. A few times now, he'd sought me out. It meant something, didn't it? It had to. Sometimes, in my fevered daydreams, it was the gateway to a wild romance. But then, in my nightmares, I decided it meant nothing at all, except an interest in getting his hands on his post. I could easily drive myself mad, seesawing between the two. I needed to get out of the theoretical realm, gain some concrete knowledge of the man.

Maybe he didn't repeat his visit to my prettily polished counter because he wasn't after a receptionist. He probably had his sights on higher things, a personal assistant, even a fellow account executive. His colleagues weren't so fussy. They flocked to me. Lounged around, telling me jokes, reporting on the weather outside, as if I didn't have floor-to-ceiling sheets of glass right in front of me giving me better minute-by-minute coverage of the elements than most TV weather girls had. Some did that general boasting men indulge in, every story coming back to their terrific prowess in football or DIY and therefore, by implication, between the sheets. My smile was a fixture, as shiny as the firm's nameplate on the door, but it meant nothing. I didn't dislike these lads, but they were puppies, frolicking at my feet.

Picture an old-fashioned musical – a girl on the desk with shiny blonde hair, and a knot of admirers around her dressed in black and white, showing off frantically with their dazzling leaps and spins. Then the hero saunters past, in grey suit, magenta tie, winks briefly at the girl, and the admirers freeze in mid-dance. She sighs and leans her head on her hand, tracking him with her eyes.

I was that girl and the lads were the cardboard cut-outs prancing around me. I indulged them, while feeling twinges of annoyance at their elbows wrecking the patina of my counter. Their attempts at flirtation didn't even bore me, I just watched them like someone parked in front of a screen, letting the images flick across my irises, not taking anything in. Yet any one of these boys would have done me fine as a boyfriend, husband.

Who was I kidding? They were all way, way above me. If they could have seen how I'd been brought up, they'd be running for the hills, no question. But my indifference was as powerful as catnip. Cracking me became their game. I gave them the shortest shrift I could, while remaining polite and cheery. It didn't do my status any harm for Patrick to see me as hugely popular, though I had to be very careful that he didn't get a whisper that I was the office bike. But act too cool, and maybe he'd be scared to approach me properly himself. I didn't want to give the impression that I'd freeze him off. On the contrary, I felt like Vesuvius, primed and ready, in the strange stillness that came before an eruption powerful enough to obliterate a thousand Pompeiis.

And, all the time, I had to conceal my passion. I knew my eyes caressed him as he sauntered through the marble hall to the lifts and back. I tried to stop myself. When he flicked his smile in my direction, I had to make sure I wasn't already gawping at him as though he was a juicy steak and I was a big cat waiting to pounce. It was hard. And it wasn't getting any easier.

The worst days were those when he was on his phone while he breezed past, hunched into the call in that way he had. Phones were smaller back then – didn't some wag make the joke that until you started getting porn on the internet, phones were getting tinier and tinier? Once filth was only a download away, the screens magically started growing again.

Well, Patrick's then was a titchy thing, the latest must-have gizmo, and when he was schmoozing a client, I could have been invisible. If it was one of those days when I'd planned my appearance down to the last eyelash, had on the carefully laundered, lovingly ironed blouse that had seemed to elicit more of a response when I'd worn it last week, I'd be gutted if he didn't even look my way. To some extent, it made me admire him more. Look at the way he gave his all to his work! Mind you, for all I knew, he could have been chatting to his bookmaker, his mum or even, banish the thought, a girlfriend.

I told myself he was just a really hard-working guy, but I couldn't shut myself off entirely from the possibility that Patrick, unlike me, had a life outside these glossy walls, that yes, he did have a girl or even a fiancée waiting somewhere in the wings, a significant other that he did all the fun things with.

I was hazy about what these might be, never having had what you might describe as a sunny life thus far, but I'd read my share of romances, hadn't I? And I'd walked around my hometown, seeing the happy couples, like a child, nose pressed up against the sweetshop window. Strolling in parks, boating on lakes, feeding each other spaghetti. That sort of thing. Though if it applied to other people, I found it a little revolting. It reminded me of my mother, throwing herself all over the latest scumbag. But the idea that it might, one day – one day soon – be me and Patrick mooning around, hand in hand, brought a smile to my face. And that's how he caught me, one day.

'Hey, gorgeous? Hope you're thinking about me?' He sauntered past, that wink perfectly timed to flip down over his blue, blue eye just at the end of his jaunty line. I was so startled that I sat up, bolt upright, like a total idiot, and lost the misty, smiling gaze that had finally tempted him into speech again, so long after those cursory enquiries about his post. Thank God I just managed not to spill my coffee. That would have killed all my attempts at insouciance stone dead. As it was, the sound of his heels faded away and all I could hear was the blood pounding in my head. If he'd turned around, he'd have seen me looking poleaxed, nothing like the girl of his dreams after all.

That episode convinced me that I had to get a grip, somehow. Give up. Get him out of my system. Or change something. At the moment, I might as well have had a sign above my head reading, 'take me, I'm yours,' every time Patrick walked past.

He was blind to it, but my dread was that someone else would see my yearning for what it was – and would tell him. The shame, the humiliation, didn't bear thinking about. I had to make myself less vulnerable. And I had to be a lot less available. There's nothing people like more than a bit of a challenge. Watch kids in the playground. They all want the same toy. One picks it up, and it's suddenly the hottest thing in the sandpit. Meanwhile, a hundred identical toys, just as good, lie unwanted and unseen.

At the moment, I was like a discarded plastic bucket, aching for Patrick to pick me. I needed to stir things up, make him see me, realise that I was a must-have. And feel that he had to fight to get me.

Or I had to contemplate something much more difficult. Something terrifying.

I needed to accept defeat and move on.

Chapter 15

Now

Becca

Becca stared straight ahead, kept her eyes on the sitcom, just the way her mother liked her to. She could sense her mother's gaze coming to rest on her occasionally when the canned laughter rang out, checking she was smiling. Becca stretched her mouth obligingly, but inside, she was thinking. She'd have to stir things up. If she was right about Louise – and she was – she'd have to make others see it. Because at the moment they were blind.

This was the easiest way to be with her mother. Let it all wash over her. And if Mum wanted to have her say about Becca's life, the telly was the referee. All points were made via the set. 'Doesn't she just look lovely?' *Compared with the state of you*. Her mother sighed as a 20-year-old with a size-six body wafted across the screen.

'That mother is so kind, isn't she?' *Why can't you stop being a bitch?* Becca countered, as the cosy TV matriarch poured out more tea, apparently without the whiff of martyrdom hanging over her every action.

They sat in a silence that passed for companionable for a while, then Becca burst into speech. 'Would you ever think that she'd be capable of murder?' she asked, jabbing a biscuit towards the sitcom daughter.

'Murder?' Her mother's eyes were as round as the coasters on the coffee table. 'But why would she need to kill someone? She's got everything, hasn't she? Look at that boyfriend, he worships the ground she walks on, you can tell.' *Why haven't you got one?* Her mother was tutting, shifting in her chair. Becca knew the signs, realised glumly she ought to go. These Saturday nights were never easy, at the best of times. And now, with her mind so occupied with thoughts of pulling that one trailing thread that would make Louise Bridges unravel, well, she hadn't got the energy to play her mother's games.

Suddenly, her mother turned to her, actually looked straight at her. 'It's not like before, is it, love? You know, when you got everything . . . out of proportion?'

Becca stared at her. She thought they had a pact never to mention those dark months, the medication that had kept her tethered to her bed, as secure as any strait jacket. '*No*. No. Of course not, Mum. Why would you say that? I'm better now, that was ages ago. All in the past.'

'It's just . . . you've got that expression again. You know, that look on your face . . .' Her mother was still gazing at her, checking for something, Becca didn't know what. She shook her head.

'You've got it wrong, Mum. Just busy. Busy at work, you know. But it's great to be here. So relaxing after a hard week.' Her fingers gripped the armrest.

Her mother subsided. So willing to be reassured, so glad to have her fears laid to rest. She didn't want that trouble again. Becca didn't blame her. It was . . . well, it was a hole that she had fallen into. But she had crawled out of it, too. This wasn't the same at all. Back then, she obsessed about anything. Everything. Light switches, lampposts. Yes, she could see now that it wasn't healthy, she'd needed help. But this time was different. She was looking into something, legitimately. A concern. A desire to protect the public. And this time, she was *right*.

On the screen, the soundtrack erupted into guffaws again,

then a smattering of applause. Becca chuckled obediently, felt her mother's eyes rake her face again, smiling this time. Becca slumped back in her chair, forgot about escape. She let the evening wash over her. She'd play the game her mother's way, for once.

Chapter 16

Then

I assessed the rest of the herd. Yes, they all played at wanting me. But it was just a game. They were little boys, compared to Patrick. I sensed, though, that Patrick would only make a move – say a few more words, even – if he thought there was real competition.

There were possibilities, all right. So many men, and all of them apparently so single. While Patrick remained immune to my charms, the rest of his floor was mine for the asking. But that gave me pause. Did I really want to foul my own nest? Risk a recommendation scrawled in the gents? I, of all people, knew what men could be like.

At the moment I had an ice queen reputation. That gave me an odd kind of status, that I surely didn't deserve by virtue of birth, education, or anything else much. If I unbent enough to date one of his cohort, would Patrick forever see me as tainted? I thought he might. Men can be territorial. I'd seen that often enough with my mother. It was fine for them to stray, make it clear they'd lost whatever interest they'd had, but if she put a foot out of line, started sizing up the next Mr Oh-So-Wrong, well . . . It was never pretty.

I wasn't saying that my lovely Patrick was anything like the scum Mum chose to hang about with. But still. I wanted everything tidy, above board. Letting him see me with another guy from work was a risk I wasn't willing to take.

I decided, instead, to try to get a little bit of practice elsewhere. For now, I'd accept that things were going nowhere with Patrick, that he was just out of my league. Instead, I'd make the day of one of the blokes in my French class, just by trying a bit of light ooh-la-la flirtation. Because, despite having seen enough rounds of the battle of the sexes to write the book on it, thanks to my mother, I actually had no direct experience.

This was in pre-Tinder times, when dating advice ran along the lines of, do an evening course or die alone. Do you know anyone who met their life partner learning to upholster or gleaning the basics of car maintenance? No, of course not. But still the advice got dished out, as though there was something deeply erotic about adult education centres. There wasn't. They were basically schools used after hours, and most of the time we were all sitting on those piddly orange plastic chairs that are big enough for you to swing your legs like metronomes in Year One but pretty well cut off the circulation in grown-ups. How could anyone think of sex while scrunched up like an old crisp packet? Must have been desperate. I know I was.

True to form, I would hunch there once a week, vacuuming up information. I was always trying to claw my way up. But there were a couple of guys on my course who'd already sidled up to chat, and not just about whether *dimanche* came before *lundi*. Perhaps they'd been given the 'join an evening class' spiel by a well-meaning parent or friend. The next time one of them came over, I told myself I'd try not to blush, stammer or freeze. Instead, I would chat. Heaven knew I could do with a few more moves, which would hopefully stop me needing a defibrillator every time Patrick spoke to me. If he ever did again.

The first of the likely lads was Mike. A nice enough boy. He'd read somewhere – or been told by his mum – that humour was the way to a woman's heart. All those personal ads with 'GSOH essential' had a lot to answer for. His jokes were terrible. But it was sweet of him to try. I couldn't help smiling up at him after one of his better efforts, not wanting to encourage him too much – after all, he wasn't fit to lick Patrick's boots – but grateful all the same. It felt good to be seen, for once.

And here my point about the sandpit comes in. No sooner had Mike sidled up to me at the coffee break and tried to get me laughing, than Pete, the other obvious singleton in the class, was hanging around at my elbow, asking me if I wanted another coffee from the dire machine and generally behaving like a dog guarding a bone.

I joshed along with them both, then mercifully it was back to irregular verbs, something I already felt more at ease with than most regular human interactions. I managed to slip out of the class as soon as the session was over, before either had got themselves sorted out. I needed time to think about this. Vanity aside, I was a pretty girl and thanks to Jen, I was beginning to acquire a bit of polish. Were either of these lads a particularly tempting prospect? Pete was an obvious doer-upper and, by the looks of him, would be grateful to be taken in hand, in all ways. Could I face it? Mike was in better nick – but those jokes . . .

At home, I realised I was being ridiculous. And much too fussy. Here was I, alone night after night in my bedsit. I was hopelessly in love with a man who, on a good day, winked at me twice and ignored me for the rest of the seven hours, fifty-nine and three-quarter minutes that we spent in the same building. As for the great swathes of time when we weren't even partaking of the same oxygen, well, I might as well have been dead as far as he was concerned. I certainly felt that way myself.

Nope, it wasn't like I had a whole lot going for me. Pete and Mike would be wise to run a mile, once they knew the real me. At least they both seemed to have people pushing them into social situations, whereas I was pretty much alone from the moment I left work every evening to when I rocked up again in the morning.

61

Over the weeks that followed, I auditioned both Mike and Pete for the role of boyfriend. Neither was perfect, by a long way, but I was used to bringing shoddy goods up to standard. After all, I'd done it with myself – and now look at me. Being fought over, in French. Admittedly, by two slightly lame *canards*. But still. All I needed was the raw material to work with. By the time I'd finished with them, they'd be damned near ideal.

It's quite an art, to spot the person who wants to learn, who isn't too attached to their own ways or too convinced they're right. There's a certain malleability some of us have at our core. We're willing to change, if the prize is great enough. We'll do what it takes.

I dropped a hint to the boys that I liked that matelot look, and the next week Pete was wearing a striped top. He asked me out to see a new French film. I admit, I'd started this whole thing to make myself look like the pick of the sandpit buckets, as far as Patrick was concerned. But, as Pete stammered to the end of his invitation, and I realised how very much he wanted me to say yes, I felt something new. It was gratitude. And actually, that little fizz of desire. There was something very flattering indeed about me, of all people, having two lads vying for my charms.

Although the men at work drooled over me, it was in a safe way that didn't really mean a thing. These two, though, they wanted me for real. I basked in it, I really did. Finally, I'd found people who actually knew me a little bit and still saw something worthwhile. I'd never managed to have friendships, apart from Jen, and she was more of a mother to me than anything else. Back in the old days, in my childhood home, men had looked me up and down and made me feel unclean. Pete and Mike's admiration did the reverse, and I began to feel like a bit of a siren.

I was nervous, though, about taking the plunge with either of them. Maybe they were joking? Waiting for me to register an interest, just to laugh in my face, say they'd been pulling my leg. What would they really want with someone like me? But gradually it dawned on me that they were both in earnest and, if I didn't want to get in the way of all our prospects of learning more than the present tense in French, I had to make a choice.

Pete was the one I went for in the end. It was quite obvious, even to him, that he needed a woman's touch. And the way his eyes lit up every time I took my precarious seat on the orange plastic chair next to his, well, it was adorable really.

The only real trouble with his rival, Mike, was the funnies. If you don't like someone's sense of humour, there's not much you can do. It's pretty fundamental, and for me it was a deal breaker. I put up with the quips for a couple more coffees before I made up my mind, and I'm afraid that gave him hope. But the fact that I sat, stony-faced, through some of what he considered to be his best lines should have given him the nudge. Anyway, he took it badly, of course.

On the face of it, my decision was absurd. Pete was a bit awkward, whereas Mike was pretty sure of himself. But that was the trouble. Mike's veneer of confidence allowed him to plough on when it should have been clear he'd lost his audience, way back. Though he reminded me in some small ways of my beloved Patrick, always the gold standard of cockiness, this persistence ultimately only served to show me that he was incapable of learning. And that Patrick, as usual, was the real thing in a world of shabby imitations.

Pete, on the other hand, was suddenly rather presentable, when coaxed out of his nasty leather jacket. They say manners maketh man, but a reasonable selection of smart new togs can do the job pretty well. Sometimes his clothes choices had class nuances that, with my antecedents, I just didn't understand. He loved those funny deck shoes and resisted getting rid of them. Then I finally realised they were a posh thing, as was the way he often wore a cricket jumper round his shoulders. Luckily my second-hand copy of *Brideshead Revisited* showed actors from the TV version on the front, wearing similar kit. So that lot stayed.

After about a month, Pete looked so great that, dare I say it, I had almost forgotten Patrick.

Pete adored me, as I was fast discovering. To say this was refreshing would be a massive understatement. I'd got used to taking my mother's assessment of my qualities as gospel, therefore it was a wonder I didn't throw myself out with the rubbish every day.

Waking up instead with a man who thought the stars shone from my eyes was a delicious novelty. I wriggled my toes in delight when we were together, and not just because Pete had the excellent habit of bringing me a cup of tea in bed. My quest for Patrick now seemed like yet another bit of my past that I might have to move seamlessly away from. The longer my relationship with Pete went on, the more I saw that I hadn't been ready for Patrick at all. I might never be. There was so much I didn't know about all the couple stuff. If Patrick had taken the plunge and asked me out, I would have been a complete novice at relationships, and that would have downgraded me in his eyes.

No, if Patrick and I ever did get together (and I was now beginning to concede it was very unlikely indeed) I had to be a glittering prize. It was something I'd never been in my life before, until Pete looked at me, bless him. But it seemed that love was like that, elevating ordinary things into extraordinary ones. I enjoyed watching it all happen. Of course, I did my best to learn from it. There was, I realised, more and more I needed to finetune, in order to fit in with other people. Not least, my flat.

For me, home was downtime. I switched off, I didn't try, I was just dormant, waiting for my next assault on the world. It didn't matter if the place was functional, bleak even. For me, home was like the dark, empty spaces at the side of a brightly lit West End theatre set. To say the place was spartan was a little bit of an understatement. Years before it became trendy, I was more of a minimalist than John Pawson. As long as things were clean, I didn't really see the problem. And the less stuff there was lying around, the fewer reminders there were of the chaos I'd grown up in, and the better I liked it. It was where I lay fallow, on my own. To be honest, I felt I didn't deserve anything more. Comfort was something for the good people.

But the first time I brought Pete back, I saw the flat through a stranger's eyes. And we both got a massive shock.

At first, I thought the poor chap was just a bit overawed that we were finally moving on to the next stage. I'd been resisting him coming home with me for a while, not quite sensing that something was off but as always guarding my privacy. For years, it was all I'd had. Now I'd finally let him in, but things weren't going as I expected at all. He wandered around, while I made the coffee we'd allegedly come back for so we could leave it untouched and get down to basics, but it didn't take him long to inspect the place. Well, the flat was microscopic. And, as I was beginning to realise from his expression, there was something drastically wrong with it. But what? I was at a loss. It was squeaky clean. It had everything I needed. Bed, toaster, kettle, microwave, my books. Once, it had also had my collection of jewellery and fripperies, but thanks to Jen the few of these that remained fitted inside a paper bag in the bathroom.

'Just moved in?' That was the question that should have alerted me.

'Been here, oh, about three years now.' I smiled bewitchingly over the jar of instant. His eyes dropped down to the granules – the fancy kind, mind you, I'd been treating myself – and did another curious double take. Clue number two.

'I expect you're too busy to get settled?' he said, offering me a way out. But out of what? I didn't get it. The flat was pristine, orderly. I hated mess, I'd put all that behind me and I proved it every time I undid a fresh bottle of bleach. What was his problem? Because there clearly was one.

I brought the coffees over to the bench. I only sat on it to eat, so the hardness didn't bother me. I read my books in bed. He sat on the edge, put his cup somewhat nervously on the floor. I didn't think to offer biscuits. Well, I didn't have any. Extra carbohydrates were definitely not on my agenda, and the list of visitors I'd had back to my flat was short. Him. I had no graceful preparations ready, even though I'd decided tonight was going to be his night. Well, that's not quite true. I'd painted my toenails, shaved my legs. But the flat? Fine as it was, I'd thought. But I'd been wrong.

'No cushions. I like it. Uncluttered,' he said, shifting uncomfortably. I made a mental note. *Buy cushions.* 'Where do you hide the telly? Radio? Hi-fi? Speakers?'

I shook my head briefly. I'd decided against these distractions long ago. Although those Disney princesses had danced their way through my childhood, lulling me and blotting out so much, once I had the choice I opted for my books. I didn't want the drone of the telly a moment longer. There was too much to get on with to waste my time on inessentials. Sometimes it meant I had to bluff my way, when some series or other was all the rage, and it was the only topic the girls at work could talk about. Not that I hung around with them much, but there were times in the canteen or as they passed my desk. There was enough in the newspapers to tell me pretty much everything I'd ever need to know about trashy TV.

I learned to make the right sort of comments, keep the conversation going, though it wasn't really safe to offer a major opinion. The one time I had, something had been awry. I couldn't work out what – well, I'd never seen the show. Tumbleweed for a moment, a week of strange looks, then we were back to normal. But I never risked it again.

As for music, well, I'd never got it. When you've been brought up with paper-thin walls, when the dubious heavy metal choices of the man living three floors down became the beat that your glass of orange squash danced to, not having sounds in your life was a blessed relief. I wallowed in the velvety luxury of silence. Same thing went for cooking. The idea of anything that lingered

– fish, curry – revolted me. I'd hated the stenches of the stairwells. Even when it wasn't effluent, other people's cooking smelt nearly as bad to me. I loved my microwave. You only needed to use a plastic fork – prick the film, then shovel the food in. Throw the lot away afterwards, all done. How great was that?

Anything that impinged on me from outside, I hated. No mess, no fuss. Plenty of space around me, all the exits clear. After growing up in the Tower of Babel, I hardly ever raised my voice. Patrick, later, accused me of faking my tone, like Margaret Thatcher, but that was always real.

Pete, still looking around my flat like a drowning man casting about for something to latch on to, piped up at last.

'Well, I can see what you *do* like. Books.' He sounded overawed, and now I looked around in my turn. I thought of my library as a kind of comfort blanket. But maybe it was daunting, if you weren't a reader. I'd had the sense to kick the self-help section under my bed that morning, when I'd decided it was Pete's lucky day, but otherwise the full might of all the knowledge I wanted or needed was staring down at us from serried ranks of Billy bookshelves that I'd picked up from Ikea, braving the maze of families and cheap meatballs, and assembled myself – not without peril to my manicure.

'Books do furnish a room,' I said gently, knowing that, despite an education I'd begun to suspect was quite expensive, the reference would probably fly several miles over his head.

At that point, my cat, Mephisto, strolled in and saved the day. Black and fluffy, from a distance Mephs looked the business and could pass for a Persian cross. Close up, you noticed his battered ear, the gash over his eye which had left the trace of a scar, even the fact that his fur was more of a dark rusty brown than true black. Like his mistress, he wasn't quite what he seemed. But unlike me he had bags of swagger. Pete dropped to his knees and started cooing, while both Mephs and I looked on in surprise.

'I didn't take you for a cat person?' Pete said, looking up from where he was now giving Mephisto a full belly-rub. The cat had not hung about long before capitulating. He was now emitting the special low humming sound I'd thought he saved just for me.

'Mmm,' I said, non-committal. It wasn't the moment to disabuse him. I just hadn't been able to leave the cat with my mother when push came to shove. One of her hook-ups had given it to her – as a joke, I was pretty sure. She wasn't fit to look after a child, we all knew that much. Why burden her with an animal as well?

Anyway, despite my better judgement, Mephs and I had been together ever since my final flit from her place. There'd been no time to be organised. I'd just grabbed what I could and I'd run. At the last minute, Mephs had miaowed. I'd looked under the sofa, wasting precious seconds, and seen the green glass of his eyes. I couldn't leave him. I'd grabbed him and shoved him unceremoniously into my backpack, and that was that, we were together.

Unlike his namesake, this Mephistopheles had never promised me the world, just a load of hairballs and the occasional scratch to keep me in line. He'd definitely fulfilled his side of the bargain. He'd been the king of our old estate, but I'd forced him to become an indoor cat with a litter box and a view out of our new tenth floor window on the other side of town, take it or leave it. Well, I could hardly cut a cat flap in our front door. I was pretty sure it was against all the council regulations to have a pet, though I didn't look too closely. That would have interfered with my pleas of ignorance if we got caught.

Lugging cat food home with my frozen lasagnes was a chore. But I loved the old dear, and I'd thought he was equally discerning. I now saw, as he writhed and purred for Pete, that he was a shameless old tart who'd go with anyone. *Wonder who he got that from?* I thought sourly.

But Mephisto's appearance had saved the day. Pete relaxed completely. Keeping an animal had, oddly enough, proved I was human.

If tonight had told me anything so far, it was that my flat was seriously scary for men, and probably for anyone. And it had shown me that Pete was more fussed about coffee than books. This was disconcerting; I was always surprised when other people revealed that they had flaws. I was used to them all being on my side.

In the morning, Pete seemed a whole lot more at ease, and Mephisto couldn't take all the credit. We were loved up, all right. His grin was so big it even lasted all the way through another cup of coffee. But I didn't need telling twice. I needed to sort out the flat. It definitely needed some 'feminine touches', as I felt sure the women's magazines would put it. And some sort of upgrade on the beverages front. Anything that would soften the effect of two-thousand-odd classics leering down at unsuspecting guests.

Learning on the hoof, you see. That was what I was good at. And self-flagellation. I gave myself a thorough kicking for not having tested out the flat first, just on a neighbour or maybe even kindly, motherly Jen. Then I could have rectified my mistakes. I had nearly put Pete off, and if I could lose someone so keen at the first hurdle, then maybe I didn't deserve to be in this game.

I was now suddenly aware that most people would find my level of auto-didactism a serious turn-off. And that was so not the effect I was after.

True, Pete might be a special case, with some sort of an aversion to reading. He had the ability to talk about sport for hours on end, without seeming to notice that he wasn't holding even a corner of my attention. TV would have been the stopgap but now he'd seen for himself that was a non-starter as far as I was concerned. Luckily, we were so smitten with each other that the gulfs between us didn't show. To start with.

Chapter 17

Now

Louise

Being widowed is a sort of rebirth, or a sort of death. I went to bed the day before Patrick died as a wife and mother, and by the next night, I'd become something completely different. It would be much more convenient for most people if I'd died with him. It would save their embarrassment. Their inability to cope with two great taboos colliding – death, and single women of a certain age.

I sense both things. And people's eyes at a distance, almost like I'm under surveillance. There's an increasing reluctance to talk to me up close. Mums at the school gate are fed up already with having to ask me how it's all going. Those hushed tones and sympathetic expressions have fast become wearied. Shouldn't I have got over it by now? But if I show signs that I have, well, I know that will be punished even more.

Some have already forgotten, quite reasonably caught up in their own lives. They stumble with every accidental mention of husbands and fathers. Confusion in their eyes, tripping over their own tongues, almost apologising that their own other halves aren't dead. I can't say, *that's fine, yours can be alive while mine isn't*. It's better if we all try and brush past Patrick's inconvenient corpse, somehow pretend that my children were the products of immaculate conception and that those little tear-off sheets from

70

the school asking for attendance at parents' evenings and sports days are addressed to me only.

It's fine. I don't mind all the *faux pas*. Not too much anyway, because my focus, as ever, is the kids. The only thing that guts me is when their own friends say something that stabs. They often blunder onto that huge sore spot which is still only lightly camouflaged with smiles and jokes. Underneath, the ulcer of my children's grief still weeps on.

A few of the well-meaning single mums tried to take me under their wing, get me to go out on their prosecco-and-innuendo nights. A kind thought, but too soon, I murmured, reminding everyone that I need special treatment. They are divorced, separated or alone by choice. I am widowed, and that's a different calling.

One even nudged me, asked me when I was going to start dating. I don't think she'll ask me that again.

Chapter 18

Then

I'd begun to notice that people seemed to find intensity worrying. Whether it was a thirst for learning or a serious effort to reach certain goals, people would much rather you shut up about it and talked inconsequential nonsense instead. I wasn't sure if it was a sexist thing. I was a girl therefore I was supposed to have nothing in my head but heel heights and lipstick shades. Or did they consider any sort of striving to be too try-hard, and therefore a bit suspect? As usual, other people's thought processes were a complete mystery to me.

Why was it good to know the plot of *Hollyoaks* backwards but bad to be interested in Machiavelli's *The Prince*? Most of this unthinking prejudice against knowledge was based on ignorance. Inevitably. There was an irony in being glued to the antics of some telly-based love rat manipulating everyone around him, and yet shunning the original work that told you how those levers of power operated. Still, it was their loss, and I wouldn't have worried about it – except that my erudition was yet another secret I had to hide.

Sometimes I'd watch my contemporaries float down the street and wonder if they knew how lucky they were. It was always worst in summer, when a girl my age, from the proper background and

72

with the right level of education, could just prance around the place in a pretty summer dress and wait for someone to come along and marry her. So easy. Whereas for me, it was a dance of the seven veils, whatever I was actually wearing. Hide my hardscrabble background. Disguise my awful accent. Soften my ambition. Pretend total ignorance. Never show how hard I was working to better myself. It was exhausting. Winter was much easier. Everyone was muffled up against the British climate. There was a solidarity in our layers of wool. And no one looked happy.

But, for the moment, I actually was. Things were jogging along so nicely with Pete. I got quite addicted to doing all the couple things. Big brunches on a Sunday. Wandering around hand in hand. Going to the movies. He liked scary films. It was a macho thing; he enjoyed pretending he was really tough. And of course, he loved it if he thought I was frightened. I'd cling to him obligingly. But I felt him jump at stuff that didn't even make my pulse flicker. I'd seen worse.

I always wondered if I'd bump into someone from my old life out on the streets. In the normal run of things, I kept to my flat and to the office, and the occasional posh bar with Jen, and was pretty sure no worlds would collide there. But wandering around the town as I now was, hand in hand with Pete, the chances had to be good that I'd see someone from before. Whether they'd recognise me was another question.

I would have loved to have seen the girls from my class, who'd shunned me so thoroughly back then. If they could see me doing all this happy stuff, surely they'd have felt bad, for the way they'd treated me? But I was probably over-estimating the impact I'd made on them. A pathetic little misfit like the girl I'd been would have faded from their memories many moons ago.

As time wore on, Pete showed himself to be excellent boyfriend material, if you could overlook the obsession with football. But I had a feeling that was a universal failing anyway. Occasionally, as we drifted around the town, his arm round my waist, he'd linger in front of a homewares shop or one of those sofa places. At first, I wondered what on earth was going on. But never slow on the uptake, I realised he was giving me gentle hints, trying to make my flat less grim. I don't think it was even because he hated sitting on that rock-hard bench. He genuinely wanted to make the place nicer, for me.

Of course I took the project on, as I do. Bought books on the principles of design, became an expert on interiors through the ages. I still loved the clean lines of my place, but I could now see that no one else in their right minds would. The first time I sidled into a cushion shop, I was blushing. Wooden owls wearing spectacles fashioned out of wire, what were they even for? Signs saying Live, Laugh, Love in curly writing. Surely other people just did that stuff naturally, they didn't need orders. Or did they? Rugs that Mephisto would take great pleasure in shredding or moulting all over. But I bumbled around, trying to work it all out. I must have looked so ill at ease that two assistants came up to ask me if I needed help. Terrified, I insisted I didn't, though I did, and then I bolted. I had to return the next week to pick up a couple of cushions, though I still shied away from the owl and signs.

Gradually, I got there. I moved the bench into the tiny kitchen, got a small sofa. It was so much more comfortable that I wondered why it hadn't occurred to me before. Then I realised. The disgusting old couch at home had been the place from which my mother held court. Upright, when things were going well, but more often prostrate, and with a hand or leg hanging off life-lessly on a bad day. I'd hated walking past, in case a vice-like claw darted out and grabbed me, or in case she or a boyfriend tried to trip me up for laughs. Sitting on my own sofa, with Mephisto or Pete, or both my boys, took the sting out of the memories. I felt silly for having been scared of soft furnishings, when it was people – some of them – who deserved my dread.

Once the cushions were in, a trickle of small changes followed. Cheerful mugs and plates picked up cheaply in the market where

I'd once bought my tatty jewels. They added something to the place, I could see it now. Colours that had been so wrong in my cheap skirts and nails could actually work in the flat.

And, as usual, I enjoyed making myself an expert, and leaving the drab world I'd been born into even further behind.

Chapter 19

Now

Louise

The Victorians had a system for mourning, and I thoroughly admire them for it. For about four years after a husband's death – or forever if you felt like it, like Queen Victoria – a widow would wear her grief on her back; mourning clothes. At least the first year, preferably two, would be in full black, head to toe. Then half-mourning kicked in; the gradual reintroduction of colour, moving from lavender to grey and then lilac. Anything less hinted at a flightiness, a willingness to entice the opposite sex with bright plumage that was most unseemly. You were a walking symbol of your sorrow.

I have chosen black as my talisman. To be honest, I wore it plenty before that day. Who doesn't? Goes with everything, looks slimming, or so they say. Perfect with blonde hair. And since my days with Jen, my colour palette had always been fiercely restricted anyway. What could be more elegant than black, white and maybe an occasional hit of sizzling hot pink? But I'm not making a style statement anymore. I'm retreating into black's all-encompassing lack. The flatness. The deadness. It suits my halfway state, between Patrick and my children.

Nowadays, I shun reds, for obvious reasons. Lilac seems much too frivolous. Lavender, I'm growing fonder of. Grey, I can see myself in, given time.

I like the codification of my state, the reminder of my condition. It's not that cheery, granted. But I sometimes think people need a visual prompt.

Of course, I don't extend the scheme to the kids. In fact, I'd be happy if they wore brighter colours. If I could see my Em in a sugary dress, my heart would skip a beat. But I'm more likely to see a flock of piglets flying past our chimney pots. Giles is happiest in sludge, khaki or browns, like a suburban guerrilla blending in with the back gardens. Boys' clothing is as dull as ditchwater anyway. Even his dad only managed the odd flash of colour, a periwinkle shirt, a jaunty stripe.

I remember with a sudden jolt that I once bought him a lavender polo shirt. It was destined to lie unworn in his cupboard, a sartorial step too far for a man who didn't mind jumping over lots of other lines.

My eyes fill with tears as I wind a lavender scarf round my throat.

Chapter 20

Then

While all this brunching, loving and remodelling had been going on with Pete, what, you may ask, had been happening with Patrick in the office? Well, some would have said a big fat nothing. Although I'd scaled down my expectations and had pretty much accepted it was hopeless, I did still automatically keep a carefully calibrated mental tally of our interactions. Some days, when he'd twinkled really heavily at me, were marked in my memory with a gold star. Others, when he'd brushed past, intent on the day's work or an evening doing heaven-knew-what, were black dates, where I would have plunged into despair without Pete.

But I'd been right. The distraction of having a real-life boyfriend had made my reactions to Patrick a lot more controllable when he sauntered past me twice a day. The breathlessness, the wild flushes that used to sweep up from my toes and suffuse my entire body with embarrassing scarlet heat, had subsided. I met his eyes coolly these days. And, sometimes, I *didn't even look up*.

This was my masterstroke. No one as cocksure as Patrick likes to think they're losing it, whatever 'it' may be. A sale, a contract, or, in this case, the potential of an easy lay. OK, so Patrick had never bothered to avail himself of all that I was offering, but we both knew for a while back then I'd been his for the asking, and not worth the dirt beneath his feet. Until suddenly, I was playing him at his own indifferent game.

I'd sowed the seed, of course. I knew that Patrick's curiosity would eventually be piqued. He'd ask around. So I'd cultivated Trish, one of the secretaries in his part of the firm. Despite all my attempts to better myself, my bid to move floors still hadn't found favour with the powers that be. Fully staffed, so they kept on saying, though I suspected in my darker moments that they just didn't think I could cut it. So if I couldn't be there, I needed someone else to keep a bit of an eye on Patrick for me. Just for old times' sake.

Trish was a lovely bit of posh. One of those plump blondes born with a pony between her thighs. She had it all: the accent, heavy as a bag of gold coins, even the casual contempt for her mum and dad, the milk and honey of her upbringing.

We started off just having a coffee in the canteen on one of my breaks. By this stage, I'd been allocated a junior, Sal, who sat at the desk with me, on sufferance I might add. The idea was that I was training her up, now that everyone was working flat out on new contracts. I think it was a sop to me, too, to compensate me for not getting promoted to Patrick's golden uplands.

I didn't show it, but I was pretty grumpy about this, as I'd seen how this played out before. Jen and me, at the beginning, right? I'd come along, Jen had fashioned me into her own image, and then she was out, on her elegant behind. The last thing I wanted was a repeat performance. I loved this job. And though I now had Pete, I would have been devastated to leave. That would have been giving up on Patrick for good.

So Sal was getting a minimalist induction into the ways of the firm, and doing what she did best, sitting around, pouting, studying her pimples in a tiny hand mirror and allowing me finally to grab the odd five minutes away from the desk. Though I didn't love the way she'd been foisted on me, I was happy enough to have the freedom. It gave me more scope to see how the land lay. Posh Trish was my open sesame.

One day, Trish and I were sitting nursing the dregs of our drinks up on the third floor. Everyone called it the canteen with a bit of a sneer in their voices, but for me it was still one of the swankiest cafés I'd ever been to. The tables were buffed to levels of spotlessness that even I, with my eagle eye, could find no fault with. Hot dishes, salads and snacks were served at great long shiny counters, and the staff were courteous, wearing strange little white puffy hats with apparent pleasure. OK, it was a tiny bit like a school canteen, except that here everything was pristine and edible, and no one despised me.

People complained non-stop about the food, but I loved it. I had to concentrate hard to do as the others did, make airy conversation while eating, lift my eyes and my fork from my plate, and not jam my elbows out to the side and scarf the lot before someone else did. I would have been entitled to free meals at school, if my mother had got her shit together for long enough to fill in the forms. That was the way authority so often outmanoeuvred people like her. Benefits were there, for the taking, but you had to have the concentration and the application to jump through a few hoops. Jump? She couldn't get off that couch most days.

People did laugh about my addiction to ketchup – I even had a good blob with the salads – but that was passed off as a cute little foible, not the mindless addiction of the guttersnipe I actually was. You could choke down a lot with ketchup. And even now that I didn't need to, I couldn't help myself. They always had proper Heinz, and I loved that salty-sweet fizz on my tongue.

As usual with Trish, I was listening, she was talking. I'd got the reputation for being quite shy – enough to make me snort with laughter, frankly. No one seemed to realise I was quiet only because I was taking things in. I wasn't diffident. I was just biding my time, and happy to do so. You never knew when someone would let slip something useful. If you're brought up without any template for normal human behaviour, you either resign yourself to being an oddity, or you try to make up for what's been lost, copy what you can. You can't do that by being the one to talk.

Besides, if I let my mouth run off, I found myself saying things that I thought were run of the mill, but that others found deeply odd. I could tell by their expressions, but by that stage it would be too late, my careless words couldn't be recalled. I didn't want to reveal all the crevasses inside me that were empty. I wanted my shameful secrets to stay just that – secret. Every now and then, I'd let something slip despite myself, though. And then I'd bitterly regret it. Like that time with Jen in the bar.

She'd been saying how unrealistic some cop drama or other was, how all the lead character had done was fiddle under the dash for a second to get the car going, how it couldn't possibly be as easy as that in real life. I just said my piece, and her jaw hit the table. 'Come on then,' she said, trying to drag me out. She only wanted me to demonstrate on her own cute little runabout. I had to reel back in, pretend it had been the drink talking. She didn't understand that hot-wiring involves ripping up the transmission. It does only take seconds, but once I'd yanked those wires out into the light of day, her Mini would never have been the same again. When you think about it, no one who starts a car that way is bothered about popping to the supermarket in it tomorrow, picking up their granny the day after for a prayer meeting. It's a one-time only deal, and probably the only useful bit of information I ever got from one of Mum's lowlife men.

That's the way it was. I had skills, but they were the kinds of things that were hard to explain and were not welcome in polite society. Better to stay silent and absorb the lessons others had to teach instead.

But it worked in my favour. I was extremely refreshing company for girls who were used to being interrupted all the time by their boyfriends, scarcely listened to when it was finally their chance to chime in and then expected to shut up and smile while their partners rode off yet again on the hobby-horse of their choice. When I was listening, I *really* listened. Head to one side, serious expression on. I gave every conversation a sort of confessional air – irresistible. People almost always ended up telling me more than they'd ever planned to.

OK, I didn't give a lot back. But with Trish, diets were 90 per cent of her conversation anyway and if I'd been her boyfriend, I'd definitely have blown my brains out. He must have had his sights set firmly on that stately home she was bound to inherit. Me, I put up with it for various reasons. And if I had views on the best way to lose weight, I kept them to myself. Pretended that eating pineapple would definitely do the trick. Food combining? Cabbage soup? *Oh yeah, that's bound to work.* For God's sake, eat less, move more. Was it really that hard to understand? But Trish, like so many women, much preferred to believe there was a magic bullet out there that would do all the willpower stuff for her, so she didn't have to. That was the trouble with being brought up on fairy stories. *If the glass slipper fits, you'll become a princess.*

In the meantime, interspersed with details I didn't need to know about her latest crazy weight loss scheme, involving enough fibre to keep her own pony going for months, and her marvelling about my own inability to put on weight – it wasn't rocket science, I hardly ate – I was getting lots of useful info from Trish.

I was careful, as usual, not to signal my interest too obviously. But Trish understood, or thought she did. In her view, she had a privileged position, as she was up there on the first floor with all the account execs, providing their admin support services.

Trish was smart enough to do the account exec job itself, but that wasn't in her world view. Just the admin was fine for her. She was only marking time before sashaying up the aisle, when her life would change and curtain fabric would become the most pressing item on her agenda. Her private education had probably cost as much as a detached house in Chiswick, but both she and her parents were relaxed about chucking it away like this.

I envied her; I did. So much that it sometimes hurt. I didn't wish her ill, but I couldn't help thinking how much better a job I'd make of her life, if it were all mine.

Still, that got me nowhere and I did my best to shrug it off. She could help me now, that was what I had to concentrate on. Because she actually knew Patrick. And she could feed him the information that I was now seeing Pete.

This had been my original scheme. To be honest, I had rather lost sight of it, recently. Pete and I were just having the loveliest time. We weren't doing anything earth-shaking, we were both at the beginnings of our careers and didn't have much money to spare, but we'd spend weekends lolling in parks, or I'd drag him to visit a gallery or a museum, and he'd try and get me to watch sport on TV. We were hand in hand, laughing ourselves silly, and it felt great. But I still somehow wanted Patrick to know I was taken.

I'd often wondered if Patrick didn't just think he was that bit too far above me in the scheme of things. Of course he was right, but that wasn't the point. During those few golden moments when he'd leaned across my desk and given me a bit of the old chat, he'd made me feel there might be a chance. But was I aiming much too high and destined to fail, as my mother had always said? I'd sometimes felt as though I really knew Patrick, that he was in every fibre of my being. But he wasn't. He was a stranger. Now that I *did* know Pete, I realised my obsession with Patrick was just another fantasy, the sort that had got me through my childhood but that was something I shouldn't cling to anymore, now I was supposed to be grown up.

All right, Patrick had made that one throwaway 'hey, gorgeous' comment just before I'd taken up with Pete, but apart from that our entire relationship consisted of desultory chats about missing correspondence, plus him winking and me alternately going up in flames with my blushes, or trying to style it out with a cool nod. Anyone would have said the bad, bad, lad was leading me on. Time to make a puny attempt to even the score by letting Trish drop the news that I had a boyfriend. She didn't bat an eyelid; didn't express amazement that anyone would be interested in a girl like me. Sometimes people's reactions, or lack of them, astonished me.

'Given up with Patrick, then?' she asked shrewdly. I shrugged. I couldn't help still thinking that she was the luckiest girl in the world, well-bred idiocy and an extra stone round her middle notwithstanding. Trish actually talked to Patrick. On a regular basis.

'So what's he really like? You can tell me now I'm seeing someone else,' I prodded. As soon as it was out of my mouth, I regretted it. I felt disloyal to poor Pete. And how much like a lovelorn schoolgirl did I sound? But Trish didn't point and laugh. She actually looked sympathetic. She had a history of having crushes on men who, despite her money and hoity-toity looks, were never going to reciprocate – one had been gay, one was about forty years older than her and married to boot. She had everything going for her, but had still managed, by virtue of being the worst picker since Mrs Bluebeard, to know the pangs of unrequited love from the inside out. I resolved to help her – once I'd drained her of every scrap of information she had that could help me, of course.

'Nice guy, what can I say? Bit of a jack the lad, but cute with it, you know?'

To say I was disappointed with this summary didn't come close. Trish had hardly plumbed the psychological depths, had she? On the other hand, perhaps there wasn't much to dredge up. And that was all to the good. Patrick and I couldn't both be complicated. I knew I was never going to get to the bottom of most of my problems, and that was with the advantage – or disadvantage – of being inside my own head, twenty-four-seven. But I'd been looking for someone interesting, at least.

Then again, maybe I wasn't sending the right canary down the mine. Trish surely wouldn't know fascinating if she tripped over it on the way to the gymkhana. She was on an unconscious mission to piss off her mum and dad, until she finally settled for the stockbroker of all their dreams, and anyone who fit the current slightly off-kilter bill was fine with her. Patrick, it seemed, was not rebellion material so she didn't find him intriguing. But for me, that was perfect. I'd had all the living on the wrong side of the tracks that anyone could take.

'What does he actually like doing? Any idea about evenings, weekends? Of course, I'm pretty busy with my boyfriend,' I said, offhand, as I'd practised in front of the mirror. It was crystal clear what I was really asking. Did Patrick have a girlfriend? But on this, Trish could not enlighten me.

'Doesn't mention any *particular* evening or weekend plans,' she said, with heavy irony. 'I'd say he's single.'

'Really? Why would you say that? Why?'

'Whoa, give me room to breathe,' she joked. I was nowhere near her, but instantly I drew even further away, put my hands round my coffee for support. It wasn't like me to crowd someone physically. As a rule, I kept rigidly to my own personal space and was grateful – and surprised – when others followed suit. But I'd been yearning to hear this for so long.

I took a breath. Tried to pretend her answer didn't matter all that much. Started fidgeting, and promptly knocked over the salt cellar. I threw some over my left shoulder while Trish looked on in surprise. She was too rich to need superstitions to prop herself up. Abruptly, I gave up with the insouciance. I wasn't fooling anyone, least of all myself. 'Come on, Trish. What do you mean?'

Trish, annoyingly composed herself, decided to take pity on me at last. 'Sometimes his shirts aren't that well ironed. Shoes not polished. Bit scruffy. But not because he doesn't have clean clothes, more like he just can't always be bothered to iron a shirt in the morning.'

'That's it? That's what you base him being single on?' I was incredulous.

Trish shrugged her shoulders. 'Doubt me if you like, but that's the kind of thing that tells. If he were living with someone, she'd be ironing his shirts. Especially at the beginning of a relationship. At the very least, she'd be telling him he looked a mess.' I was intrigued by this insight into the role of ironing in the courtship rituals of the middle and upper classes. Needless to say, it hadn't figured heavily where I came from.

'That's not to say he's not getting any, though,' Trish added her bombshell slyly.

'Wait, really? How do you know?' I was agog again.

Trish smirked. She knew she had my attention now. 'Couple of times, he's turned up to work in the same shirt twice. Looking pretty grey in the face as well. Heavy nights and I'd say he definitely got lucky, went back to hers, whoever she might have been.'

I was silent for a moment, gutted. But I rallied myself. What had I expected, a monk? It was good that he had some experience, I told myself. And it didn't matter to me now, did it? I couldn't help asking the obvious, though. 'No . . . repeat performances, though, you think?' I asked coyly.

'Doesn't look that way. Aren't you shocked, him being out on the razzle on a school night?'

I paused for a moment. A school night? I'd heard the phrase, used ironically by people my age. It hadn't really been a thing in our household. No night was a school night, or every night was – take your pick, it meant the same. The razzle, though. That went on, regular as clockwork.

I managed a smile. 'He's a scamp. Good for him. As long as he doesn't get hooked up.'

Trish shot me a glance. 'And how, exactly, are you going to stop him?'

She had a point. From her perspective, my interest looked futile and my ability to control the situation was negligible. Yet I couldn't crush down the tiny little spark inside me that was wishing, even now, that the next time Patrick did couple up, it would be with me.

I knew it was ridiculous. I knew I should concentrate on what I did have, my relationship with Pete. Pete, with whom I was having so much fun. Pete, who had given me my first taste of a real love affair. But not long after that chat with Tricia in the canteen, I started to have that doomy feeling that things were somehow going wrong.

Ironic that I'm even saying this, given what happened between me and Patrick later. But still, you know the signs, don't you? When you're in a relationship, and suddenly things go from smooth and harmonious, to bumps in the road. You start to realise that you're more different than you thought. That you might never see eye to eye. Well, of course that wasn't me. I'd always known that Pete and I were worlds apart. The thing was, I'd hoped I'd be able to prevent him from seeing the same thing. But it wasn't really working anymore. And I sort of wanted to get in there first. I was fragile, and I knew it would be a blow if he was the one to walk away. So I decided it was better to do it myself.

I dithered about ways to administer the *coup de grâce*. Fifty ways to leave your lover, and all that. Slip out the back, Jack. That had a certain appeal – no awkward conversations, no music to face, no recriminations. But Pete and I had such a very nice time together. I owed him an explanation.

All the time I was working up to it, I was wondering if I should just keep things going a little longer. Maybe I was imagining his restlessness, his occasional recoil from the things I said. Wasn't I just cheating myself of a few more of those pleasant weekends, drifting about, play-acting at love?

In the end, deciding to do the deed and actually getting it finished did involve quite a time lag. Normally, I made a decision and that was it, job done. But this time I was dallying. True, there was another person involved, and that complicated matters. Usually I only had myself to worry about, and I was now beginning to see that was quite a luxury.

In a way, I'd been gearing up to this from the moment I met Pete. It had never been meant to last. It had been a means to an end, I told myself. But in fact, I knew I was in deeper than I'd ever wanted to be. And I was worried that it was all going to hurt. A lot.

Chapter 21

Now

Becca

Becca lurched back from her screen, hands behind her head. She moved a little too fast and the wheels on her chair shunted backwards, so she had to grab the desk gracelessly and haul herself in again. It quite destroyed her moment.

For, as moments go, it was a biggie. She'd been digging away all this time, trying to find something to latch on to. She'd felt convinced something didn't add up in this case. Yes, that woman – Louise Bridges – had been dry-eyed, and that went against the conventions. But it had been more than that. Christ, Becca herself was no slavish follower of norms, you could see that just by looking at her. Whatever Tom said, she really didn't expect every widow she met to be in floods, wearing black from head to toe, rending their garments . . . whatever that even meant. But she did expect more than she'd got from Louise. A widening of the eyes in horror or astonishment, for instance. A pallor or a flush, some physical sign of inner distress. Could you hear news like that and keep every system in your body under lockdown? Would your pulse remain unchanged? Even if you didn't feel sorrow, you'd feel shock, wouldn't you? And shock showed.

As far as Becca was concerned, there was only one circumstance under which you'd remain unmoved, outwardly and inwardly, on hearing your husband of a large number of years had died. *And that was if you already knew.*

No, that day, there'd been a watchful quality about her, the house, the kids . . . a sense of expectancy.

Becca stopped herself. Did she even know what she was saying? How could a house be watchful? She mustn't get fanciful. That didn't lead anywhere useful. She had to keep her feet on solid ground, not get carried away again. But something was niggling at her. And it wasn't just today's unfinished cream bun in its bag, which was now urgently whispering sweet nothings to her.

That place. It had been scrubbed to within an inch of its life, every surface pristine. As though its secrets had been scoured away. Either the woman was OCD on an epic scale, or she'd cleaned up because she was getting rid of evidence. And the way she'd bundled those papers out of sight. One of them with that logo Becca had recognised. She hadn't been able to help the impulse that had come over her, then. Just this one sheet, swiftly detached from the pile, when Louise Bridges had been stirring that blasted Bolognese. No one had spotted her, not even the kids. Well, they couldn't see for crying, poor mites.

Becca looked from the page to her screen. To the information that was now almost at her fingertips. This was definitely something to go on, a place where she could start. All right, it wasn't everything she needed. Not yet. But this was still epic. It was something real. Wasn't it? Something more than her imagination . . .

But how would it come over to an outsider? She had a habit, she knew, of locking her jaws around things, worrying away at them. Sometimes she got caught up. She remembered her mother's wary eyes, the other night.

Was she doing it again? But she didn't feel the same, didn't feel weighed down, as she had during that sad, dreary time before. If anything, she felt buoyed up. On a mission.

Was this enough, with her suspicions, to justify another trip to the house? See whether things were usually as pristine at Number 10 Woodwarde Avenue, or whether that display of deep cleanliness had had a more sinister meaning?

She sighed. For her, it felt like a race against time. Without even trying, she knew what Burke's answer would be. Revisiting old, cold cases was not economically sound. No one was jumping up and down saying Patrick Bridges had been killed, therefore it was in no one's interest to prise open this case. If she showed her findings to her partner, he'd be angry first, indifferent afterwards.

But what if she went up a grade or two? Showed the Sarge?

Was a little anomaly enough to get something done? Or should she dig deeper, see whether the ground Louise was standing on would hold, or whether it would develop fissures, then collapse and take those long, long legs down with it?

That was quite a satisfying picture. Becca smirked as she looked around the busy room. Everyone was working, tapping away, having earnest conversations on their headsets or in little knots at the coffee station, a reassuring background hum. No one was watching her. She stuck her head in the white bag again and tore off a tiny chunk of sweetness. Like the bitten stump of the bun, this decision was something she couldn't rush.

Chapter 22

Then

Pete's mother had invited us round for Sunday lunch. Well, she'd asked us loads of times, but he'd finally decided to give in and take me. He'd mentioned it before, but only in an offhand way, as though this was certainly something we wouldn't be doing. I'd been a bit hurt. Even I knew this was a really big deal. Magazines had just about given up on etiquette columns, but meeting the potential in-laws was still reckoned to be a make-or-break moment for a couple. If the future mother-in-law hates you on sight, then you're in for a quite a road ahead.

The fact that he hadn't been sure about showing me off was one of the things that had worried me. Yes, this whole thing had started as something to keep my mind off Patrick, but I'd had such happy times with Pete. I didn't want it to come to an end.

So when he finally said yes to his mum's urgings, I suspected this was some sort of test. Either I would pass it with flying colours, or I imagined it might be curtains. And just when I'd finally got some for my flat, too.

It was a lot of pressure. I knew there would be a lot of things I should or shouldn't do when the epic day came, and I knew there was a fair chance that I'd have no clue what they were. I'd be completely out of my depth. So I was dreading it.

But my sense of curiosity got the better of me. Yes, it was going to be intimidating, but rather than fretting myself silly, maybe I should just go in a spirit of enquiry, like an anthropologist journeying to a far country. My own upbringing had been an ordeal. But maybe it wasn't always like that? Watching the interactions of a normal family would be a total novelty and I might end up learning a lot. After all, Pete's reaction to my flat had been quite a wake-up call. I'd thought it was fine, and he'd nearly run off screaming. If anything went wrong at this lunch, I would analyse the problem and learn, as ever, from my mistakes.

Most daunting of all, the place turned out to be huge, the size of a small castle. We got out at a station on the edge of town, a place I'd never been before. Off we went, wending our way through roads that got posher and posher, while the houses got further and further apart. By the time we reached Pete's family home, you couldn't see anything of the houses at all, they were hidden behind huge walls with overhanging trees. It was making me feel a bit sick, and we hadn't even got inside.

Once we were in, I relaxed a little bit. The place was pretty filthy, all the furniture looked old and dusty and, frankly, so did Pete's family. There were dogs running everywhere and the place smelt odd.

But Pete's mum was all set to love me already. He'd told me that and I'd taken it at face value. Well, she had ample reason to be grateful to me. She'd seen the miraculous change I'd wrought in her son, from dandruffy twit to a smartly turned-out and very attractive, almost-finished product. I sometimes wondered why she hadn't done it herself – just a quiet 'no, love' when he turned up in preposterous clothes and a quick jaunt down the problem hair aisle at the supermarket. Not exactly onerous. An afternoon's work. But once we got to their house, I realised exactly where all Pete's problems had sprung from.

Don't get me wrong; his mum was lovely. But dress sense? Nope. It wasn't happening. All right, my own look had gone through a thorough re-tuning recently, but my original gear, though appalling, was better than the get-up Pete's mum, Daphne, had on. Her cardigan was stretched out of shape, as though the dogs had got hold of it and worried it half to death, while the floral dress beneath it was as saggy as a fly-tipped mattress.

I felt the instinctive contempt that the young and beautiful have for less perfect specimens. Even now, knowing as I do that gravity is a force to be reckoned with and that keeping lithe in middle age is no mean feat, I still look back on Daphne and can't help a little tut.

As usual, I was missing the point. Daphne just didn't care about clothes. She considered herself above them, in a bluestocking way that I had never encountered until then. But she was a lovely, warm person, and she'd brought up a great son. The way that she welcomed me, literally with open arms, terrified and thrilled me. I wasn't used to displays of affection from motherly types, to put it mildly. In fact, I wasn't sure I knew any, aside from Jen, who was around my age and childless. My own mother had effortlessly body-swerved the role and considered female friends or relatives to be too much like competition for scarce resources. Her reaction to me as I grew and developed was poisonous enough. So I was unprepared to be dragged into the bosom of any family. But I knew from the moment that I stepped over the threshold into Pete's friendly, crowded, busy home, that Daphne actually wanted me for a daughter-in-law.

It was a lot to take in. I just tried to absorb everything around me, and stack away the impressions to work through later, when I wasn't quite so overloaded. There was a lot going on in Daphne's house. First, even though it was as big as a barn, it seemed to be full to the brim with people. Maybe because they all had braying voices and talked over each other incessantly. Pete had two younger brothers who both had girlfriends, one already with a child in tow. Then there was Pete's dad, a bit paunchy and vague – an older version of his son – who haw-hawed instead of speaking.

Haw-haw, how d'ye do, young Louise? Haw-haw-haw. Was the haw-haw laughter or some sort of speech impediment? I had no idea. There were a couple of other relatives who'd been gathered just to meet me. Yes, me turning up was quite the occasion.

I could tell, immediately, that I didn't fit in. I was too silent, too uptight, trying much too hard. I was completely overdressed in my simple column of a silk dress. I was also immaculately made up, my nails the perfect length and matching my outfit. Bang on, I'd thought. But no. Wrong, wrong, wrong. I'd misjudged it, as usual. I looked absurd, as though I was going to the wedding of a minor Royal, or at least off to Ascot. And now I hated myself even more than usual.

The other women had bare faces, no jewellery unless it was massive clashing beads or a nasty brooch. Pete's dad's jumper had literal holes in the elbows. I didn't get it. Everyone here was richer than generations of my family put together. Yet they dressed almost as badly as anyone on my old estate. I suddenly saw that Pete, in his down-at-heel 'before' version, would have slotted in just fine. Now, he looked bizarrely overdressed. I'd thought I was saving him. Turned out I'd done him no favours at all. I even saw some of the relatives having a bit of a snigger over his nice shirt with the Ralph Lauren logo – so new it still had the creases – but luckily then it was time to eat and he steered me quickly away from them.

I was shocked at the way they picked at the food. I always devoured my meals as though the four-minute warning had just sounded and this was my chance to stock up on calories to see me through the nuclear winter. This lot took a forkful, waved it around, then put it down, while talking, talking, talking. Everything was congealing on the chipped, mis-matched plates. I thought with a pang of regret of my own recently acquired set of china. I wasn't at all sure this horrible old stuff was properly clean.

There were mountains of food on the table, all being ignored;

roast potatoes, giant slabs of meat, oceans of gravy, despite the heat. But no ketchup. I wasn't sure I could choke it all down without. I tried to use the gravy, but despite its fatty darkness it tasted of nothing.

While they ate slowly, they drank fast, sluicing away oceans of red wine. I was astonished. Where I had lived, having this many bottles meant an automatic party, which in turn meant me staying in my room for as long as humanly possible. I certainly didn't trust myself to start matching any of this lot glass for glass, even Pete. When I drank a spritzer with Jen, we sipped away and I moved on to water as quickly as I could. I'd seen what abandoning control looked like. What if I turned into my mother, blotchy and itching for a fight? I knew I wouldn't, but the prospect raised my anxiety levels. I fixed my eyes on the nasty plate.

The conversation was full of in-jokes, about an endless succession of people I'd never met. Fast, affectionate, baffling. When that finished, suddenly we were onto politics instead. I stayed quiet. Pete was sitting next to me. He kept trying to hold my hand under the table – adorable, I know – but then he'd get involved in some quasi-joshing shouting match with one or other of the brothers and would pull away. Plus, his hands were getting sweaty in the overheated kitchen of his mum's house.

Though the house was huge, the kitchen was tiny. Whereas I would have knocked through, with my newfound competence at interior design, they'd kept everything as it had been in Pete's great-grandmother's day, when this matchbox had been plenty good enough for the servants. Despite all their modern political talk, I suspected there were a lot of things they'd never change.

The windows were running with condensation, as something bubbled away unattended on the hob and the table groaned with cooling vegetables. My forearm kept sticking to the oilcloth on the table, which was patterned with the same green willow boughs that twined around the curtains and even the wallpaper, a posh take on a jungle. After a while I sat back, tried to let the whole thing wash over me. Though things were so different here, the noise, mess and chaos were bringing back bad memories. I started zoning out.

Pete mouthed '*You OK?*' to me, which was kind. It made me think that maybe I should come back to the present, make the effort. Plunge in with the chat. I turned to the girlfriend next to me, who was attached to the older of Pete's two younger brothers. She had long swathes of dark silky hair hanging around her face, and a consumptive pallor. 'Where do you work?' I asked her.

'Oh! I'm at Oxford,' she said, her tone seeming to imply that I really should have known this.

'OK, right,' I said, and that would have been that, if she hadn't seemed to feel she needed to ask me something back.

'And where are you?' At my blank look, she clarified, stretching her eyes wide. 'At uni?'

'Oh, I'm working,' I said, turning away. But she persisted.

'Yes, but where did you go? Before working?'

'What do you mean?' Was she asking which pubs I'd frequented? Or wine bars? I didn't get it.

'Which uni?' she said, as though to a simpleton. To be fair, I was giving a good impression of one.

'I didn't go to uni,' I said. At that moment there was a hush around the table. Though I couldn't swear I'd caused it, it felt as though I had. After a brief pause, both Pete's mother and father started up conversations.

'As I was saying to Peter . . .'

'Have you noticed that damned buddleia is sprouting all over the . . .?'

Now I felt overdressed *and* stupid. I'd read about people like this, I'd devoured Nancy Mitford, I'd longed to be in the Hons cupboard with them all. But I'd missed the point. You couldn't join this kind of gang. You had to be born into it. And I quite clearly hadn't been.

Pete's dad was next to give it a try. 'So, Bridges, that's your, ah, name, I gather? So, Louise, you're bound to know the solicitor, Geoff Bridges, in the centre of town. Related?'

'No, no, I don't know him,' I said. It wasn't the moment to admit that my family usually tried to give all branches of the law a wide berth.

'Or the Hertfordshire Bridges? Cousins of your lot, weren't they?' He swivelled, at this point, to look at the pallid girlfriend, who peered back at me with renewed interest, followed swiftly by polite scepticism. 'Anything to do with your family, Louise?'

My scalp was prickling by now and my face was the colour of the absent ketchup. Though there was no way they could trace me back to the shame of my roots, I couldn't sit there a moment longer.

I mumbled something, eyes on my plate, which was still lumpy with cold, dry potatoes. I risked a look at Pete. 'The toilet?' He looked at me blankly. I thought again. 'The *loo*?' I mouthed desperately.

It took me ages to find it in the maze of tattily decorated corridors, and when I did I couldn't flush the ancient thing – it still had a chain you needed to yank. The soap was a half-moon that looked pre-war and I was sure the stiff sage green towel had never been washed. By the time I sidled back, having done my best to avoid the smelly dogs milling about the huge entrance hall, the conversation had moved on, thank God. I suspected Pete had warned his dad to lay off. Anyway, everyone was up in arms that somebody had done something heinous, politically speaking, and I still didn't care who or what.

Pete's older brother had a baby, who was being pretty much ignored while people argued about taxes they could obviously afford to pay without even thinking twice. The small creature was jammed in a highchair, her mother laminating the little face with gloop from a bowl. This gloop, the mum told us excitedly, was organic, locally sourced and sieved by her own fair hand. She looked prouder of this fact than of the little mite herself.

The stuff looked like the sort of gruel Oliver Twist probably got in the workhouse. He'd wanted more, this baby definitely didn't. Scarcely any made it past the tiny pink mouth, furled tighter than a rosebud. The mother didn't seem to notice, gesticulating about the Liberals or the Tories or the who-knew-what and throwing gobs of the vile stuff around. After a while she moved on to mashed banana, with more success.

I edged away, mindful of the dress I'd thought was so suitable only hours before, and which was now just absurd. Still, I didn't want to pay to have baby-gloop dry-cleaned off it. On my other side was the pale brainiac, lucky cow. What I would have given for her chances. Nothing to do but read books for three years, then a job where people would chuck money at her. She'd be promoted when she asked, unlike me, still trying to clamber up to the first floor.

I wracked my brains for possible intersections between her world and mine, and came up with nothing. She couldn't have stuck my life for a moment. But I still had to start some sort of conversation. If I stayed mute, I might attract the attention of Pete's dad again, and I didn't want that. I cast around, looked at her closely for inspiration. Ah. An obvious topic sprang to my eye. 'When's it due, then?' I asked, with a smile of hastily manu-factured interest, flicking my eyes down to her spongy stomach. She looked at me in consternation, then seemed to choke on a spud. Suddenly she pushed up from the table and left the room. There was a babble of excited voices. Pete's mum cut across them and said, down the table, 'So, this job of yours, Louise? Tell us all about it.'

Thank God, something I *was* interested in talking about. I explained it all as briefly as I could, though by the end I did notice Pete's younger brother jogging his elbow and whispering something. I shut up abruptly and the conversation moved on, an unstoppable juggernaut of noise and laughter.

In the moment of quiet, I felt something tapping my shoulder.

I turned irritably, only to see the baby leaning perilously out of its highchair and patting me with its tiny paw, which was so liberally smeared with mashed banana that the browning substance oozed between its starfish fingers. For a second, I was incensed. My dress! But then the little creature smiled at me, and I felt myself falling into bottomless blue eyes, round and shiny with love. I couldn't help smiling back and she gurgled with delight and patted me again. All of a sudden my chest felt tight and my eyes stung, and it wasn't even because I was thinking about my silk georgette. Being the cause of such simple pleasure felt like winning first prize in a competition I hadn't even known someone like me could enter.

I'd not thought about children until that moment. I had severe doubts over whether I was competent to look after Mephisto, and he was a cat who could probably open his own tins and change his litter himself if he had to. A baby, though. I'd never dreamed I'd have one – be allowed one, almost. But maybe I was looking at it all through my mother's eyes.

There was the fear, too, that I'd be as bad at it all as she had been. But again, it would be actively hard for me, or anyone else, to be that dreadful. It was a huge responsibility, for sure. But it was something that, if I put my mind to it, I suddenly knew I could do well. And now I could see the joys to be reaped from it. A smile was enough to unblock something – either my ovaries or my heart, I wasn't sure which.

My eyes filled. I had to turn away from the baby, babbling away at me, and stare at my empty plate.

'Oh! Would you like some more, dear?' Daphne asked, her forehead pleated.

I shook my head and was about to speak when Pete leapt to his feet and started to gather up plates, though no one else seemed to have finished. Then we were on to the next course. The wan girlfriend came back for this, though she ostentatiously dragged her chair as far away from mine as possible.

We were now onto what I'd grown up calling the 'sweet', if I was lucky enough to get it. I now thought of it as 'dessert', but I knew, thanks to Jen and Trish, not to mention Nancy Mitford, I should really be calling it pudding. All those who think that the English language is easy to pick up should just ponder this one little situation for a moment. What you say is as accurate as writing your income and your social class on your forehead. Most people don't care. They've made peace with wherever they've ended up in the pack. But I suppose I still thought I had plenty of room to travel upwards. And that meant I hated giving away so many clues about where I'd started off, as soon as I picked up a spoon.

Pete's family were definitely in the pudding camp. Anyway, whatever they wanted to name it, I didn't want any of it, particularly when I found out what it was – spotted dick. The very thing that had been steaming the place up throughout our main course, making me feel as though we were in a Chinese laundry. A dish that I thought had gone out with the ark – and probably sunk it, too. From the *oohs* and *ahhs* of the boys, you'd have thought that Pete's mum had learned how to spin straw into gold. But no. Instead, she'd found the formula for translating white flour into concrete, as far as I was concerned.

I'd been trying very hard throughout this accursed meal, but I wasn't going anywhere near this. As it was, I didn't even get a chance to refuse it. No one was asked, great big heaped steaming bowls of the stuff were just passed around the table from hand to hand. It was like musical chairs. When one finally stopped in front of me, I gaped at the size of the thing. Bright yellow custard – straight out of a tin, though who was I to be snobby about such things – and another tin, a green one of golden syrup, getting stickier by the second, was now circulating like the port would here at dinnertime, which they probably called supper. Even the baby soon had syrup all over her chops, despite the fuss her mother had made over her ghastly organic gruel. I was the only one not making inroads into this mess.

At this point, Pete sent me what could only be described as an exasperated glance. He'd been such a love, sticking up for me through what had rapidly turned into quite an ordeal. I had expected him to gamely continue to fight my corner, or even be oblivious to the fact that I wasn't melding with his family. But everyone has a certain length of tether available. And it appeared we'd come to the end of his.

In a way, it was the neatest possible way of ending things.

I could see, from the moment we clicked the heavy gothic front door shut on his family, where we were going. His brothers, their girlfriends, the sticky baby and Pete's mum and dad were all still round the table, sloshing wine into their glasses and putting their very posh world to righter rights. They were still all talking at once and scoffing from a huge tin of biscuits. I was relieved to be out in the fresh air, away from the smell of dog and dinner. Pete, though, walked slowly down the road, hands hunched in his pockets. He was just far enough away from me that I couldn't easily link arms or touch him in one of the ways he'd always loved, magic him back onside like one of the tiny nimble footballers he loved to watch on TV.

I felt for Pete, I really did. He wanted to be there, in the grand smelly house, with his posh loud family. He wanted me to be one of the Hertfordshire Bridges and to love spotted dick and be a pretend socialist with a trust fund. But I couldn't do it.

Chapter 23

Now

Louise

You could say that my life now is constrained. Here am I, in my black, with my mauve bag, racing around, delivering my children to this activity or that. Then we go home, and we're alone. Just the three of us.

We have the odd break with Jill, and I admire her more and more. She no longer looks at me askance, she accepts me for what I am. And what I am is her grandchildren's mother.

She's faced up to loss. She's stared death down and decided to live on, even with her child in the grave.

She used to wonder, I know that full well. I dare say she thought Patrick could do much better. I have no doubt that he considered his own options, and I know he regularly scrutinised other people's. But now . . . now that I am black and purple like a bruise, and she is grey-haired and soft as one of the squirrels in her garden, we have come to a strange accord.

To you, my days may seem empty. Pointless, even. What do I do for myself, after all? What am I supposed to do *with* myself? Those business dinners, drinks, supper parties, all the networking, it's gone now. The network is down. I only ever had value as an adjunct, an accessory – ironic, given my propensity to get accessories wrong. Now that Patrick is not there to be sought out, to be used or to use them in turn, these people don't want to know.

But that suits me fine. They were a means to an end. It was all for Patrick, for our house, for the children – and now he's not here, I don't need them any more than they need me.

I'm happy to watch a box set, cosied up on the sofa with the kids. And when they're in bed, I head for another world with my books, as I always have. And I'm quite content there.

Being alone is a lot simpler, in many ways, than living a life that's not quite the right shape, even if you thought you were cutting your cloth to suit yourself.

Chapter 24

Now

Becca

Becca took a sidelong glance at Burke. His hands were on the wheel, ten to two. Like everything he did, it was by the book, sensible, measured. She wondered for a second whether he had the same approach to sex, like that episode in *Friends* where the girls work out all the numbers, shouting 'Seven! Seven! Seven!' She'd loved it on Netflix, binge-watched the lot. She snorted.

Burke glanced over at her for a moment, careful not to take too much time from the road. 'You all right?' he asked.

She stifled her smile. ''Course. Just thinking . . .'

'You don't want to do that, Becs. You really don't.' Burke's humour was heavy, as heavy as his hands as they crashed down on the gears, changed up. They were out on patrol. A spring day. Gardens flashed by and she caught the fresh green scent of the first mown lawn of the season through the open window. Hard to believe there could ever be trouble here. This was the plush bit of their manor, where nothing much ever happened, except for a moan or two when someone's kid's 21st party kept the neighbours up past 10 p.m. or a housewife lost control of an SUV when parking.

But of course, it was also Louise Bridges' neck of the woods. And, even if Becca hadn't been doing some digging, the sight of these homes, with their perfectly raked drives and their pruned rose bushes, would have stirred her memories of that night not long ago. Where did these people find the time to keep everything looking just so? Becca's own flat, the size of a cardboard box and still the biggest she was ever likely to have – unless all her mother's dreams came true and some kind, blind millionaire whisked her away from *all this* – was a comfortable muddle. It hadn't looked like Louise's place, well, ever, but certainly not since the day she'd officially recovered, got away from her mum, moved in and scattered her possessions around. To her, a too-tidy home suggested an owner with something to hide. She pursed her lips.

'Seeing this, all so perfect, doesn't it make you wonder what's going on behind . . .' Becca waved a hand at a stretch of privet hedging, as expertly trimmed as a porn star's bikini line. Or were they all bald down there now? Their colleagues in Vice, the ones with the haunted eyes, would know for sure, though it wouldn't be the grown women that stopped them sleeping.

Burke lifted his eyes from the road for about a second, glanced to the left and back again. He shook his head briefly, though whether in denial or just in exasperation, Becca wasn't sure.

'Keep your mind on the job, Becs. Always off at a tangent, you are. Does it get you anywhere? No, it doesn't. Just takes you longer to get where we're supposed to go, in my book.' Having delivered his pronouncement, Burke grabbed the wheel a little harder. As far as he was concerned, that was it. Discussion over.

Becca subsided in her seat for a while, mulling. She wasn't allowing her partner to shut her down, that wasn't it at all. She was just thinking.

Suddenly, something occurred to her, a way to approach Burke that might get the right response. 'You know, that night . . . I always knew something was wrong. Something about the place, the way that woman was. The way she wasn't shocked, not even a bit surprised really.'

106

'*Becs . . .*' Burke let her name out with an exasperated exhalation of air.

'No, look, hear me out, all right? Just listen for a second. We've got time, we're stuck here in the car, aren't we? We might as well talk at the same time as driving.'

'Driving me mad, you are,' said Burke, signalling left at the junction, checking both ways, catching her eye for just a moment, but resigned rather than angry. He was giving her the green light, surely as the car itself was cleared to move smoothly forward. He could drive, Burke, she'd give him that.

'The table. There was all the homework and stuff. But she'd been cooking, hadn't she? Remember?'

Burke seemed to sniff, recalling the sharp oregano of the sauce on the boil. The garlic, onion and meat, hanging heavy in the air. 'Yep. Smelled good.'

'Yes. And among the textbooks and all that sh . . . stuff,' she corrected herself. Burke wasn't keen on swearing at the best of times. 'Well, there were knives, forks, plates. Like she'd been getting ready to set the table.'

'Like you do,' said Burke heavily. 'Not a crime, Becs. Even if you're Mrs Tidy like she was. You might not bother much, but lots of people like to keep the place neat.'

Becca looked at him. Nothing like being judged as a slob by your colleagues, was there? She vowed to tidy her desk. One day.

'Yes, fine, whatever. But the plates. How many?'

'I dunno. A stack. Enough for the kids?'

'Three. There were three plates. Three. Don't you see what that means?' Becca turned to Burke, eyes wide, pleading. He flicked across to her, irritated. The big flyover was coming up. He had to concentrate. And he didn't need this.

'Go on. Enlighten me.'

'*She already knew he wasn't coming home.*'

107

Chapter 25

Then

Pete's house had seemed a long way from the station even when we'd ambled along together a few hours before. Now, on the return journey, with our relationship falling apart at the seams quicker than his mother's cardigan, it seemed twice as much of a hike. The big houses with their thick privet hedges were expensively silent, but I could imagine smug residents sniggering at me over their Sunday papers, watching me retreat, beaten. My stupid silk dress with its banana stains rustled angrily as I marched along. Pete's shoulders were hunched.

I hadn't fitted in. That was my simple crime, that was why both Pete and I knew it wouldn't work, couldn't go any further. But what he didn't realise was that it was *always* my crime. I'd never fitted in anywhere. My fear now was that I never would. It had taken so much work to get this close – and then it had turned out that I had never really been close at all. I'd worked so hard to be this version of me. How could it still not be right?

It was like being five at school all over again. Or seven. Or nine. Or eleven. No one had ever wanted to play with me. I'd understood why, at one level, but that didn't make it any easier to bear. There was something very different about me. I knew it, and somehow they did too. I wasn't sure how they were able to tell. Maybe it was the smoke. That always clung to me. In many ways it seemed the least of my mother's bad habits. Or maybe it was the way I held myself. Maybe it was the twist in my smile, something flitting behind my eyes. It was obvious that I knew too much, but it wasn't the sort of delicious secret that the girls queued up behind the loos to share. It was the sort that no one wanted any part of. Ever. The sort that I haven't spoken of, even now. I didn't fit in. Couldn't. Wasn't ever going to, no matter what I did.

Granted, I never had any of the paraphernalia that eased the way into other girls' hearts either – the must-have toys of the moment, the right Barbie, the school bag everyone else swung from confident shoulders. They boasted about pinching their mums' Fenjal bath bubbles, their clothes smelt of Comfort fabric conditioner, they skipped home to find their mums had made their favourite flavour of Angel Delight. I reeked of cigarettes and stale beer, the Chanel No. 5 of our house, and put on the first thing to hand – which was the last thing I'd taken off, or had yanked off me, the night before.

But the real problem was that I wasn't a child in the way the others were. I wasn't innocent, couldn't play happy little games. They seemed pointless to me. When you have to think of strategies to save your hide every moment you're at home – keep your back to the wall, make sure you can see the doorway, line of escape clear, listen for the sound of footsteps approaching, get to know where everyone is in the flat just by the creaks of the floorboards – then playing a game of kiss-chase in the playground seems a lot less compelling. More of the same, but on a strictly amateur level. Why would I bother with that?

Packed lunches and snacks were a problem, too. Sometimes there would be food left over at home, but it wasn't the stuff the others had – the neat equilateral triangles of Mother's Pride, carefully packed with grated cheese that drifted onto the tarmac like confetti, or smeared with disturbingly fecal peanut butter.

The girls would open up their Tupperware boxes and moan. 'Ham again! I hate it.' I'd sit there on the wall, swinging my legs, the purple bruises single spies on my shins, marching up to the battalions under my skirt. I'd pretend my stomach wasn't rumbling. On the rare occasions when there had been a big takeaway the night before, I'd sneak a foil container into my school bag, eat it in the loo. I couldn't risk being seen with something so different, so wrong. I worried about the smell of Chinese food clinging, but I needn't have. They called me the Ashtray. My mother's nervous Benson & Hedges followed me around and masked everything else.

Depending on how hungry I was, I'd forage in the lockers at breaktime. But it was demeaning. I'd try not to, and not just because there was an occasional witch-hunt orchestrated by the teachers to 'catch the sneak thief'. I hated these. Yes, I was burning with guilt, but I was good at hiding that emotion, as well as every other. And I sort of felt justified. These kids didn't need lunch *and* snacks; it was plain to see there was over-indulgence going on. Even when I was a kid, there was always a fatty in every class. Not like now, when there are three, four or five and it's become normal. But I'd generally pick the blubbery kid's food, reckoning they could do without it. The odd Penguin biscuit, bag of crisps. But I, of all people, should have known, just from watching Mum. Like any other addict, they were the ones likely to kick up the biggest fuss when deprived.

I used to dream about having a mum who'd pick up a pack of those Penguins in the shop, slip one in my lunchbox every day. The type of mum in the ads who'd smile indulgently at her daughter as they washed up together with mild green washing-up liquid, or wandered through fields of daisies hand in hand with hair gleaming from the right shampoo. An ad featuring towers of empty cans balanced on top of the telly? Spoons sticky with stuff I instinctively knew I shouldn't try to eat? They didn't tend to appear much on primetime shows. And the used condoms splatted on the settee like stranded jellyfish? When I was very small I thought they might be balloons. Not a mistake you make twice.

Sometimes, if I wasn't starving, I'd wait till I got home, hope Mum still had some money left. Sometimes I'd just stay in the cloakroom anyway, even if I wasn't pinching other people's food. Well, I had no one out there in the rough and tumble of the playground. It was miserable, pretending to be busy in those acres of tarmac. Staying in was forbidden, though, so if I was chivvied out by a teacher, I'd take a book, any book, hide away in a corner, my back always to the wall. Hunched over my portal to a better world, turning the pages, trying to concentrate. Sometimes the other girls would saunter past, giving me curious glances. If anyone did speak to me, I immediately knew they were a loser, too, and the only sensible course of action was to shun them in turn. I became good at lurking. I preferred the lessons to break time. They were less lonely.

So I'd escaped all this, become the beautiful, aloof queen of reception, and now Pete was turning me down? His rejection threatened to reverse the fairy godmother spell I'd woven on myself. It was as if the clock was striking twelve and my beautiful clothes – and my new and improved self – were turning back to rags and rubbish. When I reacted to his tactful attempts to extricate himself, it wasn't him I was fighting, but everyone who'd ever pushed me away. I was angry with him, I was angry with the world. And worst of all, I was angry with myself – for having ever dared to believe I'd be accepted.

Arguments were like life and death for me. Some people can have a nice little row, exchange points of view, come away tidily having considered the opposing side's position, reach a new accord.

Not me.

Every argument is survival. I'm fighting extinction, and it's not pretty. I need to win and I don't really care how I do it. I don't even remember afterwards. All that matters is that the other person backs down, gives in, goes away. It's a scorched earth policy, all right. Like a Russian peasant, I'd much rather burn down my own house than give an inch.

There are loads of things I've bolted on to the basic model of my personality, over time. But some things you just can't unlearn. My childhood was all about survival. The playground, the foraging, the ostracism – that was the easy bit. School was like a rest for me. No one liked me, no one played with me, but I was safe.

It wasn't the same at home. If I didn't win a fight there, then seriously bad stuff would happen to me. Even if I did win, come to that.

'What don't you like about my family?' Pete had said, hands on hips, his new shirt, thanks to me, making him look quite handsome – in my eyes anyway.

It was my starter for ten.

Opening my mouth and letting rip was exhilarating, intoxicating. I didn't risk losing my temper often. But it wasn't just that. I'd felt, when I left my mother's, that I could finally be free. But making the sort of life I wanted had turned into a trap in itself, a new series of rules that always had to be obeyed, that often seemed as arbitrary as hers had been. I couldn't really remember the last time I'd been able to give an honest answer to a question. Building my new life, my persona at the firm, being Pete's perfect girlfriend – none of it had come easy.

Having my say was a rush. I remembered my mother, when the syringe was deep in her arm. The anxiety of buying the stuff, cooking it up, tightening the tourniquet, finding a needle and shoving it in, all washed away as the smack hit her blood and smoothed her struggles into a silky road to oblivion. Was this the same? My rage felt clean, like a purifying fire.

There was no going back, of course. But that was fine. Unlike school, where the people who despised me were round every corner, there was no real danger of me bumping into Pete ever again. We'd ditched the French course once things had got going between us. We'd both achieved our aims – I'd mastered a few bits of conversational chit-chat that might, or might not, come in handy someday if I could ever bear to leave my desk and go on holiday. And Pete had found me. We'd briefly flowered into coupledom. Now that things had collapsed so spectacularly, our worlds would diverge again. He'd go back to politics and pudding and I'd spend my life sighing over Patrick.

I wish I could say I picked myself up, dusted myself down. But it took me quite a time to regroup after the Pete debacle. I always found it difficult when things didn't go to plan. The original scheme, a lifetime ago, had been to parade Pete past the building casually, so Patrick could see that I was desired. Get Tricia to drop a word. This would kindle some sudden enthusiasm for more than a sporadic flirtation which was going nowhere. Then, maybe – I was a little hazy on this point – there would be some kind of boy duel between them, and Patrick, of course, would win my hand.

But that had gone pear-shaped. I'd got much too fond of Pete, had allowed myself to imagine a future with him instead, and had then come a very public cropper in front of his family. All right, an outsider would say the blunders were mine. I'd asked that poor droopy Oxford girlfriend when she was due, for God's sake. And my panic and confusion at being cross-questioned about all those other, better-connected Bridges? Pete's dad had just been doing what his breed did, sussing out connections and allegiances like one of his own dogs sniffing a lamppost, working out where I'd been and where I was going.

Pete's family hadn't meant any harm. They weren't bad people. And for anyone else, the lunch wouldn't have been such a trial. But for me it had been hellish and all I could do was thank my stars that it was over.

I wanted to stop wallowing in this tragedy, to regroup, sort myself out, activate Plan B. But it was hard to gather myself together, push myself onwards. To the extent that Patrick kept walking past, without me even noticing.

113

Until, one day, curiosity got the better of him.

Why does it always work this way? Why is neutrality, or even indifference, so much more seductive than neediness? I suppose we're all a mass of wants, underneath our veneers. More of the same would be overload. But someone who's not bothered. *That's* a challenge.

Patrick was a typical 20-something man. If you'd cut him in two, you'd have seen the testosterone fight its way to the surface. But that didn't stop me from worshipping him. On the contrary, I found his maleness hugely attractive. I was momentarily distracted by the pain of loss, that was all.

It hurt more deeply than I'd imagined possible. Pete had been such a nice guy. There was no denying his kindness, his patience. He'd more or less taught me a new side of human behaviour that I hadn't seen before – a relationship based on gentleness and yes, respect. I'd never, ever seen this in play, let alone experienced it. Life with my mother had not braced me for love.

For now that Pete had left, I saw that was what it was. Or had been. Even the cushions on my sofa mocked me. The whole place looked a whole lot more, well, normal, since his first startled visit. By that, I mean it looked more like other people's houses – a bit of clutter, maybe the odd dirty coffee cup in the sink. Not the forensic cleanliness which had been such a comfort but which I now felt I could relax. A bit. I'd even splashed out and bought a small portable telly for him to watch football on. Luckily my concentration skills were honed enough to tune out the drone of the commentators and roars of the crowd while I read with my head in his lap. Growing up with paper walls will do that for you. And if I did get bored, well, he'd been easy to distract from even the most crucial games.

There was a framed photo of me and Pete on one of my Billy bookcases now. Us, having brunch of course, smiling soppily at each other. A waiter had taken it for us on Pete's fancy camera – no selfies or smartphones back in those dark days. Pete had got it framed for me as a surprise present. A natural homemaker I was not, not back then at any rate, but I was getting to grips with it, studying the art properly.

Pete had also bought me some silly stuff like a teddy bear, sexy dressing gown, mugs with hearts on, scented candles that I had never lit. The teddy I'd chucked in the bin as soon as I made it back from his mum's, together with the candles. The rest of the clobber, including the photo, I was in two minds over. For now, I'd put our grinning faces under the bed as an interim measure.

It was this I'd been mulling over when Patrick sauntered past. I must have been looking unusually wistful. And of course, I was taking no notice of him. He did a bit of a double take and came back to the desk. 'Cheer up,' he said. 'Might never happen.'

As any woman will tell you, there are few things more irritating than a man telling you to perk yourself up, mask your legitimate feelings, put on a smile just for his pleasure. I flashed him a look that could have scorched paint. But it was Patrick. What was I to do? Not much choice. His limpid baby blues held my cross stare. I melted, and sighed just a little.

'Seriously, everything all right, babe?' Patrick couldn't have been more attentive.

Was this all I'd had to do? If I'd known lovelorn was what he was after, I would have kept a ready-peeled onion under my desk all along, to get the tears flowing just as he prowled past.

I smiled tremulously. 'Yeah. Just been a bit of a difficult day, you know?' I wasn't sure how far to push this. My low mood seemed to have triggered some sort of chivalry in him, but would he tire of this new game if I laid it on with a trowel? Or would I miss my moment if I pulled myself together too quickly? I thought about it. Here I'd been, sitting with a pert smile on my face forever, and I'd got absolutely nowhere with him, aside from those few flirtatious chats, which had meant everything to me and nothing to him. Now I was showing signs of distress, he was all over me – relatively speaking – like a rash.

I did the only thing I could. I thought hard of Pete, and particularly that horrific, humiliating Sunday lunch, and a tear was soon trickling its way down my cheek. It wasn't hard to cry, it still hurt. I looked mistily up at Patrick, and the perfect drop fell onto my counter. I wiped it up automatically. He looked back into my eyes, and I could almost feel his heart twist.

'Tell you what, babe. Got to get to my desk now but why don't I take you for a drink later, cheer you up? Can't have my favourite girl so sad, can I?'

I nodded my head, not trusting myself to speak, and then had to stop myself from going on nodding, like one of those toy dogs in the back of a stuffy family car. With a final wink, he loped away.

As soon as he was out of sight, I flopped back in my chair, clutching my empty coffee mug, feeling as though I'd run a marathon.

Chapter 26

Now

Becca

'Look, Becs. We can't arrest someone on the basis of the number of plates they have on their table. I sometimes think you're not quite the full . . . I mean, get real.'

'I'm not saying that, I'm not. But don't you see? It proves something. She *knew*. She knew he wasn't going to be back. She knew what was coming.'

'It doesn't prove a thing! You're being ridiculous. He could have rung her, said he was going to be late, was going to grab something on the way home. Or maybe he had an evening do he had to go to. These businessmen, they're always entertaining clients.'

'Is that what you call it?' said Becca darkly.

Burke waited a beat then shook his head. 'Do I even want to know what you mean by that? You've got such a downer on that case, haven't you? I don't know why you can't just accept it for what it is. The man died. End of.'

'It's hardly that though, is it? I mean, the circumstances? You couldn't call it clear-cut, could you? Come on, with all your experience.' Here Becca crossed her fingers, hoping the flattery would get her past Burke's mental block about the lovely Louise. 'Surely you've never seen a death quite like this one before?'

There was a pause. Becca, despite herself, peered hard at Burke.

He looked as though he was thinking things through. To her astonishment, he started indicating left, then pulled the car over, flicked the ignition off and turned to her. Trust him not to want to do two things at once – cogitate *and* drive. She waited, holding her breath.

'All right then, say you have a point? What do we do then?'

Becca, bubbling with elation like a shaken bottle of Tesco's Finest Cava, tried not to show her excitement. This was major. He'd finally admitted that Louise Bridges, perfumed and perfect though she was, actually stank to high heaven. 'Well, we can look into it, can't we?'

Burke's pitying glance was like a torrent of cold water on her head. 'That's where you're wrong, girl,' he said pityingly. 'Too late now.'

'What do you mean?' Becca was on the edge of her seat.

'It's already gone upstairs. My mate Johno. CID.'

And just like that, the fizzy feeling was back.

Chapter 27

Then

I'd only gone and done it. A date with Patrick. I was light-headed. I badly needed to splash some cold water on my face. Who was I kidding, I needed to take a bath in ice. I wasn't sure if it was euphoria, or the fact that, again, I'd scarcely been able to breathe when he'd been near. I'd have to get that sorted, or I'd pass out on our evening together. All thoughts of Pete were relegated to the very back of my mind – for now.

Date! There was so much I needed to do, and so little time. Plus, I was at work. The phone would keep ringing; clients would keep arriving. Didn't they know I had far better things to do with my time? A date with Patrick, and I was stuck in these clothes and with this nail varnish and hardly any make-up and I hadn't even washed my hair, shaved my legs, plucked my eyebrows . . . My to-do list was endless and none of it involved my job. I cursed the way I'd listlessly decided to skimp on my routine this morning, little realising that smidgeon of lovelorn laziness would come back to haunt me.

Before I could spiral out of control, I gave myself a talking-to. Men never noticed clothes, or hair, or make-up. It was bodies that got them going. And it was my job to make sure that Patrick saw enough of mine – but not too much. Not on a first date.

It was lucky that I was wearing a fitted blouse, in a silky well-cut satin that had cost my last pay packet. My pencil skirt clung in all the right places and my shoes were simple but deadly black patent heels. Although the current fashion was for huge chunky jewellery, I was bucking the trend with a simple strand of pearls that might not have fooled an oyster but were fine with anything further ashore. If I undid one or two extra buttons, accidentally on purpose, and leaned forward plenty, I was pretty sure that I'd have a captive audience. My earrings were discreet little pearls, surmounted by a small golden bow. The same ones I'd been wearing yesterday, but he wouldn't clock that. Yesterday, I had been beneath his notice. Today was my lucky day. I was definitely channelling understated elegance. Would it be wasted on him?

I prayed that he went for classy. If only I'd known more about the kind of girls he'd dated before. Then I could have copied. I wasn't confident when I was trying to get someone to like me for myself. Well, it had never worked. It was much safer, and less painful, to give people what I thought they wanted, instead of asking them to accept me for who I was and am. Because no one wanted that person, and quite right too.

I took deep breaths and hid my nerves away, like I always did. I focused on an easier challenge – staying pristine until the evening. I'd never treated coffee with such arm's length disdain. As for my lunchtime crumbs, I brushed them away with all the feverish enthusiasm of one of Mary Poppin's chimneysweeps.

It's safe to say that by the time the evening came around, I was a jelly. I'd done the best I could in the loos with my make-up, having nipped out at lunchtime to replenish my stocks. I'd searched up and down the high street for an eyelash curler, telling myself it was crucial, though I had one at home and nobody needs two of those beasts. I could say to myself as often as I liked that it didn't matter, Patrick wasn't going to care if my eyelashes sprung up at a forty-five degree angle or managed the full ninety, but that didn't mean I was going to try for anything less than perfection when he came to collect me.

By five, people had started to leave, and by six, almost half of his floor had gone. I was breathless again, waiting. Each time the lift opened, with that characteristic sound like a lover's sigh, I sat to attention, then sagged as another suit walked past that wasn't Patrick. By the time he sauntered out, I'd almost given up hope. But as soon as I caught sight of his face, I knew things weren't good.

He loped along, a slight frown marring that forehead I loved so well, walking fast, distracted. It wasn't a date look. Something was wrong. Hang on a minute, he was walking right past the desk where I'd been sitting, ready and waiting, technically only for an hour and a half, but in fact for most of my life. There I was, lipstick flawless, nails hastily redone with a polish that still wasn't quite dry, hair as straight as I could make it in the loos, waiting for him to help heal my heart, which was no longer aching nearly so much and getting back to its usual burning for him. But as I watched, he just carried on walking. Quite fast.

He'd passed my desk by the time I came out of my horrified trance and bleated at him. There's no other way to put it. I wanted to attract his attention, but my mouth had gone so dry with the shock of him walking away that all I could manage was a strangled yelp. 'Hey!'

His smooth stride faltered. He wasn't used to being checked. He turned his head over one shoulder, eyebrows raised. What on earth was this about? Then he took in the gloss of my lips, my handbag poised expectantly on the edge of the desk, a bird about to take flight. Then the silly round 'O' of my mouth as I looked at him in consternation. He frowned for a second, then I could see the memory rushing in. That casual invitation, made in the moment to cheer me up, was coming back to haunt him. Regret pinched his features, then worse still, pity tiptoed in and crushed me.

There was something in him that thought less of me for taking his offhand suggestion so seriously. Doing myself up to the nines – or the eight-point-fives, as close as I could get with the limited resources to hand – had done me no favours. I looked like an idiot. I was one. A complete loser. He sauntered back over to me, put his palms flat on my beautiful pristine marble and leaned towards me. 'Babe,' he said. His blue eyes were open and honest (or looked it) as he stared down at me, beseeching. 'Babe, completely forgot about tonight. Something's come up. Urgent. I can't get out of it. Let's take a rain check, yeah?'

I nodded, smiling vacuously, though inside I was in smithereens. I blinked rapidly, hoping the tears wouldn't fall – many of them, this time, unwelcome, unbidden and each one as painful as a shard of glass – until he'd left the building. I stared out through the huge window, lost in thought, then realised he was loitering outside. Only for a moment, though. A girl came right up to him, their lips met in a smooch. She twined herself round him and laughed up into his face, and then they left. Together.

Bitch. At that moment, if I could have run over that blameless girl with a ten-tonne truck, I would have done. Felt her limbs crack and splay beneath my wheels. Heard the sickening crunch of bone. Maybe even have smelt the bitter copper stench of her blood. And then I would have reversed back over her lifeless corpse for good measure. No one should get between me and my dream.

But the pure waves of anger, misplaced though they were, were exactly the balm I needed. They swept away the self-pity, dried up the tears quicker than a forest fire.

All right, I see it clearly now. It was him I should have been angry with, not her.

At the time, all I could think was, *it should have been me.* I should have left the building with him, walked out confidently with just that little sway in my hips that was subtle, but somehow indicated interest, possible availability. I was sure he would have noticed. I should have glided past the glass doors with him – no, wait, he would have held one open for me and I would have smiled up at him and wordlessly drifted through, as though such gallantry was my due. Then I would have been standing outside the building with him. Mission accomplished. Well, not even nearly, but at least mission launched. I would have smiled up into his eyes and he would have, almost unknowingly, planted the first of many, many kisses on my eager lips.

But none of that was happening, was it? Because this cow had got there first.

I stared out at them, the anger in my eyes enough, surely, to shatter the glass. Their lips were still slobbering over one another. It was revolting. I carried on looking, my glare locked on as surely as her sea anemone mouth. I would never have made so much physical contact on a first date.

Suddenly I was sick to my stomach.

It *wasn't* their first date – it wasn't the first time Patrick had been out with this girl, whoever the hell she was.

Had I been wrong all this time? Had he actually got a girlfriend? Or was my timing just really crap? It looked like I'd split up with Pete, just at the moment that Patrick was getting serious about someone else. And he'd chosen the exact same moment to get my hopes up again.

That was when I should have started hating Patrick.

123

Chapter 28

Now

Louise

I've taken to drifting around the house when the kids are at school, just picking things up, putting them down. In anyone else, I would diagnose boredom, or restlessness. But I know that it's my way of stroking this place, as though it were a large black cat, as though it were my Mephisto come back to life.

Years before Marie Kondo told us to pare down our homes, I realised that a few loved items stood out better without background noise. It was partly fleeing my mother's home with so little, and partly a personal preference not to be drowned in other people's tastes.

I've developed faith in my choices, since revamping that first flat. Now I'm happy for them to stand and be judged. I wander the children's rooms, picking up the dirties, tucking away the clean. I pass by a journal on Em's desk.

She's my daughter, my flesh, but in so many ways a mystery to me. What is going on, as they say, in that pretty little head? She is like a locked box of secrets. So I can't resist sitting down and thumbing through this.

Soon my head is bowed, and I'm unable to read through eyes that fill up faster than I can dash away the tears. I'm crying like her at last, my face wet, make-up sluiced. I hold the book away, worried that tell-tale drops will pucker the pages, alert her to a stranger's presence here in her private world.

It's little memories about her dad, the things he said, the times they had. So many more than I remember, all with significances I didn't see or ignored. I'd worried they'd forget him, so I'd dotted those pictures around. Made sure they knew they had two parents, not just one imperfect mum.

I needn't have worried. He's in them, with them, every day.

Chapter 29

Then

If there was one thing I'd learned from my mother, apart from all the stuff I was doing my best to forget, it was that a wingman would only slow me down. My mother had had me, and goodness knows she'd made it plain enough that my presence had wrecked every aspect of her life, from her vagina to her future.

I had a long way to go, and it was faster travelling alone.

I missed Pete. I ached for what had been lost. And the humiliation of that family lunch still felt like bitter ashes in my mouth. But I had to tell myself that I could do better. Once again, I dared to lift my eyes to the prize. Patrick. In many ways, I couldn't believe for a second that he'd ever look at me seriously. He hadn't minded having a quick flirt, when he'd had time on his hands, but I was pretty sure he never seriously thought there was any mileage in me. Now he'd let me down so badly. Who could blame him? I wasn't sure I could. Despite my best efforts, I'd made it too obvious that I adored him, and where was the fun in that? We both knew he could do so much better.

I knew that even Jen and Tricia were distractions. Yes, I loved meeting up with Jen, now getting edgier all the time, tripping on her asymmetric hems, trailing arty scarves, and clutching *Brides* magazine as though it were the Holy Bible. We'd still carve the weeks into laughs, play out scenes for each other. She was nostalgic about 'the Desk', as she called it reverently, remembered the foibles of everyone in the firm, always thirsty for the gossip. And she loved telling me about her place, was always trying to get me to jump ship, 'improve myself' as she put it.

She was only a few years older, but she knew the ways of the world that I so badly wanted to be a part of. She was generous in encouraging me to believe I could reach out and touch my dreams, however ridiculous they might be. I hadn't known her all that long, but in many ways, I felt Jen was the one who'd finally brought me up. She'd showed me the way to go about things. She'd been so much more interested in my development than anyone else, from my actual mother to every social worker on the team.

My relationship with Tricia was more tenuous – but she was useful to me. She worked more closely with Patrick than I did, she had that window on his world, being in the same open-plan space. She wasn't under any illusions about why I sought her out. She could probably sense that we weren't so much chalk and cheese as a thoroughbred and a sewer rat. But though she had the background, she was busily damaging her looks with her alternating Mars bar/cabbage soup diet, while I was morphing more and more towards her style. As far as outward appearances went, that was. I still had 'damaged goods' written all the way up and down inside, like Brighton rock.

I think she found me interesting, too. For her, it was a safe way to peer into corners she'd never dare look at in the dark. All right, my accent was less full of sudden jags and lopped-off edges than it had once been, thanks to my tireless efforts. And I almost never wore manmade fibres anymore. But Pete had shown me forcibly that I still wouldn't pass in her home counties universe – nor would I really want to. My drive wasn't all about snobbery.

I just wanted a good life. Still do. That doesn't have to be about being posh, though the two often go hand in hand. The things I want – need – are stability, the ground solid under my feet, a clear view of all the exits and no one bad coming through them anyway, no surprises lurking, no one owed money or a favour that you have to grit your teeth, or some other part of your body, to pull off. Autonomy. Self-respect. Safety. If you've never known what it is not to have those things, then you probably don't realise how hard you'd work to achieve it.

Odd, I suppose, that I'd fixated on gaining all this through someone else – through Patrick. Someone I still hardly even knew. I could have made it on my own, been my own little island, secure in myself and not risking the cruel brush of someone else's disparagement, disrespect, or much, much worse. But I was braver than that. Or stupider. My hormones led me onwards, where my brain told me to stay back. And perhaps I was always looking for someone, someone who'd look after me, someone to care.

Perhaps there was more of my mother in me than I've ever dared to admit.

I can't help looking back on those years as a golden time. Many would look at where I was a few months ago and envy me. But, despite it all, it was those early years that were the most fun. Fun, because of Patrick, but also because of the sense of boundless possibilities open to me.

I'm not sure anyone else would see it that way. I was on quicksand, after all. One false step and I'd plunge down, down. But I was so careful. And people only see what they want to see. They don't look too carefully, unless you give them cause. We all love watching the meringue-white swan glide across the pond. No one stays to watch it heft itself out of the water and waddle like any old lardy goose over the grass.

OK, I'll admit, I was angry with Patrick, after the damp squib of our date-that-wasn't. It had been so degrading, and although I was used to knockbacks, this one really stung.

He wasn't to know about all the hours I'd put in to ready myself during the day, thank goodness. That would have made things even more mortifying. But he'd seen my consternation as he'd breezed past. Worse, he'd seen my attempt to cover it up, gather some tatters of dignity over my naked disappointment. I was well and truly on the back foot, and it was horrible.

I should have been angry with him, his faithlessness, his lack of consideration, the emptiness of his gallant gesture, which he'd probably forgotten all about before he'd even left the lift that morning. But I was good at not laying blame at the right door. It had taken me years to see my mother for what she was. She'd brought me up to believe that everything that happened to me was my own fault, that I somehow invited it and definitely deserved it. She'd told me that a thousand times, and I'd also deduced it for myself. Children are logical, and there had to be a reason why she punished me the way she did, why the bad stuff kept on happening to me. It was clear. I was evil and was getting my just desserts.

I'd made excuses for her for years, but eventually the worm had turned. I didn't know it, I can only see it now, but the same pattern was starting up all over again in my head with Patrick. I should have been angry with him then. I should have felt let down. I was right to feel slighted.

But instead, I swerved round him, and I re-routed my juggernaut of hatred. I directed it straight at the girl he'd kissed that night instead.

When I saw Patrick in that clinch, with that girl, outside *my* marble foyer, going on *my* date, I felt my anger lap across my marble counter towards her, a bile-green tide of corrosion. If I could have slapped her round her pink-and-white cheeks, I would have done. How dare she be standing there, kissing him, when it should have been me? There are times when we all feel perilously close to the edge, but I felt my grip on sanity slide.

There was nothing I could do, though. Nothing, except take home a bottle of cheap Chardonnay with my Tesco ready meal and tuck into both with the deep hunger born of misery. I even ate the dollop of stodgy rice that clung to my chilli, for once. I could just about have stood it, seeing the girl he really liked, if he hadn't dangled the prospect of our own date in front of me. But he'd shown me the path to heaven, then slammed the door in my face. Although he couldn't have known the true extent of my obsession, he did know I had a soft spot for him as wide and deep as the ocean. What he'd done was cruel.

But the red-hot current of my hatred stuck its thorns deep into the girl, not into him. Why do we do this to our own side? It's unfathomable. We should have solidarity against the common enemy. Maybe you do. I'm coming round to it myself. Back then, I admit, I blamed *her*, even though it was all Patrick's fault. He'd made a promise he wasn't interested in keeping, like so many men before him, and sauntered away from the devastation he'd wreaked. But instead of wanting to get my own back on him, it was her I focused on. She became the nexus of a perfect storm of rage. Oh, my mind's eye. It was hardly the 'bliss of solitude', as advertised by poets.

I blame my mother for this. As you'll have gathered, she is responsible for much of the crap that it was my life's work to crawl away from. An unreasoning faith in men, despite all the evidence that they would fuck her, and then fuck her over, had taught her nothing when she brought me into the world, and continued to teach her nothing over the years of my childhood. She always believed everything a man said to her, but questioned every word that came out of my mouth. From puberty onwards, she treated me like her deadliest rival. It was exhausting. It was unfair. It was the blueprint I learned and, until I had my own daughter, I carried it on.

It was not good and I apologise for it.

So, instead of deciding he was a waste of time, I decided to find out everything I could about Patrick's girl. Today, that would take less time than it did to type this sentence. An idle click at my laptop, and I'd have her laid bare, like a pathologist at a post-mortem. In those days, it wasn't so easy.

My first port of call was Tricia, font of all knowledge about Patrick's floor. Trouble was, I was angry with her as well. Why hadn't she given me the heads-up? Told me he had a love interest? I refused to call this . . . creature a girlfriend. Surely it hadn't got to that stage. And he had better taste than that. Or he should have.

Tricia was shamefaced. She sat opposite me, in the firm's café, the next day. She'd tried to weasel out of meeting, but I wasn't having any of it. To say I was on edge was an understatement.

'The thing is . . .' God, how I hated the weakness of those three dribbly, mealy-mouthed words. Excuses, pathetic excuses. But I hid my fury, schooled myself to listen like a good girl. Her vowels had never been so plummy, never had such trouble tumbling out of that prettily lipsticked mouth. I gazed, fascinated, at her small, even white teeth, the product of regular trips to the dentist and Mummy standing over her every night wielding a toothbrush.

My hatred for Patrick's chosen one almost spilled over. But my anger was just a mask for sorrow. I was bleeding, weeping inside, as Tricia told me all.

It turned out that she had seen the whole relationship developing, right under her nose. The girl was only one of her friends! I admit, I loathed Tricia and all the rich bitches of the world at that point – and their closed club that I would never, ever be a part of. I bit my lip inadvertently, blood flowering in my mouth. It had all been going on while my back was turned. My face twisted, though whether this heralded rage or unstoppable weeping, even I couldn't tell. I lifted my coffee cup up to disguise it, tried a wobbly smile instead.

The girl, this *Jane*, had come with Tricia to an office party. Something I hadn't even known was happening. And there she had met Patrick.

Where had my invite been? In the bin, with me, of course. For a few moments, the dark clouds swirled, then I took a breath, rationalised it. At the time, a couple of weeks ago, I'd been with Pete. I'd been busy, distracted. Tricia explained it was just their team, celebrating some big contract or other with a few best mates. She hadn't thought to mention it. I did feel this was a total dereliction of her duty, knowing my feelings towards Patrick, but I had to let it go. Had to, though it hurt. Just so I could keep on dragging information from her.

Anyway, it seemed the party had gone the way of all office shindigs. Started off with lame conversation round the desks, crisps and tragic bits of repartee falling over people's keyboards like dandruff on a middle-manager's shoulders. Then, thanks to umpteen lukewarm glasses of white wine, served in those plastic cups that crack if you grip them too hard, things had loosened up. To the extent that Patrick, my Patrick, had last been seen snogging this girl Jane round by the photocopiers. At least they hadn't taken lots of A4s of their bits. But they had been the talk of the office. Obviously.

At this point I couldn't help giving Tricia one of my looks. It had been designed to stop grown men in their tracks. Tricia wilted. Even while her doting mother's back was turned, her meanest au pairs had never glared at her as I was doing now. But she blustered.

'What could I do, Louise? It was too late. The deed was done. In the loos, John from Accounts said,' she added, leaning forward and even smiling, as though I was just after the prurient gossip. As though my world, or the one I had been very much hoping to construct, hadn't just shattered.

I sniffed. For one very dodgy second, I thought I might actually cry. But I managed to suck all the hurt back up into myself, and the steel shutters of my rage clanged down hard instead.

Chapter 30

Now

Becca

At first Becca had loved coming to the office. Gliding past the punters reporting their stolen bikes and their grudges against neighbours, flashing her pass at the desk sergeant, being buzzed through into the behind-the-scenes bit of the cop shop. She'd even liked the jauntiness of that name – and being able to shed a layer or two of her cumbersome uniform was definitely good news. But now she could safely say the novelty had worn off. Being out there, on the streets, expecting the unexpected, never knowing what strange kettle of fish you were going to be radioed into, that was the buzz. Hard to explain to a civilian. But it beat filling in forms any day.

Except times like this. She stared at the screen again, just checking she hadn't imagined the email exchange. It had been so much easier than she'd thought. She'd assumed an insurance company getting a request out of the blue from the police, would demur, want to check, ensure everything was kosher. Question her credentials, at the very least. She knew she would have done.

But it was a small firm. Not one of the conglomerates around these days. Was that why Patrick Bridges had chosen it in the first place? Or maybe Louise herself had made the selection?

They could be understaffed, they could just be lazy and not

want to bother making sure she had a right to know. Whatever the reason, they'd rolled over. Admittedly, she'd had the account details, via that letter she'd filched. That was the in. And the heap of figures they'd sent in return was overwhelming, all-encompassing. All the payouts and premiums for the whole company for years were here, in a jumble. But Becca not only had the time, she had the concentration and, all right, the obsessive attention to detail required to ferret nuggets of gold from this pile of dross.

And here was what she'd wanted, needed, prayed for. What she had been sure of, all along, was hidden there. Right in front of her, in black and white.

Today had to be the day when she'd finally say something to Burke, get him to pass it up to his mate Johno. Because what she'd dug up, well . . . surely it wasn't just her? Surely it showed something was seriously amiss in Louise's world? Like a skew-whiff gold frame in a stately home, it was the tiny detail that revealed the whole picture was a fake.

OK, technically speaking, she didn't have the authority to have got her mitts on this. Morally speaking, maybe she didn't have the right. But judicially speaking, in her view, someone had to. And the sooner the better. Every day that passed, Louise Bridges was getting away with it, getting further from her crime, burning through anything that could tie her to the truth. Continuing that sickening pose, her grieving widow act. For Becca, that felt like the real travesty. The woman's hypocrisy, it was revolting.

Becca had known, still knew, the real pain of losing someone she loved. Her dad. Now here was Louise, aping that heartbreak, pretending she cared, dragging those poor kids around with her to bolster her performance. Well, it wasn't on. Everyone else might be fooled. But she, Becca, had seen right through it. And she was going to put a stop to it.

Chapter 31

Then

I sat across from Tricia in the staff canteen and let her flannel on. Until she'd produced enough of the stuff to kit out every bathroom in the land. When she'd run dry and took to giving the remnants of her lipstick nervous little licks, I put my head on one side.

'So what's this Jane like, then?' I tried to keep my tone neutral, cool. But I could tell from the way that Tricia scraped her chair back a bit from the table that I hadn't quite got it right. No matter. I still wanted the answer. The lengthening pause between us made that transparently clear.

'Jane?' Tricia faltered. *Who do you think I mean? The Virgin Mary?* That's what I nearly said. But I was admirably restrained. I just gave her my long, level look. I tried to keep the flames from flickering, tried to keep the canteen clock from ticking. The silence stretched between us like a prisoner on the rack.

Then Tricia cracked. 'Well, I know her from school. Hadn't really seen her for years, then we bumped into each other at a drinks thing the other day . . . so I thought I'd ask her along to the office do . . .'

My shoulders sagged. It sounded all too depressingly clear. Girls like Tricia never stopped going to 'drinks things', never

135

stopped meeting people they had links with – schools, relatives, neighbours. Maybe it was just that all their lovely crisp fifty-pound notes in the bank were friends with the other person's equally enormous piles of money. Tricia found connections wherever she went, a gilded parachute designed to keep her from ever touching the filthy pavements where the likes of me slogged along, trying to scrape a living.

It really pissed me off. My life was all about hiding from anyone who'd known me on the way up. My first action, when the glorious day came when I finally felt I'd got to safety, would be to pull the ladder away, keep all those ghosts with their ashy fingers from crawling after me. God alone knew when I'd get there, though. And this news felt like yet another setback.

It was ridiculous. Everything in my head started to protect Patrick from the consequences of his actions, and it was all her, this *Jane*, this interloper, who was the spanner in the works. I was much more willing to blame her than him, though the truth was I still didn't know either of them. How was it possible to love someone as completely as I loved Patrick, and yet never to have exchanged more than the most basic of conversations with him? Every fibre of me still yearned towards him, although I now suspected that he was no more to be relied upon than any other man.

I still had palpitations each time he passed. It got to the point where I could tell when he'd entered the building, even if I didn't look up and see him. If only he'd stop. Say hello. Ask a question, like he used to do. Toy with my affections, get my hopes up. But I had the feeling that our abortive date was now coming between us.

The others started to try their luck again; the junior execs, making their way. They'd lope my way, bold eyes flicking over me. Luckily, I was so polished now that there was nothing their eyes could snag on. Not like the old days of cleavage and thigh. Now their eyes slid away, thinking they were way out of their league. They weren't, of course, but I wasn't going to let on. And it didn't stop them trying. When has being outclassed convinced a man he didn't have a right to have a go? They'd lay their meaty forearms across my marble, lean close with breath that was either minty or sandwich-laced, depending on the time of day. Just a smile, a bit of fun. I'd know one was smitten when I got gusts of aftershave. I was polite, but firm. No dates. Banter, just to show I wasn't stuck up. But nothing more. And not one of them gave me even a moment's flutter.

Patrick was the one.

I despaired. Every morning, I preened myself for him, made myself gorgeous, tried my best for irresistibility. And every day he kept on sauntering past. Yes, there was the flick of a smile, but it was automatic now. And the wink, though I began to wonder if it was just some sort of facial tic. Because that was it. Nothing more. Not a word, these days. As though we'd never had those flirty little exchanges that had meant the world. As though we hadn't trembled on the brink of dating. As if *she, evil fucking Jane,* hadn't got in the middle and ruined things.

That wink, was it even meant for me? Perhaps he didn't even realise that Jen had left, that I was the new her. Maybe our chats had just been candyfloss to him. Had I done too good a job of filling Jen's shoes, become indistinguishable, just another chic blonde with a coquettish smile? Because smile at him I did. It was the only weapon I had left in my arsenal. Though I felt so shy, so humiliated, that I wanted to duck and hide under the desk, I made myself give him the full beam, all my practice here in the ladies, having carved out a dimple that I was damned sure ought to reel him in. *Look, no grudges! Don't worry about the fact that you left me in the lurch, feeling like a prize idiot. I'm still here. Still waiting. Still lovely,* I told him every single day with that grin. I might as well have been talking to the marble counter itself, for all the response I got.

From the outside, I probably looked as though I'd resigned myself to the status quo. Pete and I had split up – irreconcilable differences, all right – and Patrick was going strong with Jane. Nothing much I could do about any of that, right?

Then one morning Trish came into the building, mascara everywhere, sobbing, and more or less collapsed on my lovely desk. I rushed to pat her as best I could, proffer tissues (and clear away the worst of the smears) and volunteer to take her for a coffee. I was even happy to leave the desk to the tender mercies of my underling Sal for a few minutes.

Sitting opposite Trish that day, our coffees cooled on the table between us as she haltingly sobbed out the story.

'It's Jane,' she blurted. Her brimming eyes met mine and went a curious triangular shape with grief, before more tears started spilling out everywhere.

'Jane?' I said blankly.

'You know,' she said, 'My friend who dated Patrick.'

'Oh. *Jane*. That Jane.' I paused.

'She's been run over.' Trish started hiccupping again.

'No! What happened?' I wanted every detail. 'Run over? How? An accident?'

'Hit and run. No one saw anything.'

'My God. The roads are crazy round here.'

I sat back, conscious that I was just mouthing platitudes. But that was what you did, right? Tricia certainly seemed to find it comforting. The flow of tears was slowing. Now she dabbed her poor eyes.

'No, it was where she lived. Right near her house.'

'Oh yes. And that's . . .?'

'One of those little streets, the edge of town.'

'God, how awful. When did it . . . happen?' I asked gently.

'Just last night. In the rain. Poor, poor Jane. I wonder if she knew what was happening. Do you think . . . do you think she would have felt anything?'

'God. Let's hope not. Don't torture yourself, Trish,' I said. 'I'm sure it would have been quick. It's dreadful. Patrick will be *so* cut up,' I added. Trish nodded, but was too choked to speak. I passed her another wad of tissues, patted her hand for as long as I could before the inevitable happened, and Sal barged into the canteen with a problem only I could sort.

Patrick *was* cut up – a little. Really not as much as you might have expected. Of course, he and Jane had not really been an item, in the true sense of the word. But still, I would have thought there'd have been misty eyes, a bit of soul-searching at someone his age departing this earth so young. But no.

The truth was that Patrick seemed to have all the depth of the last spoonful of soup in the bowl. Either that, or he'd never really felt a thing for Jane. I knew which I wanted to believe. I watched him leave work that evening in a bit of a daze. The next morning, his face was pale and he was distracted – no wink. But by the day after, the spring was back in his step. I could more or less see him parcelling the whole sorry Jane business up and stacking it in the 'never to be opened' section of his brain.

Strange, then, that I didn't realise there was a time when I, too, would be just another box that was wrapped round with heavy-duty packing tape, a problem to avoid lingering over at all costs. But we each think we're special, don't we? The one who can unlock something no one else can bring out.

And that was that, as far as Jane was concerned. Poor girl. Wrong place, wrong time. And wrong man.

Chapter 32

Now

Becca

It was a bit like plunging into the school swimming baths long ago, thought Becca. Her eyes would already be stinging with the chlorine, her hair trying its best to work free of the cruel rubber cap, but worst of all was looking down and seeing her own chubby white flesh, puffing over the black suit, wobbling with the fear. Still, she preferred that exposure to the moment when the harsh turquoise water closed over her head and she was sure, every time, that she was going to drown in a sea of her careless contemporaries, all swimming like seals.

She looked around the room. Everyone was busy, occupied, carrying out their legitimate tasks, not questioning things that didn't need prodding at. Why was she different? Pointless to even ask, she just was. But this wasn't like before, the depression, that business. Besides, everyone admitted to stuff like that now, there wasn't a stigma anymore. It hadn't been a big deal anyway. A few pills and she'd been fine. Her mother had blown it out of all proportion. Now she was a different person, completely. She was all fired up, ready to dive. Or just put one foot forward.

And yet still she couldn't quite do it.

Even now that she'd cracked Patrick Bridges' emails. The terminals that had once hummed with his correspondence might be charred and melted out of shape, the filing cabinets that had housed his records were burned past recognition. But once she'd lifted his email address from the insurance correspondence, given her IT skills, her endless patience and yes, all right, her acres of free time, she'd managed to worm her way in through the cracks. In cyberspace, she was a lot more limber than in real life.

Was it strictly legal? No, if you looked at it like that, she supposed it wasn't. But was what Louise had done legal, either? Or moral? Not in Becca's book, it wasn't.

Maybe there was another way in. Something easier, something more . . . defensible. She wondered again about Burke's chum, Johno. She couldn't wheedle her way round him, could she? *Wheedle? You? Never,* said her mother's voice in her head, even more scornful than usual.

But there was a first time for everything.

Chapter 33

Then

In the end, it was a random courier who came to my rescue, broke the ice that had packed in tight around our fledgling relationship. Strange, the part they've played in my life.

It was a Wednesday, a little while after Jane died. I can even remember the weather, though it was so many years ago. That's because I remember my outfit. Do you do that? Significant days, key events, and I can recall what I had on, sometimes down to the underwear. And on this day, every detail was important.

I signed for the package, thinking nothing of it. Some days all I seemed to do was sign. It was like every day was Christmas, but all the presents were for someone else. Just like it had been back with Mum. I never got to open anything. Mind you, even the people these packages were destined for weren't really interested. No one wets their knickers for biros and notebooks, do they?

So this was like every other day. Except that the courier seemed to be taking his time. It was before they got the little digital pads that you scrawl on with a stylus. They had notebooks back then, and biros too. The bloke was making a big play that he couldn't find his, patting down his leather biker jacket and heavy leather jeans. Of course, all the patting drew my attention to his body, which did look pretty good. There's something about leather, isn't there? It's just sexy. Not if you think about where it came from, literally off the back of some poor cow. But if you keep your mind away from that, look at the supple, semi-matt sheen, smell that rather delicious spicy scent of new handbags, posh cars and squashy sofas, then mm, yes. It just gives you a flutter.

I looked up at him, my interest suddenly piqued. And then he took off his helmet. It was a bit like one of those shampoo ads, where someone shakes out their hair, usually in slo-mo. He lifted away that great big black thing, like a bowl on his head, and there he was. Not with waist-length blonde tresses; that would have been silly. But with messy, slightly overlong, gently wavy chestnut hair, just brushing his shoulders. It looked silky. It was all tousled up, but if I'd run my fingers through it . . .

Despite my lingering sadness at the way things had ended so catastrophically with Pete, despite my yearning for Patrick, I caught myself looking at him in *that* way. You know, speculative. His eyes matched his hair, chestnut, but they had an extra something – a fleck of green. Unusual. I was pretty sure my own pupils would be dilating involuntarily, swimming in those knowing depths. It was like he'd choreographed the whole thing. Maybe he had. After all, his job was to deliver brown paper packages to bored girls like me, all over town. If I'd been him, I would have definitely worked out some strategies to liven up my day.

Just his luck, but Patrick walked by as Motorbike Boy finally opened his mouth to speak. His words fell on deaf ears as my head whipped round, almost of its own accord, to track the saunter that haunted all my dreams. Patrick was perfectly capable of passing by without so much as a glance in my direction, I knew that to my cost. But today, perhaps the activity at my desk drew his eye. For whatever reason, he changed path. Started coming straight towards us.

Motorbike Boy, bless his bulletproof arrogance, was still leaning over my marble, trying to maintain that deep and meaningful eye contact, whispering seductively about how he was always losing track of his pen. I just bet he was. But the second Patrick had stepped out of the lift, the biker boy had started to fade away. By now, with Patrick within yards of my desk, he was the invisible man. I could still smell his shampoo, but I wasn't seeing him anymore.

On the face of it, it didn't make any sense. Motorbike Boy had it all – the physique, the strut, the raw nerve. Patrick, by contrast, was a stuffed shirt who had led me on and who, when he'd had a chance to be my knight in shining armour, had let me down so badly that I still woke up shaking. But you could shout that as loud as you liked; my heart wasn't listening. And, what was more important, while there was another man at my desk, transparently finding me irresistible, Patrick's interest had suddenly gone from nought to sixty. I'd done it. God knew how, but I had. I was suddenly the best bucket in the sandpit.

Patrick walked over at a fast clip that had his heels snapping on the foyer tiles and leaned into my space. He ignored the courier, who by now was sadly putting his pen away. I wouldn't have been surprised if it had gone all droopy.

Patrick fixed me with those eyes, those eyes I'd fantasised about so long and so hard. 'Drink? Later?' he said, as though we did this all the time.

The questions wind-milled through my head: *Me? Really? And so soon after Jane . . . Are you sure?* But more importantly, *What time?* And *Where are we going?* But I kept my mouth shut. And smiled. And nodded.

I couldn't believe my luck.

Chapter 34

Now

Becca

Becca knew she wasn't really built for sidling. And considering her dearest wish was to move into plain clothes, she wasn't that great at subterfuge either. Luckily, it turned out she didn't need either skill. No sooner had she approached Johno in the canteen than he'd suggested a quiet coffee, just the two of them. For a moment, she shot him a sidelong glance. If she hadn't known better . . . but she did. Thanks to her mum, and her ten-tonne hints, Becca knew there was no way in hell that she could appeal to a bloke like him.

Mind you, she told herself quickly before she could feel the sharp smack of rejection, it was mutual. His sleek porpoise body, with the gently curved gut, his smooth features, fresh-faced as David Cameron before Brexit, well, safe to say he did nothing squared for her. Still, she'd do her best to keep that from him. A dented ego was less prone to chat; she knew that much.

When they finally settled into their seats, their original pre-lunch coffee had been shunted several times until it had become a quick half down the pub after their shifts had finished. Both had been busy at the original appointed hour, and all stops in between. But, as Johno swung onto the stool with a self-satisfied smile, and pushed the brimming beer her way, Becca realised this was all turning out rather well.

That wasn't to say she loved pubs. The smoking ban had improved things but the sticky tables, yeasty smell, the preponderance of IC1 males, they all still made her feel out of place. But needs must, and this was definitely home territory for Johno. He'd be relaxed. And that could make him a lot more receptive to what she had to say. She picked up the beer mat and started tearing at the edge, working out her approach. He leapt in.

'So, it's about the Bridges case, is it?'

Becca put down the mat. 'How did you know?'

'It says "detective" on my payslip,' he said with more than the ghost of a smile. Before Becca had a chance to speak, he'd started up again. 'Plus, it's the only case where we've got an intersection. You did the knock, didn't you? With The Burke?'

She bridled at the nickname. She might have her doubts about her partner sometimes, but that didn't mean she was happy to sit by while others took a swipe. But she'd let the remark go for now. 'Anyway. There must be something about it that you're not happy with. Otherwise, why agree to meet?'

'Why indeed?' Johno twinkled at her over the rim of his glass. A filigree of foam was already clinging to its sides; he'd polished off more than half at one pull. When he put the glass down, she could see his smirk unimpeded. But she realised that there was an attraction there, despite all her attempts to tell herself otherwise. She wondered if she'd finally bitten off more than she could chew.

'Seriously, what do you think of her? The Bridges woman?' She leaned forward.

'Sure you want to know?' His chuckle was X-rated. Becca sighed inwardly. This had started so promisingly. *Please don't say it's going to turn soul-destroying.* She didn't want to listen to another man lusting after Louise Bloody Bridges. Nor did she want to spend her evening coal mining with a plastic spoon, for dribs and drabs of information.

'No, but seriously,' said Johno, dropping the banter and fixing her with a shrewd glance. 'You might be on to something. Tell you what, I've got to dash now, but let's have a proper chat about it . . . day after tomorrow? Curry in that place by the station. 8 p.m. OK?'

Becca's stab of disappointment that the talk she'd been waiting for all day was suddenly over, gave way rapidly to surprise, and then pleasure. A bit too much pleasure, she realised, as a pink glow spread over her cheeks. She found herself nodding. Too many times. She consciously stilled her head as Johno grabbed his phone and keys from the table and got up, tipping her another practised smirk as he left.

She looked at his empty glass, only a swirl of foam left in the bottom. She gingerly took a sip from the top of her own, trying not to slop it everywhere, winced at the taste, and pushed it away. She should really get going, but she took stock first. Things hadn't gone as expected. Not at all.

Well I never, she thought to herself. *If I didn't know better, I'd say that I'd just got a date.*

Chapter 35

Then

Passing the bar that night, you'd have looked in and seen me glittering atop my stool and you'd have thought, *pretty girl, looks happy.* Those four words summed up everything I'd been striving so long – and so hard – to achieve. The love of my life was about to drop into my lap. Plus money, status and respectability, of course, but they were secondary to my adoration. The days spent like the Little Mermaid, walking on knives, the nights like Cinderella at five to twelve, were all now worthwhile. It was perfect. I felt as though I was holding the world in the palm of my hand, instead of just Patrick. And like a delicate glass bauble on the top of a teetering Christmas tree, everything was poised to shatter.

He was captivated. Of course. I always brought my A-game. And tonight had to be A-star times A-plus. I was in a bar with the man of my dreams! I had to be more careful than ever. I put everything into seeming not to make any effort at all.

Yes, I was paranoid, but I had good reason. An unguarded remark, at any time, could expose me for the snivelling parvenue I knew I was inside. I couldn't help remembering how I'd mispronounced the name of a wine only a few weeks before. I'd pointed at a high bottle, asked a shop assistant to reach it down for me. The triumph in that pimply git's voice as he'd trumpeted, to the whole shop, 'what, you want the *bewjollies*, do you, love?' At that instant, he was transformed from a lowly shelf-stacker to the victor, standing over me in the gutter, and pissing on me for good measure. Every little helps, indeed.

But I tried to banish such morbid thoughts on this, the crowning night of my life so far. The ached-for date with Patrick. I was flying high; I would not look down.

Everything I said, every gesture I made, was exactly on point. My jokes sparkled, my little *aperçus* were clever but not so brilliant that he was outshone. In truth, it's not hard to get a man's attention. All you need to do is have breasts and nod. But I suppose I was still young then and wanted him to love me for myself, not just for the way I looked, or the way I reflected him. As I say, I had a lot to learn.

And what did I find out about him? That night, nothing. I was just blinded by the joy of being with him at last, having his attention, or more realistically, sitting there giving him mine. It was clear he liked what he saw. All the little signs I'd read about were being deployed; the eye-meets that were just too long, the casual brushing of my hand when he refilled my glass. It was a wonder I didn't fall off that stool with the sheer delight of it all. I was seriously out of my depth with him, and all my usual checks and measures, my desire to stay safe, within my own comfort zone, started to whistle away into the wind. I was his for the taking.

The funny thing was, he seemed just as keen as me. I didn't have enough brain cells going at the time to notice, but once the first few heady days had passed and I could catch my breath, I realised that this was a two-way thing. He was every bit as smitten as Pete had been – before his family had got involved.

It was a shock. And a check on my feelings. What did this mean? It was obvious why I was so much in love with him – he was everything I wasn't, had everything I didn't. He was so attractive he made my ribs ache. So confident that I finally felt safe. He was upwardly mobile, he was smart, the real McCoy, with a solid background and enough wealth to make all his efforts at work laudable, not desperate like mine.

I did wonder what he could possibly want with me.

But I cursed myself for even thinking it. Why would I taint this, the purity of our fledgling love affair, which had taken so long to start but was now progressing with wildfire speed? We didn't need doubt to creep in under the door, with all its insidious sidelong glances.

So I shut my ears to the questions, and was soon distracting myself with our stratospheric sex life, followed rapidly by the gorgeous dilemma of who was moving in with whom.

Mephistopheles was in his cat basket before you could say Whiskas.

Chapter 36

Then

For my next trick, I had to win round Patrick's parents. We were into our third month now, and things had settled down a little bit. We were living at his place – it was big enough for about 50 per cent of my books. I'd told myself I was long overdue for a clear-out, but secretly I mourned the loss of each and every volume. I'd already had to take the self-help books down to the local Oxfam during Pete's brief reign.

There were some genres I was really attached to, and I thought long and hard before letting them go. The true crime books were in this category. They were already tucked away, out of sight, in a secret layer behind other books on the shelves, even though visitors to my flat were still virtually non-existent. I felt obscurely ashamed of my addiction to them, though I wasn't sure why. Was it worse than all those fictional killings that old ladies were happy enough to borrow in their thousands from public libraries, and chat about with their chums over a custard cream and a cup of tea? Why did the fact that the deaths in my books were real make them somehow revolting, my interest perverted? The completely unrealistic deployment of a blunt instrument in a library was fine, whereas a genuine life-and-death struggle was shocking?

I didn't get it, and I resented my own shame – but not enough to wean myself off true crime, until I had to up sticks to Patrick's. Moving the books would inevitably expose them to his curious glance. I didn't want to see the question in his eyes, have to fumble for a justification for my interest. And what would that even be? I wasn't sure I could put the fascination into words. Yes, I found it intriguing that the men who'd killed Jill Dando and Rachel Nickell were still wandering the streets. I wasn't alone. The fact that the books existed at all showed there was a market.

But in the end, I whittled away at the collection for weeks, splitting it between the various charity shops in the nearest high street. Luckily there were plenty of these moving in as the economy dived. And soon, the books were the least of my worries. Because Patrick's parents wanted to meet me.

After the debacle at Pete's, which had led inexorably and immediately to him casting me off without a backwards glance, this news filled me with dread. Why did people have to involve their parents in their lives? God knew I'd never wanted my mother dragged into anything, and as for my father, well, good luck trying.

But Patrick was close to his family. And, worse still, it was a two-part summons. One invitation from his dad, one from his mum. I couldn't even get it all over with in one fell swoop. His parents were divorced, so it was very much separate lunches. I did a little digging with Patrick and it seemed the divorce was 'amicable' – or, in other words, a polite, middle-class affair that didn't involve the restraining orders and black eyes so popular in my old stamping grounds. Nevertheless, it wasn't so amicable that one lunch table was big enough for the both of them. It was his dad's go first.

I had a feeling that this would be the easier of the two meetings. Men were always willing to overlook a lot when they saw blonde hair and a good figure. I'm not saying it was fair or right, it was just the way it was. Patrick's dad was no different from the rest of his sex.

He was a doctor, a GP no less, pillar of the community, lovely man. Bit of a gleam in his eye, which explained the young – very young – wife and new brothers for Patrick. Patrick seemed fine with it all. How he could be, I didn't know. I couldn't imagine having that sort of emotional ballast. His dad was all over the younger boys, throwing them in the air, joshing with them. Yes, it was in that way that suggests rarity – a man showing off his daddy credentials in front of an audience. I'd have been spitting. But Patrick wasn't riled at all. Mind you, my mother couldn't have drummed up a parenting skill if you'd given her a month's notice, and my father was just another stain on our sofa.

I got through it all without disgrace, though there was no obvious interface between his dad's world and mine, except that my mother had often been in need of medical assistance. The young wife was nice to me, scrutinising me a little bit harder of course, but unable to find any chinks in my armour. I'd dressed down, after the train-wreck at Pete's. Jeans, sweater. Form-fitting, simple. And, thank God, irreproachable this time.

Besides, she was too wrapped up in the boys to spare much interest for anyone else. Patrick she treated as a sort of big brother, which was odd when he was actually her *kids'* brother. But as long as you didn't think about any of it for too long, it was all fine. Maybe this was how the middle classes kept their sanity. Maybe, also, this was why they spent so much time discussing the far shores of politics and other crap that meant nothing but kept one's mind off emotional shipwrecks closer to home.

His mother, of course, was the main event. I was dreading this one. It was key. Meeting Pete's family had been something that both Pete and I had put off for as long as possible. The way I'd crashed through it so disastrously showed my instinct had been right. Meeting Patrick's mum was crucial to my future happiness and I couldn't avoid it, but neither could I put a foot wrong. I'd created a God-like image of Patrick in my own little head, I sometimes felt I existed only to please him. The prospect of losing him thanks to his mother's legitimate disapproval gave me so many sleepless nights I had to buy a new, thicker concealer for the bags under my eyes.

The trouble was that I'd started freezing now, when I was stressed. As a small child, I'd rarely suffered from nerves. The more worrying the situation I found myself in, the more I usually chilled out, my thought processes remaining clear and unhurried. Now I couldn't rely on that anymore, and what was worse, stress brought its own special showreel of other awful times with it. Flashbacks, sometimes horribly vivid, of moments I thought I'd papered over or 'done a Patrick' with, shoved them right to the back of my memory cupboard.

It was as though the burden of damage was cumulative. For a certain amount of my life, I'd been able to cruise along, managing desperate situations with reasonable aplomb. But then, just as I grew into adulthood and really wanted to glide, these icebergs had started to bob up again from the deep. This time, with Patrick's mother, I was seriously worried that a whole bunch of ghosts would be coming with me on our visit, not least the look on Pete's face as I saw him for the last time, and the relief palpable among his family as we closed the front door on that ghastly lunch. I was beside myself that I might somehow mess this up before I'd even set foot inside her door.

I needn't have worried. The fact that Patrick was now trailing well into his late twenties, and had never brought a girl back before, had started to freak Jill Bridges out. Thank goodness, the very last thing she wanted to do was frighten me off. I didn't know it then, but she'd started to worry that he might be gay, which shows you how far off the mark she was. Not that she was homophobic, she'd have been fine with it all. But in those days, a gay son meant no grandchildren, which she would have found hard to take.

Jill was a solicitor. The idea that I'd be sitting down at a table with a lawyer, yet without a single police uniform in sight, not so much as a caution wafting through the air, had been one of the things that had had me taking the odd deep breath. In the event, I was too busy taking in every aspect of her home to stress too much about the legal side of things. It turned out she only did the boring bits of conveyancing anyway – nothing criminal. Of course. The Bridges were much too well-heeled to get their hands dirty with scum like me.

But the house. This was suddenly what I wanted. Though it was too cluttered, too untidy for me ever to feel really at home in, it was a first glimmer of what I wanted down the line. It wasn't pretentious, but you could tell that money had been spent. It was comfortable, but not luxurious. It was very well judged. And full of that middle-class taste that is so quintessentially English – a pile of well-thumbed newspapers, a working fireplace, a tray of tea, books lying cracked-spine-up all over the sofas. There was even a chubby marmalade cat, who'd clearly had a better time of it than my own poor bandit Mephisto, currently home alone and no doubt clawing Patrick's sofa to shreds to pay us back for going out.

I dragged my attention back to Jill. She was interrogating me, not like a brief but like a concerned mum. I liked it, as I liked everything about her, from the slightly spongy tum pressing at her jeans under the hastily wrapped cashmere cardi, to the quarter-inch of grey peeping like a shy fieldmouse from her parting. She had the confidence to let herself go. It wasn't a surprise that she hadn't remarried or found a boyfriend, in the wake of Patrick's dad's departure.

But, though I wouldn't, *couldn't*, contemplate looking like her for a second, I admired Jill's nonchalance. It was unfair, I suppose. Pete's mum, Daphne, had also abandoned all efforts to beguile, like a rubber band stretched to its limits and then failing to ping back, and I'd just despised her for it. I was basically a terrible snob back then, desperate to rise above the chaos of my own beginnings. Jill seemed relaxed, her attitude full of the natural ease I lacked, and therefore intriguing. Pete's mum seemed wilfully unattractive and I didn't get it.

Jill was a kind woman, and welcoming. True, she did fix me with narrowed eyes every now and then. I had to watch the shape of my vowels very rigorously when she was around. One sign of a muffin-topped diphthong and I'd get a sidelong glance. Nothing more than that, but it still terrified me. And I'm not sure she bought my handy story about the hit and run that had squished both my parents one dark night, even though I'd practised all the details specially.

If I hadn't known better, I'd say the odd doubt has flickered across Jill's mind over the years. Luckily, she's too well brought up to voice it directly. That middle-class code that I came to love so well, was and is my best friend. It's prevented her from calling me out.

One of the main bones of contention stemmed from that first meeting. 'Where did you grow up, Louise?' she asked, her sharp eyes veiled by puffy lids. Her GP ex-husband might well have diagnosed too many hot toddies by the fireside of an evening – but he'd legged it. Not his problem anymore.

'Oh, you know, in London,' I said, vague as a pea-souper fog. 'Love that picture over there.' I wandered over to study it closely. Both Patrick and his mother looked surprised by my enthusiasm. I soon gathered it wasn't the done thing to comment on concrete objects – the china, the curtains – as signifiers of other people's taste.

'Whereabouts in London? Patrick has cousins in Battersea . . .' And we were off. If there were loads of taboo subjects that had to be avoided for no good reason I could see, one of the areas you could delve into forever was other people's family trees. I didn't really get it. To me, it seemed a lot more personal than praising someone's taste in soft furnishings. Unfortunately, my background was more rock pool than gene pool. And I didn't want to lift any stones, for fear of what might creep out.

'Oh, nowhere near Battersea. Is that a magnolia?' I was getting desperate, had moved over to the French windows, which gave onto a neglected and scrubby area the size of a football pitch, liberally strewn with uncollected leaves. But I had unwittingly struck gold. Jill was off the sofa and frog-marching me out into the cold to look at her herbaceous borders before I knew what had hit me. It turned out that lawns, for some reason, you could rave about until the cows came home, though you must never, on any account, mention carpets.

'No, dear, it's not a magnolia, it's a lilac tree, but you probably knew that, didn't you?' Jill tucked her arm beneath mine as soon as we were outside. I was disconcerted but did my best not to pull away. And I knew better to insist on my ignorance. The garden was dank and, as far as I could see, a total waste of space. You could have built twenty-five, maybe fifty, flats on this footprint, if you were going straight up. Or four really big, really swanky ones. My head swam at the likely value. That wasn't going to happen, though. Jill much preferred old leaves to fresh banknotes.

'What a good idea to get outside and have a chat away from my son. Clever girl. Now, what do you *really* think of my boy?'

I admired Jill for what she did that day. She might well have had her doubts about me – frankly, I would have seen myself off the property with a shotgun – but she cut to the chase. Did I love her boy or not? And I did. Too much, if anything. As soon as she got that information, she relaxed. Perhaps that's what being a nice person is all about. Allowing others, however unworthy, to have a chance.

Once I'd consciously unstiffened my arm, I remember enjoying the stroke of her kitten-soft cardigan against my skin, the faint, tired waft of Rive Gauche from her body. Her face was gently lined in close-up, pale as parchment, her mouth already thinning. She'd slicked on some lipstick in my honour and it was feathering out, like ink in water. I still believed, at that age, that wrinkles were the fault of their owners, but I loved the way Jill embodied graceful surrender.

She patted her pocket and produced a battered pack of Benson

& Hedges, offering me one. It explained the delicate fan of lines above her lips, crackles on an antique vase. I declined nervously, unsure what the right answer was. But as an addict, she couldn't have cared less. She bent her head to the cheap garage lighter and breathed in deeply, gratefully. 'A small sin. But we all have them, don't we, really?'

I loved the way she said it on an exhale – 'really' becoming 'rarely'. I tucked away the soundbite, not to use – people would fall about if I tried it – but just because it was such a treat to hear something so genuinely posh. I still had trouble remembering to tack every single H back on to its stem, words were always hacked like headless hydrangeas where I came from. I could never aspire to swallowing my 'e's. In my old block, that would have meant something entirely different.

Chapter 37

Then

Did he live up to his promise, this man I had waited so patiently for? Was the game worth all I'd staked on it? Oh, the answer has to be every bit as ecstatic as the one I gave when he asked me to marry him. *Yes.*

As soon as I'd said it, I plunged into planning a wedding that made Jen's little do look like an elopement. And after it, far from feeling like an anti-climax, our progression from first flat to little house to, finally and gloriously, Woodwarde Road seemed as smooth and perfect as the oyster satin of my wedding gown (spaghetti straps, bias cut, a beautiful caress of a dress that hit the floor the moment the hotel door closed behind us).

Thinking about our early years now makes me smile. Waking up, day after day, with the man I loved just didn't get old; nor did seeing his blue, blue eyes over breakfast or catching sight of him in the corner at a party. I'd loved him from the first moment I'd seen him, and he could still make my pulse flutter even now. My heart would hammer as I realised, yet again, how lucky I'd been. The man I loved, loved me back. There's nothing better. We were together. Such simple joys, but I resolved never to take them for granted.

Then, just when I'd thought things could hardly be more

perfect, I got pregnant. It wasn't planned, but immediately Patrick was as thrilled as me. We'd swirled the possibility around, but had always thought it would happen later, when we were more settled, more securely on our way. But life has a way of turning even the best-laid plans upside down.

Having kids together, that's the glue, isn't it? The cement that holds a man and woman together, makes individuals into a family. With one of each, a boy and a girl, we got the perfect result. It seemed to be yet more proof that we were invincible. From the outside, the four of us looked solid. It was as though we all held up our own corner of our lovely house.

And I was good at pregnancy, too. I'd thought I'd hate it, the loss of autonomy, the sense that someone else is in the control room all of a sudden, making you put on shedloads of weight, grow ponderous and swollen, steering a path you can't see or alter, that leads inexorably to the delivery room and the very, very bad idea that a fully formed human can emerge from your vagina.

But I got through it all. We sniggered our way through the antenatal classes. The lessons in huffing and puffing, the enthusiasm for water births and whale music. Even the ridiculous notion that it was somehow more noble to have this eight-pound object emerge from your nethers if you did it without an anaesthetic. Luckily, we had private medical insurance by that time and I managed to convince my consultant that a caesarean was the only way to go. By this stage, I was most definitely too posh to push, thank God.

It wasn't until after the births that I realised what the real point of the antenatal group had been. To introduce you to other women who were going through the same new-baby experience, at the same time as you.

I'd avoided all Stacy's overtures at the original classes. But then I'd arrived home with my first little shrivelled screaming baby. I looked down into his squinty, raging ink-blue eyes. The love I had for Patrick, huge though it was, was but a shadow of this new, all-consuming passion. But I needed so much help to get through this. In minutes I was searching out Stacy's number and begging her for a coffee.

I'd seen, even while she was pregnant and the size of a blue whale, that Stacy was going to be brilliant at this motherhood lark. I badly needed someone to copy. Jen had been fabulous at getting me this far, helping me transform myself into Patrick's wife; now I needed another example to help me become Giles's mum. Motherhood was a bit of a crisis for me. It could have gone so wrong. I could have lost sight of my perpetual mission, to be better, to better myself. I could have just followed the vile pattern I'd been set. It would have been a lot easier.

Instead, I did everything I could to carve a different path. It's hard doing that single-handedly. I already knew several shedloads of stuff I shouldn't be doing, from mainlining drugs down. If I could pick up some useful tips from watching Stacy, a woman who seemed incomplete without a child attached to her like a limpet on a rock, then so much the better for everyone.

I'd never gone in for lots of friends, it was like a language I didn't speak. Most people learned it young, in the playground. But it had never crossed my mind to bring anyone from school home. Why would I want a witness seeing what my life was like? Even if there had been a single person there who'd have said yes. Even if my mother would have let them over the threshold.

Jen had been a wonderful mentor. There'd been Trish at work as well, and even Sal, my number two on the desk, I suppose. That had been plenty. It was only when I was home with babies that I realised how much I actually needed the company of other women. Although technically I wasn't alone anymore, with a baby in the house, I'd never felt so dangerously isolated. With so few clues to go on, I needed to see how this motherhood lark was done first-hand. And Stacy, messy and chaotic as she cheerfully admitted she was, became my accidental role model.

Without her I'd have found it so much tougher. Unless you've been faced with the crescendos of wails, those unrelenting hours with a small, anger-filled blob, poop at one end and sick at the other, you just don't know how hard it can be.

I loved them so much, but it's a fine line, finer than a silent movie star's eyebrow. There's nothing like another being's total dependency on you to make you realise your power – and your responsibility. I now saw how astonishing it was that I'd ever made it to adulthood. I decided that my mother must have just zoned out a lot of those years, with the aid of the ever-handy drink and drugs, while I'd brought myself up, a truth locked so deep I couldn't remember it.

I, of course, wanted to do things differently – perfectly. Not for the first time, I wondered about my absent father. Maybe he'd levered himself off that grim sofa and then put in an eighteen-hour day somewhere else. Because someone, somewhere in my background had a strong work ethic. It certainly wasn't Mum, so could it have been him? Maybe he was a perfectionist too. It would definitely explain why he hadn't hung around at our place.

Thanks to the way the world is skewed, as the children grew I spent my days at home, acting as a taxi service to my growing children, ferrying them from ballet to football and back again, while Patrick was out there, in the workplace, earning ever-greater fortunes – and doing lots of other things as well.

I always loved my part in our little equation. My kids, the home. Our life. It seemed more than enough, to do this well. And, to be honest, I was never qualified to do much else, on paper at least. After escaping my mother's house, any letters after my name were always going to be AWOL, not PhD. So, when I briefly considered going back to work after having the kids, I realised it would be crazy.

I loved what I was doing in my small domestic sphere and, though I felt a tiny bit vulnerable, not having a Plan B, why did I need one? After all, Patrick was my Plan A. He would always be in my corner. Why wouldn't he be? I was his greatest fan, and his support system. Clean shirt? Dinner on the table? Cheerleader and groupie? Tick, tick, tick, I took care of everything at home and made it oh-so-easy for him to leave it every day. My hero, conquering the outside world.

So, once I was pregnant, that was that. I earned little enough from my job anyway. Certainly wasn't worth the hassle of finding another, once the kids were here, to pay a pittance straight into some other woman's pocket. If anyone was going to be doing the child-minding, it would be me. And, because I'd seen how not to do it, at very close quarters, I was going to be the best mum ever. Hands down.

Of course, I hadn't really reckoned with the reality. Pushing swings, for example. The minutes drag more heavily than the arc of the rusted chains, the creaking of the frame is the yawning stretch of time. And how do you discipline children, when all you've ever known is the sharp sting of the slap . . . or worse? It was tough.

Crying babies did my head in, toddlers outwitted me, the whole applecart was in danger of tipping. But then, as usual, I resorted to something that had never let me down, in all my lonely years on the planet. Books.

Toddler Taming. I wished. *The Contented Little Baby.* In my dreams. *Positive Parenting.* Ugh. But gradually, the kids grew, and I did too. My skills developed, one step ahead, most of the time, and we scrambled through. It helped a lot that I wasn't a helpless junkie and alcoholic. And that I loved them so, so much.

Chapter 38

Now

Becca

Becca took a look round the Indian restaurant and snapped off another bit of the poppadum in front of her before sneaking it into her mouth. Anxious, she'd left too much time for her journey, found the place too quickly. And now he was late. It was still almost empty, snowy tables beautifully laid and expectant, teenage waiters loitering around the back, whispering in their magenta waistcoats. She wouldn't have worn one for love nor money at their age. The music was muted, the lighting was dim. She felt like a right pillock, sitting here. Lonely splendour, they said, didn't they?

She didn't bother with the little dips. The red one was usually ferocious, the green one too gloopy, and the chopped-up onion . . . Well, was there a reason why she shouldn't have onion breath tonight? She squirmed inwardly, loath to admit her pathetic longings, even to herself. She'd been so sure she didn't fancy him. But as soon as there'd been a glimmer . . . she slapped herself down, mentally. *Get over yourself*. But would onion help? She put the tiny spoon down.

She sighed a little as the poppadum disappeared. Why did food always do that around her? She checked her watch again. Then her phone. No message since the one fifteen minutes ago. *Held up. There in 5.* 'In a minute' had been the childhood phrase her mother had fobbed her off with all the time. *In a minute* meant twenty, thirty or more. Now five did too. No wonder she was so bad at maths.

She was just finishing off her second glass of white when Johno sauntered in. 'Well then, Becs. Started without me? No, no, you're all right,' he laughed as she jumped to explain the mess of poppadum crumbs, the glaringly empty silver platter, the glass, ditto. The chopped onion looked forlorn. 'I'd have done the same. You ordered yet? Or just eaten all the starters?'

Once they were through the menu palaver, they both resettled themselves and Becca took him in, really took him in, for the first time. He'd spruced himself up. Was it for her? She couldn't quite believe it, but the freshly slicked hair, the shirt with ramrod creases down the sleeves, even the occasional waft of aftershave that reached to her across the table like a diffident kitten's paw. They all suggested preparation – preening, even.

She, by contrast, had made little effort. Well, little effort for a girl. She was clean, and so were her clothes. But they were the usual – sweatshirt, jeans. All right, jeggings. The hoody was her favourite, from Hollister. She'd had it forever but it had been dead pricey, once upon a time. *That doesn't count*, she told herself. *He's all gussied up and you aren't.*

Well, so what? There had never been any chance, anyway. She eyed him covertly. No. He was just too . . . successful for her. Successful with women, that was. Career-wise, he was only a couple of rungs above her, and she'd barely got started – and intended to go as far as she could. But on the personal life front, it was clear that he'd outstrip her any day of the week. He had that look, like he knew the inside of a pair of knickers all too well. He might actually be married, she hadn't made enquiries. That would be like getting a megaphone and shouting her interest in the incident room. It was a big station and they worked very different areas. No gossip about him. That she'd heard, anyway.

There was no ring on his finger. She looked closely. No indentation, either. Still, she felt a little on the back foot. Should she be flattered by his efforts? She just felt flummoxed. *Typical,* her mother's voice hissed in her ear. *Over-thinking. Just make the most of it, girl.*

She pinned a smile to her face. 'Busy day, Johno?'

'You know how it is. Always happens when you've got one foot out the door, doesn't it? I'd been waiting all day for this report, then suddenly it drops. Had to look at it.'

'Oh, no, I wasn't . . . I didn't mean . . .'

'You're all right,' he said again. 'How about you? Lot on?'

Becca sighed. As always, there were mounds of chores on her desk. But so few she was interested in. It reminded her of why she was here, why she'd got into all this in the first place. Louise Bridges.

The waiter appeared with a stack of plates, started polishing them with a purple cloth and putting them down in front of them. His colleague wheeled over a trolley groaning with dishes. Becca winced. She'd probably over-ordered. Again. The fragrance of cardamom and ginger fought briefly with aftershave and won. They both leaned forward, Becca's eyes wide with greed. There was a silent tussle over the yellow mountain of rice and she retreated, mortified, only for him to give way, sit back with a smile. They chewed until the silence seemed charged. Becca leaned forward earnestly, lifted a fork to her mouth, put it down. Fiddled with it. His eyebrows rose.

'Do you ever get a case, or not even get it, just find yourself on the fringes of it, and it's just . . . so much more interesting than all the stuff you should be doing?' she burst out, plucking at the stiff linen of the tablecloth. She saw his eyes tracking her fingers and moved her hands to her lap. She didn't want to give too much away.

'You mean like the Louise Bridges case? Why's that got under your skin?'

Bingo. He hadn't forgotten. Becca flushed. But it was hard to explain, even to herself. 'There's something about that woman. I just don't think she should . . . get away with it.'

'With what, though? No sign she's done anything,' he said, almost absent-mindedly, ladling the thick reddish sauce from his madras onto his plate then pushing the dish her way.

She shook her head. 'No sign she's done anything, *on the surface*. But then, no one's really been looking, have they? There are reasons why I'm interested.'

'Reasons? What sort of reasons?' She'd got his attention back from the food now, but he was looking at her as if she was one mushroom short of the full bhaji.

Becca rolled her eyes. 'Reasons for her to have done it, of course. What is it about that woman? Anyone else sitting on a pile of money after the sudden, unexplained death of their partner, and we'd be digging away. With her, it's "how would you like your money, madam, gold bars or a cheque?"'

'Hang on a minute. It's not unexplained. It's all been neatly labelled, filed away. And why would she kill him? Father of her children, sole breadwinner?'

'Don't say you lot haven't looked into it at all? The insurance?'

He leaned forward, one hand absently pulping his naan bread.

Becca took a breath. This was her chance. If she could convince him, maybe they could look into the case together . . . She started her spiel, left nothing out. Those papers, the way Louise had hidden them, what they'd actually said . . .

'Wait. You mean you've pulled up the papers? How? On what authority?' Johno was staring at her. She felt her colour rising. She wouldn't mention the letter she'd stashed away that night.

'Well, I've done some IT training . . .' She said it vaguely, hoping it would cover a multitude of sins. But he was immediately electrified.

'You're kidding, right?' He leaned across the white tablecloth, now splattered here and there with yellow dollops of turmeric. 'That's illegal,' he hissed.

Becca wasn't sure what to say. She was astonished at his ferocity. On the one hand, yes, she knew it wasn't strictly ethical. She was a police officer, for God's sake. On the other hand – look at what she'd found. She stared at him, half a child with a hand in the cookie jar, half a professional who'd been vindicated by the evidence. Gradually, vindication won out. She sat up straighter, held his stare. 'What's really illegal is that bitch trying to get away with it.'

'Oh. Here we go,' he said, sitting back, relaxing.

'What's that supposed to mean?'

'Just, you know. This is one of those women things, isn't it? You don't like her.'

'I don't like anyone who breaks the law. And I don't like to see people getting off the hook – not *like this*,' she said quickly. 'Can't you see? She's up to something.'

'Looks like you are, too,' he said, glancing at her then turning his attention back to the food.

They ate in silence for a few minutes. Not even the smoothness of the korma sauce could appease the ache Becca felt, though. This wasn't how this had been meant to go. Suddenly the world felt heavier, darker. Like it had before. She stabbed a chunk of chicken viciously with her fork, chewed it unnecessarily thoroughly, looked all round the restaurant – anywhere, but at him.

After a while, he gave a little cough. She turned back to him reluctantly. He was smiling, and the smile broadened as she caught his eye. Then, slowly, she was grinning, too. 'Look, let's not fall out about it. I'll keep a watching brief, how's that?' Johno's head was on one side, as though he'd promised a favourite niece a trip to the fair.

Becca nodded warily. But inside she was exultant. This was what she'd been after. True, Johno didn't seem convinced that

Louise Bridges had done anything wrong. But, with more eyes on the woman, she was bound to make a slip. Becca would bet anything on it. She toasted him with her now-lukewarm wine. He smirked and signalled over to the waiter for more.

Chapter 39

Then

Shopping. It was supposed to be what I was good at. My profession, if you like. Or so Patrick used to say, after a glass or four. But there were times when it was just another chore. One trip sticks in my memory, for all the wrong reasons.

Life in the suburbs, with Patrick, with kids. It had been a golden dream for so long. But the children were soon at school, and Patrick . . . well, he was off doing whatever. I needed someone, and there Stacy was. After the NCT, we'd chosen the same nurseries. Then we were at the school gates together, and busy hanging out in between drop-offs too. I'd moved on so far that I was the one who was the mentor, the Jen in our little relationship. I won't lie, it felt good.

'There's never anything here to suit me,' Stacy always wailed when we shopped. This time was no different. She was flipping through the racks, jangling the hangers in a hopeless, angry way, too fast, too indiscriminate. Her emotions always seemed to be on the surface. Like braille but much easier to read, in a way I could never afford to be. She made me laugh, too.

'No rush. What about this?' I held it up. An embroidered cardigan. Deceptively simple, just that bit of embellishment lifting it. It glinted in the overhead lights, catching the eye. In fact, I quite fancied it myself.

'Oh, didn't see that.' Stacy held it up against herself, spread out the sides awkwardly, seeing if the fabric would stretch, the hanger tucked under her neck. 'I don't know, it's really not my colour.' Stacy jammed it back on the rail.

I picked the top up, sauntered over to the mirror. Perfect. Then I caught sight of Stacy. Try as she might, she couldn't keep the downward drop of her mouth from giving her away.

There was no need for me to rub it in. I popped the top back decisively. 'Not for me, either. Here, try this.' I disentangled another, this time in a rich emerald that would take the heat out of permanently flushed cheeks. And this was the right size. Stacy was as happy as a Labrador with a new tennis ball, whisking off to the changing room with her find. Correction: *my* find. Not that I'd take the credit, you understand. But sometimes it gets tiring, nudging other people in the right direction, correcting their mistakes – half the time, stopping them from making them in the first place.

Female friendship is like that, as I'd gradually discovered. Alliances, sometimes stronger than steel, sometimes spun from finer silk than a spider's web. Affection, sometimes with a dash of venom on the side. Worth the effort, absolutely. It's all credits in the favour bank, isn't it? I knew there'd come a time when I'd need this goodwill. A pick-up from school at the last minute. A playdate when I had to be somewhere else. In the world I'd found myself in, or had hammered out – the jury was still pondering which it was – women needed to stick together. Against our better halves. If that was what it took.

I sighed and selected something for myself. A substitute. Not the cardigan, though that was still tempting me. A little top instead. I couldn't pretend I needed this, either. It would just be another shopping scalp, cluttering up my already over-stuffed dressing room, never likely to make it out in public again. I shrugged it on, indifferent. Of course, it looked great. I'd have to buy it. But maybe I'd order the cardigan I really wanted online,

171

save it for times when Stacy wasn't around. That way I'd be having my cake and eating it too.

Not that I would ever dream of doing *that*. How long had it been since I'd sunk my teeth into a sponge, felt the pippy sting of jam, the smooth ooze of cream? Thing was, I was more in love with the full-length mirror in this cubicle than any pud. Simple as. I'd hated communal changing rooms when I was really young, my body as unformed as the dough in a tube of JusRol croissants, no friends to screen me from curious glances. But then I hit my stride and realised I could change all that. If I just put in the effort. I wasn't born tall, blonde and beautiful. Well, tall, yes. The rest was all my own work.

The mirror showed that I'd got what I always wanted – the figure, the look, the hair and everything that went with it, from bag to shoes. Bag to *husband*. I suppose you'd like me to say it was tough. It wasn't really. It was a waiting game, and you had to have discipline. *Just say no.* Though I loved food, and still always wolfed it down too fast, nowadays it was salad on my plate. I'd turned down fatbergs of junk, enough chocolate to solace the heartbroken for decades. Second helpings, cheese, doughnuts – nothing passed these lips. Unless I was out with a girlfriend and had to push a bit of cheesecake around my plate, just to show I didn't need to try.

Was it worth it? Well, yes, absolutely. Look at all I had.

I gave myself one last smile in the mirror, the ghost of a wink even, then threw back the curtains and stepped out to join Stacy. Of course she was taking the emerald-green number. She bustled to the till first, then it was my turn. We were chatting, arranging that Stacy would pick the kids up from swimming (see what I mean about favours? Would that have happened if I'd got the cardi I wanted?) and I was keying in my number, when the machine squealed.

I remember that sound like it was yesterday. Not just because Em's scream hit the same high note, when she answered the door on the worst day of our lives. And not just because the card reader squealed again, when the shop assistant, apologising profusely, took the card and tried swiping it through herself.

CARD DECLINED came the message, and suddenly the girl was a lot less flustered. The look she gave me changed from embarrassed to sour. Just like that, I'd gone from being a very good customer put out by the shop's incompetence, to a chancer trying to defraud her. That was the point at which I started wishing they'd turn the thermostat down in that place. I could feel Stacy's eyes on me, inquisitive beetles, but despite the throb of heat in my cheeks, something inside me had frozen. I knew I should be passing this off airily as some weird mistake, implying the machine had a glitch, but I'd shut down. It was too much like old times.

'Have you got another card you'd like to try?' the chit on the till asked me, breaking into my thoughts, a mocking half-smile playing somewhere behind the apparent concern. Stacy turned away, her attempt at diplomacy, and fiddled around with some scented candles. I shuddered inwardly, looked in my purse, the serried ranks of possibilities, AmEx, MasterCard. But I didn't want to take the risk. What I wanted, really wanted, was to run.

Suddenly I was 7 again, in the supermarket with my mum. Her face was often flushed, too, a roadmap of veins tracing the journey from morning remorse to afternoon bottle. Everything on the conveyor belt, that I'd so optimistically stuck in her basket while we chugged round the shop, was now negotiable – except the booze. Goodbye Sugar Puffs, farewell crispy pancakes.

'Don't you want it now?' tutted the shop girl loudly, exasperated. I'd turned away from her, my face and neck stained with this shame, and the memory of so many others. Stacy's head shot up but she didn't spin round. I tried for offhand. 'No, I've decided against it, bit last season,' I said. But we all knew, the three of us, that the truth was different. Simpler.

I couldn't afford it.

But why? While I busied myself appearing normal, striding from the little shopping arcade to the bay where we'd parked our cars, nodding along to Stacy's drivel about her kid's clarinet exam, my head was full of noise. What was Patrick playing at? *The fucker*. How could he let me down like this? Show me up? In public? And in front of Stacy, too.

I knew I should have said something to her, shrugged it off with a joke, been my usual self. But I couldn't. It cut too deep. This one slap in the face joined up with all those other humiliations. It dragged me under. With my mother, I'd come to expect it. But Patrick?

This wasn't part of our deal.

I was the stay-at-home mum, making sure his shirts were ironed, meals on the table. Mundane enough. But I was also the glossy advert for his success: the MILF on his arm at all the corporate dinners, my killer heels impaling the tongues of all the other men. Not as easy as it looked, but I'd played my part, learned the rules. My clothes were now almost always perfect, on this side of glitzy, but well on that side of frumpy. It was a balancing act that I tried to achieve without ever looking down. Fifty years ago, a woman my age would have opened the door wearing curlers and a nylon housecoat. Now here I was, looking younger than I had a decade ago and even skinnier too. He didn't know how lucky he was.

And yet, he wasn't holding up his end. What was going on?

Stacy was chuntering on about the exam. I played my part mechanically. *Yes, music theory was always the most difficult bit. Terrible, the way the examiners tried to catch the kids out.* All the time, my mind was whirring. How could she care so much about this crap? Yet I knew that on any other day I'd have been fired up too. Em had only passed her last piano grade by two marks. Stacy's Violet had failed by one.

The fact that I'd always felt sorry for Stacy before made all this so much worse. She was the loser these days, not me. But now I'd been humbled – and in front of her.

174

Beside my consternation, another emotion was growing, like one of those time-release films. A tiny crimson speck was opening into a blood-red rose. Anger, with its scalpel-sharp thorns.

I've never been a fan of tables being turned. Unless I am moving the furniture myself.

Chapter 40

Then

I couldn't tell you the day when I fell out of love with Patrick. It wasn't the same as falling *in* love – that moment when I saw him for the first time and I knew, just knew, that I was his and he was mine.

This was more of a creeping realisation.

There was the first problem – that he loved me, really loved me, initially anyway. That meant that I had to doubt him. In my book, it meant he had to be a) an extremely bad picker and b) fundamentally flawed himself. I struggled against this analysis, I really did. I kept on track, wrestled down the side of me that immediately said this made him as trashy as me, not worth bothering with. I decided not to devalue him, just because I didn't value myself.

And it worked. The rustlings of my dark soul were stilled by the sheer pleasure of our time together, especially before the children came along. That sounds bad, and I've said before they are the loves of my life. Nevertheless, not even the most devoted parent would pretend that kids make things easier with your spouse. When they came, what they did provide was a distraction, a new focus.

Unfortunately, Patrick, for all his sterling qualities, couldn't cope with not having my undivided attention.

There was another truth which grew inexorably over the years, just gradually seeping out from the sides of my consciousness.

It was that Patrick was the type of man who was not capable of faithfulness.

Even if he'd married, I don't know, the hottest porn star on the planet, who turned out to be a brilliant cook, housekeeper and nanny into the bargain, and also looked just right at corporate dinners, he still wouldn't have been able to help himself. He always had an eye out for other women.

You might say, *don't they all?* Is there a man alive who is true and pure and devoted through and through? And women are no better. I'd given the odd sideways glance, over the years, for sure. But I would never have acted on those fleeting impulses, and there Patrick and I parted ways. Who was it who said, 'No man is a hero to his valet?' And certainly no wife looks at her husband and thinks he is a paragon – or not for long. The closer you get to another person, the more clearly you see their flaws, the bits missing, the chips and cracks.

Don't get me wrong, it wasn't anything dire with Patrick. He wasn't a beast. Just the usual. He left the loo seat up. He dropped his clothes on the floor and didn't touch them again until they were safely laundered and stowed away, apparently by fairies for all the thanks I got. He couldn't take a joke directed at him, criticism cut him to the heart. He was just a man, no more, no less. Lazy, ungrateful, sometimes boorish, but, as I often reminded myself, the man I loved.

But he gave other women the eye and was surprised when I took it badly.

I used to think it was just a reflex, meaningless but annoying, like a propensity to belch. But, as time went by, I began to suspect it was a lot more than that.

Our sex life inevitably suffered, thanks to two children and a busy life. I did my best, running to keep still, staying available and alluring despite my exhaustion. I suppose he simply tired of

177

me, though I tried my hardest to keep everything up to scratch. Beauty treatments, manicures, the works. Pilates, yoga, kettlebells, spinning, Zumba, there wasn't a fitness fad I hadn't mastered. I read the newspapers to avoid getting too boring and mumsy. Knew more about the FTSE 500 than he did. I even joined a book group, though the rest of the bunch were happier swilling wine than getting to grips with the chosen novel. But he turned away from me more and more.

No one is perfect. I'm not, as you may have gathered by now, and nobody I've met on my way here has been either. Some are a lot nicer than others. Maybe some hide their bad sides more effectively.

Patrick was a nice man but flawed. That was about the size of it. But for me, the day when I admitted that might as well have been the day the sky fell in. I'd been fixated on him so long that, to finally see him for what he was, well, it was devastating. Especially when I'd staked so much on him.

Of course, he wasn't to know how serious a game we were playing. But I felt he should have guessed.

Chapter 41

Then

So there I was, in my perfect home, with a life carved out of nothing and two beautiful children. It was all I'd ever wanted, and more.

But I'd wanted Patrick in this picture too. Perhaps I'd been greedy. Certainly I'd been unrealistic. Because it turns out you can't have it all.

As soon as I took my eye off him, he was off. With another woman.

So, in some ways, I had managed to replicate my dear mother's pattern after all. I'd chosen an unfaithful mate. I'd only picked the one, mind, whereas hers formed a disorderly queue.

The first time I caught Patrick out, I seriously thought the world would end. I thought my heart would break, thought the marriage was over. I'd never felt such pain. Are you sitting there, feeling smug, thinking it'll never happen to you? Don't get too cosy, will you? If it happened to me, then I hate to say it but yes, it could happen to you.

There are always signs. Different with every bloke, I suppose. With Patrick, it was an attentive/argumentative thing. The guilt would make him buy a bunch of flowers on the way back from the sex. He'd enjoy my delighted surprise and gratitude, it would make him feel great about himself, help him brush off the remorse. But once I'd said thank you as much as anyone could, he'd start getting annoyed with me. I wasn't grateful enough for the real present he'd bought me, the one hiding behind the bouquet – the fact that he had come home at all. I'd taken that for granted, not realising it was negotiable, that he felt he might have a world of more interesting options open to him.

And my worst sin was that I wasn't *her*, whoever the *she* of the moment was. His deep resentment, that I was too tired to listen to him talk about himself with the usual degree of sparkling interest and, what was worse, now had a child hanging off my tit, would then make him pick a fight.

At first, I was mystified. There I was, up to my neck in Pampers, longing for conversation with a grown-up, and instead I'd get all this. But then things started to add up, like heavy beads clicking into place on an abacus. Even though I didn't really want to see the truth, I couldn't avoid what was going on.

Working late, that old classic. Then his phone would be off for crucial chunks of time. Texts coming late at night, that he'd announce too loudly were 'just work'. Calls he had to take behind a closed door. A certain look in his eye.

For a while, I clung to the hope that I was imagining it, due to the sleep deprivation. But eventually he relaxed enough to leave his mobile unguarded and a lovey-dovey text pinged in. I was able to read it before the screen went dark again. No need, even, to hack in.

Didn't say a thing. Just felt my heart shatter into a million pieces.

'You're quiet,' he said, in that new, accusing tone. I immediately went into chatty mode, while inside I reeled. How could he? When here I sat, with his tiny newborn son, the wife and mother he'd always wanted. That I'd yearned to be. For so, so long.

It was a low blow. Even thinking about it now makes me cry. There I was, at my lowest ebb, struggling with breastfeeding and hating it, spending hours a day on my own with a baby that only seemed to sleep when it was least convenient to me. The occasional coffee with Stacy was great, but there were still great swathes of time when the world was just me and Giles, neither of us convinced that I was cutting it as a mum. And now Patrick had done this.

He'd kicked me when I was down, and it took me ages to get my head around it. But gradually I pulled myself together. It would be even harder to manage a newborn without his daddy. At least Patrick did stuff around the house . . . well, he stomped around putting the empty wine bottles out once a week. Without him I'd be doing that, as well as everything else.

Eventually, I got my head around it. Even saw where he was coming from. I'd let things slide. True, it was only a few weeks after Giles's birth when I found him out the first time, but obviously our sex life had flatlined. I gritted my teeth, took the dressings off my caesarean scar, and did the necessary. Good job it hadn't been a vaginal delivery. Anyway, my shadowy opposite number disappeared overnight. I felt a pang for her. No chance that he'd come clean to her and admit his wife was dragging herself round the house with a colicky newborn and had been temporarily too tired to do the nasty with him. Because that would have made him look like the louse he definitely was.

Should I confront Patrick? I weighed it up. This was another of those occasions when a close group of female friends might have come in handy. I sized Stacy up over one of our coffees, deliberated getting her take on it. But in the end it was too painful, letting my humiliation out into the light of day. I did what I'd always done; curled round the hurt, waited for the ache to go away. Considered my options. Once I'd thought hard for a bit, I came to a conclusion I was happy with. Well, something I thought I could live with, at any rate.

I let it go. I could see that Patrick was struggling now he was not my number one priority. It was silly, but true. Men are so keen to prove their virility, get you pregnant, produce a son and heir, aren't they? And then, the realisation hits them. They've created their own replacement. For, as much as I had adored Patrick, my little boy Giles was now top of the heap. Even when he was yelling blue murder. So Patrick had to prove himself to some other woman.

She was the first but, of course, not the last. Now I saw the signs coming, billboards along a familiar stretch of road, I counted those girls in and out. Another popped up when I had Em. And there were many more, studded through our marriage like those ugly silver lumps on a Rottweiler's collar.

Somehow, it never suited me to make a big scene. While I didn't confront the issue, it could be pushed into the background, when his latest had lost whatever allure had snared him in the first place. I even felt a tiny bit magnanimous towards the girls, I really did. I knew, none better, what it was like to yearn for this man. And I also knew the real Patrick. No one else knew him better.

For them, it would be breathless excitement for the first few weeks, when he'd promised he'd leave me – us – for them. Once he'd had them a few times and the novelty had worn off, and once I'd braced myself and done my conjugal duty again, things would start to go pear-shaped for the poor old girlfriend. There'd be lengthening pauses between calls, then the excuses would come tumbling out, and the horrible truth would dawn. He'd never had the slightest intention of leaving home for them. My heart bled. Not.

Often they were actually doing me a favour. When we'd first got together, I'd thought there would never come a time when I didn't want Patrick. But the reality was that two children, hot on each other's tiny pink heels, was a massive passion killer. Sometimes I was too tired for sex, and sometimes it just came right down on my to-do list, after scraping the hair out of the shower plughole and descaling the kettle.

I liked to feel I could reel him in though, when a fling had gone on too long, when it suited me to take him back. I consoled myself that this gave me a sort of power. And this always worked very well. Until he went and overstepped the mark.

Meanwhile, I had the kids to bring up. Don't get me wrong, he was involved, but it's the mum that sets the tone, isn't it? And this mum didn't really know, at first, which tone to adopt. As usual, I fell back on my tried and tested method of decoding the human race – my childcare books. Unfortunately, the kiddie gurus seemed to delight in contradicting each other. Leave the baby to cry, but don't, feed on demand, but stick to a rigid four-hourly schedule, give rewards while potty training, or go straight to hell for it. Which do you pick?

Most people have an inner compass, set by their own child-hoods. I didn't, and I freely admit I made mistakes. But then, as Larkin pointed out, all parents fuck their children up. They don't mean to, but they do. They don't even need to have endured a shit upbringing themselves. Sometimes complacency can make you the worst sort of parent. I watched people in the park, I studied the remnants of my NCT group as we all got on with our lives, and I judged other people's parenting ferociously, mainly so I could assess how I was doing myself. Once, I overheard two mums on a bench saying that too many blankets could contribute to cot death. I rushed home and threw half of Giles's bedding in the bin.

Watching other mothers cooing over their babies helped me too. While I loved mine to bits, I was quite happy not being in the same room as them for much of the time. But this seemed wrong, from what I gleaned. I'd just wanted a bit of time to myself. But once I worked out this wasn't done, I really took to togetherness, and we were quite the sight as I took them for airings in their state-of-the-art prams.

Celebrities now make such a thing of snapping back to their pre-baby size the moment the bundle of joy has been extracted. Believe me, I've been there, done that, before they even thought of it. I made a point of being back in pre-pregnancy jeans, scars

183

and all, as soon as humanly possible. I used to think it was probably one of the reasons Patrick didn't leave me sooner.

One of my best sources of feedback on my mothering performance was Jill. As a professional woman, and a no-nonsense
person, I hadn't been expecting much granny gushing from her.
But she surprised me by going baby-crazy. Maybe she'd hadn't
had the time or inclination when Patrick had been small. Or
maybe she was just gaga for her grandkids. But she showered
Giles and Em with love and with surprisingly soppy blue and
pink babygros, which I only put them into when we were on
our way round to hers.

As a newly minted granny, and Patrick's mother as well, I
wasn't expecting her to be neutral on the way I did things. If
I was messing up, she'd surely let me know. But, aside from an
odd pause in the conversation every now and then, I felt she
was giving me a solid eight to nine out of ten on bringing up
babies. True, she'd try to be tactful even if I was doing badly,
she wouldn't want access to her beloved babies withdrawn. She
knew that I was in charge of the social calendar and there could
be many bleak months when we were terribly, terribly busy if she
put even a toe of one of her funny posh pumps out of line. But
Jill was cleverer than that.

We were sitting there one day, in early spring, in her garden,
She'd either falsely got the impression that I loved the great
outdoors, from our very first meeting, or she couldn't resist
rubbing my nose in that early subterfuge, I was never sure which.
I certainly wouldn't have put it past her to know full well that I
didn't know one end of a rhododendron from the other, and to
be indulging in a long-running dig at my expense. But I didn't
care. It gave us something to chat about, as we cooed over little
Giles, asleep between us in his car seat.

'Will you be planting a tree for Giles?' she asked that day.

Naturally, I just looked at her as though she were mad. True,
we did have a patch of garden at our house, not yet our wonderful

forever home, as people say these days, but still a solid family place that was evidence of Patrick's gradual ascent – with me shoving him on from behind, of course.

It was not long after I'd made the discovery of his first affair, and to say I was a bit off him was an understatement. 'A tree?'

'Hasn't Patrick told you? We did that for him, and his grandfather did it for his father.' As usual, Jill sounded a bit wistful when talking about Patrick's dad. Divorce was still spoken of in hushed tones in families like theirs. For one thing, it screwed up inheritance so badly, she'd once confided in me. 'I'm so sorry for Patrick, having to share with those . . . other children,' she'd said, and it was as close to venomous as a woman like her could ever get.

Sitting there, that day, still inwardly digesting the knowledge of Patrick's betrayal, I heard the tale of the trees, remembered her words about the divided estate, and vowed then that I'd keep our marriage together. For as long as I could, anyway.

Chapter 42

Now

Becca

It wasn't a surprise that Johno had turned out to be such a waste of space. Becca couldn't honestly remember a single man who hadn't – apart from her dad, of course. But she'd had such high hopes. Again.

When would she learn? She tutted to herself as she stared into the depths of her terminal. She'd expected to hear from him, after their . . . well, she wouldn't call it a date, exactly. Although it had been so like one. She remembered his aftershave, his shirt. But nothing. When she'd seen him in the corridor last week, he'd all but blanked her. *What do you expect, wearing that hoody?* her mother would say.

In the desk opposite, Burke's neighbour whispered to him. 'See? She's off again.' He shrugged his shoulders, but gave the woman a quick complicit grimace.

Becca lifted the polystyrene cup to her mouth, oblivious. Sipped up some of the sweetness. She ought to cut out the sugar. Tomorrow, tomorrow. For the moment, it was helping her keep going. Yesterday had been another late night, following Louise from one corner of the internet to the other, and then a turn waiting outside her house as well, to see what the woman was doing in person. Well, that was precisely nothing at all, last night. The lights had been on when Becca got there, then they'd gone off, and that was as exciting as it got. If Becca didn't know so much better, she'd say Louise had a quieter life than her own.

But that was just a smokescreen, she knew it, had always known it right from the start. She'd sniffed her out, and now it had been proven. Bugger Burke, bugger Johno. She'd been vindicated. Patrick Bridges' email was a rich seam that she was mining, deeper and deeper.

She shook her head as she thought about it, and then was seized with a ferocious yawn. Even the milkshake couldn't pump enough glucose into her system to keep the tiredness at bay. She could do with a break. But that was what Louise wanted, wasn't it?

No, she wouldn't give up now. Just when she was so close.

She had to keep going.

Chapter 43

Then

We'd tried it before, and it had always done the trick. A weekend break. Time away, from the kids, from the stresses and strains of normal life. And, in Patrick's case, away from whoever it was that was currently threatening to bring the whole edifice of our marriage down.

I suppose if we'd gone to the same place every time, then we might have been able to settle more easily into the routine. But would it have come to symbolise every other time our marriage had been in tatters? Would I have counted the months, preferably years, between our stays, remembered what, or rather who, the last weekend had been expressly designed to forget? No, it was better to find a new spot every time. Pretend this was just another lovely treat in a life filled with luxury and abundance, not my desperate attempt to oust the latest piggy-in-the-middle from our marriage bed.

This hotel was lush, I had to admit. I looked around the bedroom and whistled. 'Business must be good.' He'd booked it himself, this time. I should have realised immediately this meant a conscience that was even more heavily overloaded than usual.

Patrick winked at me – yes, he was still doing that, after all these years. ''Course it is, darling. You know me. Strength to strength.' He loped over, almost wading through the velvety pile of the carpet, skirting a four-poster bed piled high with pointless cushions that were destined to hit the floor pretty soon. 'I know how to show my special girl a good time.'

I bit my lip. There was so much I could say, wanted to say. So many reproaches, now. But that was contrary to the spirit of our agreement. I'd made my decision, way back when Giles had been a tiny squirming thing in his Moses basket. I'd kept my mouth shut then. I'd keep it shut now. Whatever it cost.

Somehow, I'd turned myself into a politician's wife – the poor sap who makes tea for the journos door-stepping her unfaithful husband, who keeps a bright smile hoisted no matter what scandal lurks below decks. How had I got here? How had I become something I couldn't help despising?

But there was still so much of my life that I loved. My home. And yes, I'll admit it, my status. The way the other mums' eyes followed me, as I showed up with my bag and my boots and my BMW. I enjoyed knowing how far I'd come and seeing other people take me, now, for what I only appeared to be. And like a river running deep and strong under these superficial streams, there were my kids. They were behind everything I did and endured.

Was their security still reason enough to keep this going? I took a deep breath – difficult, when he was squeezing the life out of me, then getting handsy in those old familiar ways.

Despite it all – the humiliations, the disappointment, the betrayal – it seemed the answer was yes. Here I was, and my body still responded. He was the one I'd chosen, till death did us part. This lovely hotel room, his undivided company for a change, our life continuing on together . . . these were all things I wanted. I let myself giggle up at him, coquettishly, moved my hand to the buttons of my silk shirt. 'Come on then, show me,' I said.

Later that afternoon, I ran a bath in the deep, white tub, and threw in the entire bottle of Jo Malone bubbles. Why not? There'd be another replacing it in the morning. I was padding around in the white velvet robe, enjoying the feel of the plush carpet between my toes, peeping out onto our magnificent view – actual peacocks on the lawn this time, though the male was sullenly dragging his finery after him, refusing to shake a tail feather at his mangy-looking mate. 'Don't blame you,' I whispered to him. Well, she could have made a bit more of an effort.

Patrick was downstairs, ostensibly watching the footie in one of the innumerable lounges, probably trying to ring his latest floozie. I smiled. He'd have a job. I'd silently removed her number from his contacts while he'd been asleep, counting on him not to have memorised it. Well, I didn't want her disturbing our little break.

I stretched luxuriously, thinking again how magical sex was. I'd been pretty sure I'd be faking everything, today, feeling so stressed and threatened, but it didn't take much for instinct to override little things like irritation and anger. Now that we'd reconnected, I felt a lot more charitable towards Patrick, despite his lying, cheating ways. He was still mine, after all.

I padded into the bathroom to turn off the taps. Damn, I'd run the water too hot. Occupational hazard with hotels. The plumbing was always an unknown. I turned on the cold tap, shoved up the sleeve of my robe to fish out the plug. Didn't want the bath overrunning.

That's when I heard it. Wasn't sure, at first, over the roar of the water, the thuds from the pipes. Old buildings always had air bubbles somewhere in the system. But no, there it was, an insistent, artificial little tune, just rising above the din. I shut the taps off as quickly as I could. That wasn't my ring tone. And Patrick had his phone on him. I ran into the bedroom, wet feet marking the carpet, and looked around frantically.

It wasn't coming from my holdall or Patrick's, just by the door where he'd dropped it. I bent down and, somewhat ridiculously, looked under the bed. Not so much as a piece of fluff. This was what Patrick was paying stratospheric rates for. I flung open the wardrobe doors. Suddenly it was louder.

I'd unpacked already. Yes, I'm a tidy person, we know that. But if you stack clothes neatly in a suitcase, then getting them out and putting them on a wardrobe shelf is no big deal. I lurched forward to flip through Patrick's neat pile for our stay, sweaters, shirts and trousers. Nothing. Just then the sound died.

But not before I'd realised where it must be coming from. Patrick's briefcase, in the bottom of the wardrobe. Tucked behind our shoes. I hadn't put it way back there.

I took it out and looked at it. It was a fancy number I'd bought him a couple of Christmases ago, from Coach. The smooth tan leather smelt divine. It was bloody well locked.

I rocked back on my heels, thinking hard. His keys.

Patrick was no James Bond. This was about the most devious bit of subterfuge I'd ever caught him in. With one corner of my mind, I was impressed. The rest of me was plain angry.

Now I just needed as much information as I could get. I ran to the bedside table. A creature of habit, he'd emptied out his pockets before he'd emptied himself into me. Along with his small change and some crumpled-up receipts, there were his keys. And at the end of the bunch was a weedy little one. Gotcha.

Within seconds, I had the case undone and the phone in my hand. It was light, cheap, the type they sell you at dodgy market stalls. I couldn't quite believe Patrick was stooping to this. But, on the other hand, he knew me so well.

I'd begun to pore through every manifestation of his flings, I scrutinised his careful pruning of messages. Not at first. But over the years, I'd decided that if there was something going on that was supposed to be out of my control, I wanted to have as much of an overview as possible. While we never discussed any of it, he had to know that I always knew.

But he'd been getting more secretive recently, making it harder for me to follow his tracks. And now he'd really taken things a step further. A step too far.

The phone's screen said it all. 'One missed call.' And the number? There it was, large as life. I blinked.

No. *No.* I couldn't believe it.

It was horribly familiar. It was a phone *I* rang almost as often as, apparently, he did himself. I collapsed into a heap on the absurdly plush carpet.

Stacy. My best friend.

He really was outdoing himself this time. *Two* bits on the side. The first was nothing, just some intern at work. I realised that he was probably dumping her even as I sat here.

But this? Stacy? This was *my best friend.* I looked at the phone for a minute, as though I'd never seen one before, feeling like Pandora. Should I look? Could I face it? But I had to. There was still the faintest possibility that this was innocent, despite all I knew about Patrick. Maybe they were planning some sort of surprise for me? I pressed the *message* button, not sure if the phone would be code protected, but a line of texts popped up obediently. I scrolled through, nausea rising. Oh, Stacy had been planning some surprises, all right. But not for me. Just for her Big Boy.

It hadn't been going on long, but it had got serious very, very quickly. From jokes to nicknames to – and this I could hardly believe I was seeing – words of love. Words he'd never used with one of these women before.

I couldn't help myself, I hurled the thing at the wall, and bits flew everywhere. I let them. Patrick wasn't playing by our rules. He wasn't supposed to bring anyone, let alone *her*, on this make-or-break weekend, was he? No, most emphatically not.

And Stacy. Behind my back, with my husband? While still pretending we were such great friends. My mind wheeled and whirred, worse than my mother in one of her stupors. I was stunned. Apart from anything, it looked like she might be a better actress than I was.

For a while, I froze, then the flashbacks started. I breathed heavily, wrestling for control, trying to get my pulse back down to regain some semblance of calm.

Eventually I succeeded. My mind cleared. And I looked down and thought. The fact that he was screwing Stacy was shocking enough. But if he was sinking, suddenly, to these depths, what else might he be capable of? I looked through her messages again, though it turned my stomach. Some of the most gushing ones were thanking him for a necklace. For a moment or two, I hoped that was just smutty talk. Then I realised, with anger, that he was buying her serious presents. A necklace. A bracelet. Earrings.

This was new. The intern, for example, wouldn't have got much more than the dubious pleasure of rushed sex with Patrick for roughly six weeks, the odd dinner if she was lucky. But lavishing gifts? On Stacy? I was quivering now.

The fling was plenty bad enough, don't get me wrong. This was enough to turn my world upside down. She'd been my friend; the one person I'd relied on most as the children grew up. The pain cut me, right to the heart. Maybe this was why I found friendships so hard. When they went wrong, it hurt so much.

I realised wearily I'd have to rethink everything about my routine, the children's activities; so much of it involved me and Stacy jogging along together. Swapping lifts, swapping rounds of coffees, swapping gossip, swapping laughs. That had been my life for years, now. All that was going to come screeching to a halt.

But, while that was a disaster and a betrayal of the worst order, a knife in my side, Patrick was mooning over her. Saying stuff he'd only said to me before. And spending actual serious money on her. That was yet another escalation. That was our money; mine and the kids'. It wasn't to be frittered away on his floozies. And wait a minute, my own credit card had just been declined, while I'd been out shopping with Stacy. Had Patrick spent so much on her that my card had been blocked?

I was now getting a very bad feeling. How much, exactly, was he wasting on Stacy? What was he playing at? We were comfortable, yes, but that didn't mean he could throw away our hard-earned cash like this. I had to find out what he was up to, how much he was spending. What other dirty secrets had he dragged along to our cleansing weekend? If he was capable of this, then what wouldn't he stoop to?

I crawled back to the unlocked briefcase. I took out an unfamiliar laptop. It looked brand new, its sleek iron grey the colour of a shark's back. He had a huge Mac at home, its twin at the office. He had an iPad, his smartphone and this burner. And now, a third laptop. Why did he need this?

Twenty minutes later, I knew all too well. The business was in trouble.

Chapter 44

Now

Becca

The evidence was stacking up so beautifully now. Becca couldn't quite believe it herself, the way things had started to fall into place. Yes, she'd always known it had to be there, but she was amazed that Patrick Bridges hadn't hidden things better, or got himself out of the godawful mess that had been threatening to engulf him.

What had he been playing at? It was as though, for years, he'd been riding high on a bubble of charm, of reputation. Then, from nowhere, that had burst. This wasn't so new. Becca had seen it in her lifetime, with far bigger institutions – banks, investment houses, once bestriding the business world, then suddenly crumbling into ruins.

Everyone usually professed to be astonished. Then came the tales of incompetence, over-valuation. Patrick had failed on a smaller scale, but in a similar way, and the devastation he'd been about to wreak on his family would have been total.

Becca now knew his email folder far better, clearly, than he had himself. Once she'd done her initial delve into it, she'd come up with sheaves of correspondence from disgruntled companies that either weren't getting paid or weren't having their projects completed. She knew she shouldn't be proud of how she'd wormed her way in. But yeah, she was, actually.

Motive. That was one of the sacred triumvirate. Like the pointy bit of an isosceles triangle, it stood proud of the other two elements. Means and opportunity, well, diligent police work would normally give you those. But without a proper motive, a really good reason for murder, no one was going to poke around in a posh bird like Louise's life. Burke had made that plain enough.

But now they had cause.

Becca unwrapped a Wispa bar and sunk her teeth into the delicious first couple of centimetres, feeling the initial resistance and then that airy melting on her tongue. This time, there was no flicker of guilt. Smiling with sugar-coated teeth, she knew she deserved it.

Chapter 45

Then

It was the worst moment of my life, by far. Worse than the realisation of his first infidelity, worse than this new horror that he
was fucking my best friend, worse even than several incidents in
my childhood that I really didn't want to revisit.

I sat there, in the quiet hotel room, shaking my head, trying
to understand what my husband had become. What had Patrick
been playing at? How had things got this bad?

Turns out, in his new career as a two-phones, two-mistress big
shot, Patrick just hadn't had the time or the inclination to cover
the rest of his tracks properly. The laptop in this briefcase was
password protected, yes, but it was the same tired old *P@55w0rd!*
he'd always used. In a trice, I was in.

There was a higgledy-piggledy mess on his desktop. I quickly
scanned the company's accounts. It looked as though the firm
was being propped up by huge wodges of cash, being deposited
at irregular intervals. These weren't payments from clients. They
were transfers. Where from? I was getting a bad feeling about all
this. The hairs were standing up on my arms.

Among the mess of folders I saw one of those finance apps
which collects all your banking together in one place. It took me
some time to get in but I knew all the data, his mother's maiden

name, his date of birth, and there was that stupid *P@55w0rd!* again. Once I had it open, I almost wished I hadn't. Although I now had the evidence right before my eyes, I still couldn't take it in.

All the accounts were low, lower than they should have been. That was why my credit card had been declined. Healthy balances, not long ago. Then the start of a gradual dwindling process, as money got funnelled into the company and disappeared. It was a one-way trip to a seemingly huge black hole. If I'd ever been looking for an illustration of how to throw good money after bad, this was it.

I went over to his email. A trail from his broker showed that the house had just been re-mortgaged. My house. The place where my children lived. Which I had assumed was debt-free years ago.

Then I saw another finance app. Why would he have two? But the idea that he did, and this would be the one where all the money was stashed away, safe and sound, stopped my heart pounding for a moment or two. In a flash I was in again. Then, in the jumble of accounts with negative balances, I saw two in the children's names. My heart nearly stopped. I'd set these up, one for Giles, one for Em, when they were small. That's where all their money had been safely tucked, over the years. Christmases, birthdays, chunks here and there for special milestones, starting at secondary school and doing well in exams. I'd even got serious, as the big money started to roll in for Patrick, and set up a feeder from the joint account. That dropped a few hundred a month into each as well, to top up. And every now and then I'd added a bit more for luck.

The idea was that we'd present this to them, with bows on top, at some point in the future. Whether it was for their eighteenth birthdays, or for uni, or even for when they were 21, that bit wasn't clear. The thing that was absolutely definite and crystal in my mind was that they would be getting a proper start in life. They would have what I had not – a sure foundation, a nest egg, a deposit on a flat. You could call it what you liked, but I knew exactly what it meant. Security.

And now it was all gone.

There was not a penny left in Giles's account. When I clicked feverishly on Em's, it was the same. Empty.

I pressed my fingers into my temples as hard as I could. I needed to feel some physical, external pain, to escape from the turmoil within. Although I was sitting very still, my eyes were darting restlessly from side to side, like searchlights. When I closed my lids, trying to get some respite, I saw rows of zeros dancing mockingly. I forced myself to open my eyes again, and there was the screen, its desktop mess no doubt a reflection of its owner's mind. What else was lurking here, in this tangle? What other surprises? But I knew that there just couldn't be anything lower than this. Stealing from his own children. Snatching away their futures. Because the more I thought about it, the more I realised how much was about to disappear. Their expensive schools. Our holidays. Music lessons, tutoring, outings. All the things they wanted all the time – phones, clothes, parties, presents.

OK, many people manage without this stuff and maybe they are all the better for it. But I had made a deal with Patrick, and with myself, that things were going to be different for my kids, that they would have everything I'd lacked.

By raiding their accounts, trying to stem the haemorrhage caused by his own incompetence, he'd not only betrayed my hopes and dreams for them. He'd also made these sweet kids, our wonderful children, as vulnerable as I had been. I'd sworn they would never be on my tightrope with no safety net, afraid to look down. But now, at a stroke, there they were, up there, exactly where I had been.

I'd been so determined that they wouldn't come from nothing, have nothing, that they would always have something behind them – but instead, I had unwittingly given him a lovely pot to plunder. When it came down to it, when it was his skin or theirs, the coward had chosen himself. His selfishness took my breath away.

No. No, I wasn't going to have it. After everything I'd worked for – that we had worked for – he couldn't take a wrecking ball to their lives like this.

What if he couldn't keep up these payments? We were going to be out on the street, and soon. It was where I'd started out, but I would be damned if it was where my kids would finish up.

I didn't need to look through anything else. I'd got the picture. This had been a long time coming. Things had been slipping, it seemed, for years. But he hadn't told me. He'd not so much as whispered to me, never asked me to stop spending, never mentioned the car crash that was hurtling towards us, not even a distant threat, but imminent now, round the next bend.

I rushed into the bathroom and threw up. In the loo, of course. Even in extremis, I was tidy. But this was the destruction of everything, of my life, of my children's futures. And he'd said nothing. *Nothing.*

The smashed Nokia lay where it had fallen, unimportant now. What was Stacy, some stupid lay, compared with the ruin coming for us? It was like making a fuss about a peck on the cheek at a party, while an orgy raged next door.

I tottered to the mirror, wiped the hair off my sweaty face and looked deep into my own eyes. Could I have seen this coming?

There'd been the incident when my card had been declined. I'd had it out with him, and he'd waved it all off. He was so plausible, that was the trouble. You'd think I'd know better, now, but I fell for his guff every time. How stupid was I? How gullible?

It should have sounded alarm bells. Well, it had, but I hadn't joined the dots. I'd assumed the serial girlfriends were the worst of it. He'd played me, leaving that stuff in plain sight to occupy me, while all this was going on behind the scenes.

The lying fucking bastard.

God, I hated him now. I wanted to hurl the laptop the way

I'd thrown the phone, but this was bigger than just the type of row that leads to a divorce. The stakes had grown immeasurably higher. I had to think very hard, and quickly too. Curbing all my destructive instincts, I tucked the laptop back in the briefcase as gently as though I was putting one of my own babies back to bed. I scrabbled around under the dressing table and picked through the soft thick pile of the carpet – noting again with horror how much this weekend must be costing – and reassembled the cheap phone, before stuffing that away too. I replaced the briefcase behind the shoes, where the lying scum had half-hidden it. Then I trudged to the bathroom.

Tears had been running, unheeded, down my face and trickling down my chin. I rubbed them away irritably, wiped the steam off the mirror to see, in close-up, just what devastation really looked like. Yup, not a pretty sight. I put the loo seat down and tried to take deep breaths, regain some measure of calm, focus. It was so hard.

All I saw in front of me was the flat I'd come from, the place where I'd lived with my mother, all those unhappy, endless years, laid end on end without end. The grim stairwells, the concrete balconies, the leering neighbours, the black mould in the bathroom and kitchen, the paper peeling even after I'd tried to superglue it. The feeling of being trapped. In the wrong place.

I wasn't going back there. Not with my children, I wouldn't do it.

All the safety I'd felt, in my palace of a home, all the security I thought I'd bought for my children, the careful blind eye I'd turned to Patrick's unfaithfulness, the unspoken bargain we had made – everything was whisked away from me that afternoon, as I sat in a five-star luxury bathroom, with Jo Malone's basil tickling my nose. That smell still makes me want to throw up.

Chapter 46

Now

Becca

Becca sidled in through the police station door. Yes, it was a bad sign that she was having to go in sideways like a crab, she hissed back to her mother's voice in her head.

Would her mother be shocked in real life, if she knew that she provided this constant negative commentary in her daughter's mind, day after day, hour after hour? Or would she just be sorry that Becca seemed to take so little notice? *What do you think you look like? Are you really going to buy/eat/wear that?* Becca knew her mum thought of herself as kind and believed she was endlessly supportive. She didn't realise that every pinching of her nostrils, every forced smile shouted disappointment louder than words ever could.

Becca didn't blame her mother. Yes, she knew a lot of her decisions were questionable, but today, she finally felt she was doing the right thing. Even if the way she was doing it was a little, well, dodgy. First, she walked straight past the lift, and opted for the stairs. Virtue, already. But then she carried on, hefting herself upwards, past her own floor, to places where she had no business being. Up, up to the giddy heights where Johno worked.

She had a pretext – she wasn't a fool. After all, as he'd pointed out, they were all detectives up there. Paid to have suspicious minds. Or, some would say, in this day and age, paid to fill quotas and cover their backs. Not enough money in the coffers to do a proper job, and always at the mercy of the politicians and their sharp little scissors, snipping budgets everywhere.

But the plain clothes lot would certainly look askance at some junior bod like her prowling in their exalted midst. So she had a sponsorship form she'd knocked up. Couch to 5k. People were always coming round with stuff like this. And sure, they'd have no trouble believing the couch part. The 5k would be more of a challenge – but of course she had absolutely no intention of going through with it.

She'd delved a little into the rotas last night. There was never high security on these – who cared about office hours, except those who had to slog through them? Johno was scheduled to be safely away from his desk this morning. The perfect opportunity. And, as she'd got here so early, she was willing to bet few of his colleagues would be putting in an appearance either. There wasn't an active case on. Though the DCs all walked around with a swagger, each of them like Horatio Caine in their own private version of *CSI: Miami*, the truth was this was a quiet little backwater. The biggest thing for years should have been the suspicious death of Patrick Bridges. Except that they weren't treating it as such.

These thoughts kept her occupied until she reached the final landing, hauling herself up by the iron bannister and stopping for a moment to catch her breath. Coming in this way, instead of via the lifts, she had a better view of the open-plan area where Johno worked. She peeped in through the safety glass panel. As she'd thought, the sea of desks, separated here and there by a half-dead pot plant or a battered hessian divider, was mostly empty. At the far end of the room were the few offices used by the high-ups, and a large meeting room for live ops, but the rank and file spent most of their time here in this dusty, godforsaken wasteland.

Only a few desks were filled, mostly women on shift work, heads down, nondescript, diligent. She might be reading too much into it, but she felt as though they were trudging through the hours before getting back to more important bits of their lives. If she could just channel that weariness. The last thing she wanted to do was breeze in, be remarkable.

She cracked open the double doors, hesitated, but it was too late, the head nearest to her had bobbed up, brown eyes questioning. She sidled again, trying to tread lightly, repel that steady attention, look purposeful but bored. Anything but nervous.

'Yeah, where does Johno sit?' she asked, going for a faintly irritated tone. It seemed to hit the right note. The woman's mouth twisted slightly and she gave Becca a knowing look. 'Just over there, the one by the window. Best seat in the house. Wouldn't you know it. What's he been up to?'

'Oh, nothing much . . .' Becca seemed to falter. Now she could look as nervous as she felt. 'Just got to leave this here for him,' Becca brandished her sheet of A4. It trembled slightly in her hand. The woman raised her eyebrows, but she didn't look unsympathetic. 'Go for it. Want me to pass a message on?'

Becca didn't have to act to look horrified at the very idea. She shook her head, probably too many times. 'Nah, you're all right. I'll catch him later.'

'Catch *something*, more like,' the officer said, under her breath, but again she was amused rather than disapproving. It looked as though Becca wasn't by any means the first fluttering moth drawn to Johno's flame, though judging by that smile she might be the most unlikely.

She stepped forward more boldly, winding through the workstations until she got to Johno's. Then she was brought up short. A framed picture of a woman was in pride of place, right by his phone. It could have been anyone, a sister, cousin, she thought wildly. But of course, it was his wife. She knew it with a heavy certainty. Bastard.

The officer was still watching, less benignly now. Becca was sure she must look gobsmacked. She thought quickly. Despite everything, she had no intention of messing up this opportunity. She refused to bottle out, drop her bogus sponsorship form and run. There was too much at stake. And discovering that Johno was hardly footloose and fancy-free, well, it made no difference. There'd been no chance anyway, she knew that really. She thought fast, then caught the edge of one of the untidy piles of folders stacked high on his desk – wouldn't she have known he'd be a fellow slob? – and pushed it accidentally on purpose to the floor.

At the crash, several more heads bobbed up. She lifted her palms, looked gormless – *didn't have to try too hard*, said her mother's voice – and got to work, not before making sure the first woman was shaking her head in resignation, and signalling, 'Nutter, what can you do?' to her colleagues. Becca knelt down, killing her knees, and swished her hand in the pile of documents until she found what she was after. With her back to the room, she slid out her phone and took a quick series of photos.

Huffing upwards moments later, she plopped the files back on the desk, neatened the edges of the pile, and that was her, done. She turned to go, relieved.

And came smack up against Johno's amused smirk. 'Well, what have we here, then?'

Chapter 47

Then

The question was, what should I do next? Yes, I was devastated. Yes, part of me would never recover from the shock. But did that help? Would I gain anything by lolling around bemoaning the luck that had made me fall for this idiot, this waster, liar, thief? No. I had to find a solution to this situation. Like Houdini, my eyes had always fixed themselves on the way out, and this, though it was the most appalling blow of my life, because it impacted my children more than me, was just another exit I had to manage.

I wrapped myself in the white velour robe, registering its sumptuousness with nothing but irritation. An hour ago, I had luxuriated in it, and allowed it to convince me that Patrick, despite all the evidence to the contrary, still loved me and felt I was worth splashing out on. But now I knew he was just recklessly chucking money away, money that we didn't have. The way he'd been doing for *years*. Stupid bastard.

This weekend had gone from being an essential, a make-or-break situation, to an absurdity we couldn't afford. *I* couldn't afford. After the first headlong panic, seeing the numbers, I now had to click into another mode. I couldn't afford to be a headless chicken. I probably couldn't even afford to *buy* chicken anymore – not Waitrose's organic corn-fed, anyway. It was going to be mechanically recovered nuggets all the way now, if I wasn't very careful.

I thought back. Before finding the laptop, I'd been happy. Even the phone call from *Stacy*, which had made my blood boil, was now less than a matter of total indifference to me. She was a pesky fly that I couldn't even be bothered to swat. My main task that afternoon was to get to grips with the accounts, see if there was anything at all to be done.

I made myself tea with the dinky little kettle provided and got my head down. Made myself get that laptop out again, pore through it, but this time with the detachment of a forensic accountant, not the stone-cold horror of the betrayed wife shortly to lose everything. You might think, *what does she know?* It was true, my job on reception had been largely ornamental. But you know me. I've always been more than I seem. I'd taught myself a thing or two over the years, hadn't I? I'd been running a house for over a decade – a house that was as big and as complex as quite a few companies, I'll have you know. Cleaners, gardeners, music teachers, tutors. I employed half the area, all cash in hand, but all carefully noted.

Oh, I knew a thing or two about finance, let me tell you. And very soon, I knew as much as Patrick did about his balance sheets. His idiocy was going to make us homeless.

I couldn't let that happen.

Chapter 48

Now

Becca

Becca's eyes were fixed open so wide that it was beginning to hurt her cheeks. She tried to get a grip.

'Not that I'm complaining, it's lovely to see you, but *what the hell are you doing at my desk?*' Johno kept his expression friendly for the benefit of the colleagues ear-wigging all around the open-plan office, but the words came at her with unmistakable venom.

Becca carried on staring into his eyes, praying for inspiration to come. Her mind was as blank as virgin snow. All the scenarios she'd envisaged, had been ready for – and this was not one of them. He was supposed to be at home. *Bastard.* Her fingers quivered and her piece of A4 rustled. She suddenly remembered it.

'Was just bringing you this. Christ, chill out. Anyone would think I was burgling you or something,' she said, aiming for a bit of levity, but knowing she sounded on the squeaky edge of hysteria. She shook it in his face, hoping motion would cover up any more tremors. 'Sponsorship. That's all I'm after. Mind you, some would call it daylight robbery, eh?' *Shut up, Becs. Shut up, you don't have to come over like a second-rate comedian.*

To her relief, he held out a hand, looked sceptically at the form she'd cobbled together last night and sniffed. 'Couch to 5k, is it?' he said, looking her up and down. Any notions she might have cherished that he fancied her evaporated like mist in the morning sun. That glance said it all.

'Got to start somewhere,' she said humbly. She didn't have to pretend to be crushed, it came naturally. Then, suddenly, inexplicably, he was smiling at her, just like he had in the restaurant. 'Go on, then,' he said, fishing in his bulging pocket. For a second she wondered what on earth he was doing, and then, like a magician, he pulled out a crumpled fiver. 'Good for you, girl.'

Her smile was a little more perfunctory. 'Your wife doesn't mind you, er, contributing?'

'What she doesn't know won't hurt her,' Johno said, grin fading. Had he registered the edge to her voice? *Good*, she thought, as she turned to go. 'Hang on a minute,' he said, much more loudly. She wheeled round in dread, legs jelly again. 'Aren't you forgetting something?' She stared at him, willing him not to notice the state of his files, not to guess what might as well be burning a hole right through her phone's picture folder.

'Sorry?' she whispered.

'Well, get on with it, then. Ask the others.' Becca looked around the room. By now, several more people had wandered in, a few watching them curiously. She looked down at the form in her hand and up at Johno's twisted smile.

Chapter 49

Then

I heard the rattle of the bedroom door, Patrick's cheery, 'Hello?' It took a beat before I could reply. 'Hi, in the bath, darling.' Just the right tone, unconcerned, cheerful.

I did a bit of splashing, just so he'd get the idea, if he hadn't seen the clouds of steam pouring into the bedroom. The first tubful with all the bubbles in it had gone as cold as the grave while my eyes restlessly scanned columns of figures, my stomach hollowed out with the horror.

A bath would explain my high colour, the way I wasn't rushing to greet him and garland him with kisses, as per my usual routine on one of these make-up breaks. It might also explain a certain glitter in my eyes. The light of war.

This wasn't going to be any sort of swift battle. I'd thought we were doing very nicely, thank you, due to my hard work, striving to position him correctly, encouraging all his endeavours. Well, maybe not all of them, but certainly wining and dining the right high-ups, helping him achieve every promotion, climb all the way to directorship, to owning his own company. I'd thought he had it from there. But no. He'd fucked it all up.

Take this new mortgage he'd acquired without telling me. It was massive. Yet he'd signed it without so much as mentioning the fact over the cornflakes, between his sordid flings. It was immoral, if not actually illegal. He'd gone and torpedoed our safe harbour, our children's home. The house – *mine, ours* – must be on the verge of being repossessed.

I fumed. If the bathwater hadn't been scalding already, it would have risen to boiling point now. I hit it with my open palm. He'd played me for a fool. The water sprayed up and I had to blink it furiously out of my eyes. 'All right in there?' Patrick called. He'd already switched the telly on. Sport poured out into the quiet afternoon, jangled around my head.

'Fine. Just rinsing my hair now,' I said, drowning him and Gary Lineker out with the taps on full.

By the time I had emerged from the water and wrapped myself in a towel the size of a small country, a lot of pieces had slotted into place. Especially his pattern of increasing secretiveness, which I'd seen without really noticing. Trouble was, I'd always been secretive myself. We'd edged around each other like a couple of low-rent spies. I kicked myself for all the mistakes I'd made. My worst hadn't been trusting that sack of shit on the bed out there – I hadn't for years – but not checking up on him more thoroughly.

I'd taken my eye off the ball, that was for sure, just as Patrick's team currently seemed to be, judging from the groans coming from the bedroom. I'd really thought infidelity was the worst that he could throw at me. How stupid had I been?

I wiped my hand over the mirror, gave up as it misted again immediately, and swiped it with one of the fluffy towels instead. My image was blurred, but that suited my mood. I was a mass of thoughts and plans. Yes, I had finally worked out what he'd been up to for the last few years. Throwing our future away, making rubbish decisions, destroying everything like a wanton boy pulling the wings off a fly.

I marvelled at the fact that he hadn't said a word. This baby of a man, who whined if he had a headache, had kept this huge catastrophe from me. It was inexplicable. I could only guess that he'd become more proficient at lying and cheating over the years, hiding all the sordid liaisons from me, and that he'd used his new skill set. Just when I didn't need it most, he'd actually got brilliant, all on his own. Unfortunately for all of us, the thing he was brilliant at was hiding the enormous hole he'd been digging. A hole that was about to swallow us all up.

Well, not if I could help it. I looked at my misty reflection, blurring into a silvery film of droplets. He wasn't going to drag me and the children down too.

I combed my hair with quick, angry strokes, twisted it up into a bun, smeared on a bit of make-up – they don't call it war paint for nothing – and took a deep breath. But then, even when I got to the door, I couldn't quite go through with it. I leaned my forehead against the wooden panels for a few moments, collecting myself, willing myself on. Then, finally, I flung the door open with a dazzling smile. One long silken leg free of the bathrobe, tied loosely around my waist and ready to come off with the slightest tug. 'Well, hello,' I said.

'Was wondering where you'd got to. Thought you might have gone down the plughole,' he said with a bluff smile.

'Just wanted to make sure you were ready for me. Like I'm ready for you,' I said.

For a second, our eyes met, his wide with sudden alarm. Then my smile lulled him. He opened his arms. 'Get over here now, darling,' he said, all his Christmases come at once.

Chapter 50

Now

Becca

Safely back on her own floor later, with a therapeutic doughnut in her belly and another in a bag beside her, Becca was almost tempted to take her pulse, see whether it had gone back down to normal yet. She had fifteen ragged signatures on her fake form, and a handbag filled with money that she'd defrauded from her fellow officers. She shut her eyes briefly, lifted the bag to her lips and bit off another chunk of heavenly stodge. *5k my arse. I'll be lucky to get to the starting line at this rate.* Then she remembered, with a rush of relief, that there wasn't actually a starting line.

Even better news was that, on her phone, she had shots of the entire Louise Bridges file.

She also had a whole stack of legitimate paperwork on her desk, waiting patiently for her attention. She slid the first brown file over, opened it up and ran an eye down the form. It was the usual dispiriting collection of misspellings and half-completed information that her superiors expected her to process perfectly. She sighed. It was going to be a long day.

Back at home hours later, with her washing on and the chores done, to the extent she ever got through them, Becca was finally free to read through the Bridges file. She hadn't printed off the pictures at work, you never knew who was watching, but now she pulled a chair up to her laptop and settled down. She knew she'd purposely spun out this moment, made the anticipation last as long as possible, and wondered again what it was that fascinated her about that woman.

Partly, looking around her own home, she knew it was envy. Here she was, in rented accommodation, and destined always to be, unless she found a crock of something that wasn't actual shit one day. Her lot was always going to be cramped quarters, dodgy landlords' furniture with wonky legs and unfixable dripping taps. Even if they made her chief constable – and a girl could dream, couldn't she? – and she could actually buy a flat, would she ever have a family? She doubted it. She'd kidded herself that there had been a flicker in Johno's eye, but it had never been even a smidgeon of lust. It was always just derision.

So yes, she looked at a woman like Louise Bridges and she envied her. For sure. She'd had it easy, you could tell. Becca knew the type. Pretty, successful. There had been one in her class. Debra Elton. Six inches taller than her, Debra had always seemed to be gliding past her at school, giggling with her bevvy of friends as Becca struggled to keep her blouse tucked in and stop herself from tripping over her own feet. Yes, Becca had always had her mother in her corner, but that was a double-edged sword. 'You can do it, Rebecca, Debra may be much prettier and more popular than you, but don't you forget, you're really not bad with those computers when you try.' *Yeah, thanks, Mum.*

Louise Bridges' mother, though. She'd be one of the same breed as her daughter. Tall, slender, well dressed. A posh bitch bringing up another in her image. She remembered Debra Elton's mum, something big in town planning, a real chilly-knickers type, frosty smile that didn't even get into the same postcode as her eyes. Her own mum had been properly intimidated by her.

The one time Mrs Elton had deigned to talk to them at a parents' evening, Becca's mum had gone full-on fangirl afterwards, waffling on about what a 'lovely person' Susannah Elton was, *so*

214

well spoken. There had followed a few excruciating months when she'd badgered Becca to bring Debra home to tea. As though Becca could even get close enough to Debra to ask her, and as though she wanted the humiliation of a puzzled 'No?' to be dealt out to her at school, in front of everyone. Becca's mother didn't understand the first thing about her life. She'd felt that at 13 – and nothing much had changed.

Becca didn't have anything against posh bitches as such (*who are you trying to kid?* she asked herself). But there was something else in Louise Bridges' expression. A sense that she was better than everyone around her – and hiding a lot, too. That she'd spent years pulling the wool over people's eyes. That she was used to getting away with things.

But not murder, thought Becca. Oh no. She wouldn't be getting away with that. Not if Becca had anything to do with it.

Chapter 51

Then

So, we'd had our rekindling weekend, and I'd put on a stellar performance. My silk and lace nightdress, enough to drive the Pope to impure thoughts, had required careful handwashing and coaxing back into shape, and was now hanging up to dry on a padded hanger in the airing cupboard. Can I just stress, that's the kind of effort that I put in. It came as standard, with me. We're not talking drip-dry nylon. And then, after I'd done all that, plus finished my own unpacking and his too (the laptop having mysteriously disappeared, along with the phone), I was expecting us to get back into the routine of our lovely life.

Maybe not quite as seamlessly as we had sometimes done. There was more at stake this time, I knew that. Not only a mistress for me to see off, but a financial mess to sort out too. But these weekends usually brought in their wake a special kind of lovey-dovey unity. That would give us the chance we needed to regroup, then move on.

I'd always be quite pleased with myself, once we got back from one of these breaks. I'd be thrilled to have safely averted another potential crisis. Patrick, extricated from the clutches of the latest flooze, would be giddy with his own feelings of relief at being back on the straight and narrow, being a decent family man again.

We'd be calling each other 'darling', touching each other at every opportunity like honeymooners and the children might even tell us crossly to get a room. And then we'd all laugh.

I'd managed to convince myself that Stacy would now melt away, joining the massed ranks of Patrick's little mistakes. She'd just be one more glitch in our otherwise happy marriage, that neither of us would ever have to refer to again. I hadn't bothered to call her, confront her. Told myself I didn't need to. In truth, it hurt so much I didn't know where to start. And anyway, I was going to be too busy sorting out our finances, saving us from ruin, to worry about her.

But then, a couple of days after our weekend, just as I was mustering the courage to have a proper talk with Patrick about the company, he'd gone and left his little depth-charge.

A note. Right there, on the kitchen table. Where the kids could have seen it.

Detailing his plans to dump me and leave. Forever.

Thank God I got through the door first that day. I'd dropped my bag on the counter, immediately seen the piece of paper. He occasionally left me one. *Get more beer*, that sort of thing. Just on a Post-it or the back of a letter. But this was folded over. A sheet of A4. My name, *Louise*, on the front. It was just lying, stark and white on the black counter, where I'd see it as soon as I walked in. Me, or anyone else, come to that.

Something told me it was bad. I felt it in the tightness of my chest, a sudden breathlessness. Then, as I snatched it up, I saw the gleam of gold, heard the metallic clatter. His ring fell out. His wedding ring. He had taken it off, put it inside the note.

It was like a punch in the stomach.

Thank God my reflexes were quick. I slapped my hand down on the ring before it bounced merrily onto the floor, right in front of my son and daughter. Scooped it up and crumpled the note into my bag. Turned as they came in, my back against the counter. Nothing to see here, nothing at all. There was a buzzing sound in my ears. For a moment, I thought I was going to faint on the spot.

'Just . . . just going to the loo,' I managed, my voice high-pitched.

'TMI, Mum,' said Em scathingly.

Normally I would have ticked her off for cheek. Today I could hardly hear her above the beating of my heart. I locked the door, shut the lid, collapsed onto it, and got the note out of my bag. The ring fell to the bottom, but I didn't have time to worry about that now. I started to read:

Louise, the note began. His handwriting was sloppy. He'd used a biro. And not even a 'dear'. The words danced up and down but I had to read on.

I'm leaving. I just can't go on pretending.

Pretending? I took a shaky breath. What did he mean? Who was pretending? I read on. *We aren't right for each other anymore. I don't know if we ever have been.* I looked up from the paper. Remembered our wedding day. Remembered how I'd gazed up at him at the altar, and he'd smiled right back into my eyes, made me feel so safe. I knew then I'd come home. I had my dream man, my Patrick. He was mine, now, for good. For better, for worse. Hadn't he felt the same? Didn't he still? It seemed not. *Things haven't worked for so long.* It wasn't true. We were a team. Yes, there'd been ups and downs – the girls – but they'd just been distractions. He couldn't help himself. I knew that, I understood. I'd made allowances. *I've been so unhappy. I need someone who really loves me.*

What was this? I did love him, despite everything. I really loved him, the man he was, not the man he pretended to be or the man I'd once thought he was. That was real love. But this? This note, this nonsense. This wasn't about love at all. It was about sex, attention, novelty. Why was he looking for someone else to love, when here I was? I loved him, I always had. *I know you'll be shocked, but I have no choice.* Well, that wasn't true, of course there was a choice. He could tear this note up and we'd forget it. I could do that. I could put it behind me, as I'd done so many times before. *I don't want to go on with you.* At this point I started to hear ringing in my ears again. I put my head between my legs, praying I wasn't going to collapse, praying the kids wouldn't have to scrape me off the floor. Finally. Finally, now, I understood. It was all in what his note *didn't* say. He didn't mention her name, he didn't whisper a word about running to another woman. He had no idea I was onto them. Nor did she. They really thought I didn't have a clue. But I knew their dirty little secret.

This was all about Stacy.

He genuinely thought he was in love. Not with me. With *Stacy*. And I knew, all too well, how powerful that feeling could be.

I'm sorry I've let you down. Patrick.

And that was it.

'Let me down'? As though he were a plumber who'd failed to turn up? As though we were casual acquaintances and he was slightly late for coffee? As though I hadn't been to hell and back for him. Thank God, I felt the first flickerings of anger now, felt myself coming back from the brink.

The fact that there was no mention of Stacy, that was the most ominous thing of all. If I hadn't seen that number flash up, I'd have thought, what? Just another one of his whores?

But no. Not this time. This time was different.

It was love. That was the only thing that made sense. He really thought he loved her. And now he thought he'd just leave me for her.

Did either of them know the meaning of the word? The visceral longing that had seen me concentrate everything in my being on getting him, the passion that had made me turn a blind eye to so much, in order to stay with him? And after all I'd done for him?

I had made myself into the perfect woman, the perfect wife, the perfect mother, for him. Given him our two lovely children. Enthroned him in our beautiful house. In my heart.

And this was my reward?

The crap I'd put up with over the years, the nonsense I'd swallowed, for the good of our marriage, for our family. For the kids. I'd done more than my fair share, fulfilled my side of the bargain every single day, I'd tried to make things as good as they possibly could be, and he'd not only done the dirty on me – countless times – but now he'd plundered his own children's money and re-mortgaged the house. And this was the moment when he was going to walk out, too? And with *Stacy*, of all people?

Part of my mind just refused to compute it. It must be a mistake, it must. Because why would he choose her, over me? And over all the other girls, the shadowy creatures who'd hovered around the edges of our marriage? Surely they'd all been younger than her? And prettier?

What on earth was it about Stacy? She was my age, she'd had a child, she wasn't in great shape. She was funny, yes, she was nice – but ordinary. I just couldn't begin to fathom what the attraction was.

All these years, I'd laboured long and hard to be just what was required, to be the wife he'd needed on his arm. Looking as good as I could, saying all the right things, schmoozing the right people. And then she had rocked up, with her bunchy frumpy skirts, her straggly brows.

She was a great mum, I'd give her that, but the rest of it – no. The worst thing was that I'd always felt sorry for her, the way that she was never quite on top of things. She was always laughing that she'd burned the dinner, she was always forgetting to fill in the school forms. I'd tried to help her. And all the time, she'd been chipping away, undermining the ground I stood on. I couldn't bear it. Couldn't bear that someone was going to take him away from me, after all this time. That *she* was going to be the one to do it.

It had never actually occurred to me before, not for a moment, not seriously, that he would really leave me. Well, not after the first time, anyway. That first time, I had thought my heart would stop with the shock and the shame, and yes, I had believed our marriage was over. But it hadn't been. I'd battled my way through, brought us safely through the crisis. Since then, I'd convinced myself that it was the novelty he was after, the thrill, the chase. Not a new life. Just a way to spice up the one he already had.

But this, with Stacy?

It didn't fit the pattern.

For a start, she was someone we both knew. Usually the girls were peripheral figures, office juniors, waitresses, hotel staff. Neat and tidy, in that I'd never run into them in a million years. Separate, not allowed to contaminate his family, his home. But Stacy. That was fouling his own nest. It wasn't just that I vaguely knew her. She was my *best friend*, for God's sake. We'd had dinners together as a foursome over the years. We had a complicated system of school runs organised. Our kids had grown up in one another's houses. Did he imagine this was going to continue? Did *she*? Were they stupid enough to believe that we were all going to jog along together, as though we were in some sort of free love commune?

I had been an idiot. A change wasn't as good as a rest – a change was a klaxon. A warning. As soon as I'd discovered that his current bit on the side was Stacy, I should have done something, anything. But I had just tried to ignored it, as usual.

And all the other little things along the way, that now shouted out to me. His distraction. His concentration on her, not me. The gifts he'd bought her. Presents that had cost money, at the same time that my own credit card was being refused. This had been a clear sign.

He'd switched allegiance and I, the woman who prided herself on her hypervigilance, had not seen it coming, had let it all go on unimpeded. What a fool I was. I blamed myself entirely that things had come to this pass.

And now it was up to me to get us all out of this mess.

I sat there on the toilet seat, clammy with the shock. It was no use asking myself what my mother would have done in similar circumstances. There was nothing from her that I could draw on, gain strength from, use to help me through this, the worst crisis of my life. But I could use my own reaction to some of her worst stunts. The first time she took an overdose, a deliberate one anyway. I'd sat alone in the hospital. Waiting. Hours in a pea-green corridor, on a plastic chair that groaned every time I moved. But I didn't move much.

The busy passing nurses might have mistaken my state as worry over my mother, as she hovered between this world and the next, between the ghastly boyfriends and St Peter. Why she chose to come back to earth, I'll never know.

I can't pretend my torpor was induced by fathomless terror over my mother's fate. In her most affectionate moments, she'd shown me indifference, and as a result, my feelings towards her were a pick and mix that didn't really include filial devotion. But her condition did really worry me. With her in the flat, the authorities believed, completely wrongly, that I was being looked after. Without her loomed the unknown. I could only imagine this was bound to be worse.

I would probably have been much better off in an institution. It may not sound a great option to you, but to me the order and possible safety seem quite enticing. A bit like a nice holiday after a punishing slog at work. But as it was, the charcoal they'd pumped into my mother's stomach did its job, soaked up her latest bout of self-indulgence. She got discharged, and my relief over the future turned right back to dread of the present.

A day later, I came back to find yet another random bloke installed in our kitchen, acting like he owned the dump and my mother as well. I slunk into my room and locked the door with the bolt I'd shoplifted and fitted myself.

Why was my mind flicking back to that, right now? Was it trying to tell me I'd survived worse? Or to remind me that all

Mum's men had left, so it shouldn't be such a surprise that Patrick wanted to do the same? I'd always told myself he was different from all her boyfriends, I'd loved him for that. Now I felt doubly cheated.

Maybe the message was shorter, simpler: it was time that I stopped putting up with it. I wasn't 11 anymore, I wasn't the kid in the corridor, dreading the next few hours. I had kids of my own to stick up for. I'd be there for them. And I was going to shape the future, not just accept my fate.

There had been no dealing with my mother, she wasn't capable of learning the error of her ways. Patrick, though. Was I going to let him get away with this? Wander off, scot-free, leaving us about to be made homeless? For I couldn't pay this mortgage he'd hung round my neck. And if he wasn't going to be here, why would he?

Panic was useless to me. I needed to keep a clear head. I put my left hand to my mouth, sought out the tender pad of flesh at the base of my index finger. I bit down on it. Hard. Until I could taste the salt rush of my own blood. The richness of it flushed out my mind, clarified everything, brought the world back into focus and banished those bad old days with my mother.

We'd had a perfect life, Patrick and I. Everyone envied us. I saw the glances in the playground. Yes, I loved those little longing looks. Just as I'd loved him.

What had made him do this? After the weekend that was supposed to put the runaway train back on its tracks. Was this guilt, or was it Stacy? Was she, my *best friend*, putting pressure on him to leave?

A sudden rattle at the door jolted me back to the here and now. 'Muuum, Giles keeps pinching my ruler.' That whiny tone Em had after a long day at school. They needed a snack. We all needed routine. Or everything in the world was going to come crashing down.

I opened the door, gave Em an automatic hug, went back to the kitchen like a sleepwalker. I stood there trying to be the mother they had always known. Inside I was ashes.

I sorted out the ruler war, I chopped up some apples. All the while, my mind whirred.

Patrick was mine. I'd made vows, and I'd kept them. And I'd meant every word. Yes, till death did us part. But the simple truth was that he had fallen in love with Stacy and was no longer interested in me. It was a devastating thought. Another rejection coming to rest on a pile that reached up to the spotlights in the kitchen ceiling. But this was the very worst. More horrible even than the certain knowledge that my mother had never loved me.

In some ways, the most terrible thing about all of this was that it was *Stacy* he loved. Not a girl half his age, with the dewy skin I'd never get back, no matter how many products I slathered on. I couldn't say dismissively that he was just having a mid-life crisis – terrible cliché but these things happened, and how could I be expected to compete against the charms of a younger model? Because she was a bog-standard middle-aged mum, someone I had always thought of as warm and kind. Until now.

Had I been wrong, all these years, thinking that Patrick wanted glossy perfection? Believing that I was cementing our life together by making the best of myself? Would he actually have preferred to know the real me, the lonely misfit desperate to fit in? But it was too late now to show him my true colours, my vulnerability, the way I still craved the reassurance of his love.

It's hard to remember what it feels like to be *in* love, once it's over. Like trying to remember a beautiful dream. The edges slip away from you, even as you wake up, open your eyes. Then the middle's gone too. But that sparkly feeling when I thought of him. The gasping for air when I was actually with him. Being too excited to breathe. How ridiculous is that? Such a basic thing. I bet no other mammals make such fools of themselves, get so wound up, too overcome to fulfil basic bodily functions. Just being with him, so close, was once enough. I'd go light-headed. My chest would heave – I'd worry he'd hear it.

Then it goes. The magic evaporates. The back of his neck, that I used to have a special thing about, suddenly was – just a neck. Thickish, red. Only flesh.

Yet though my infatuation with Patrick might be over, my deep love for him never would be. The thought that he had left me brought back the old breathlessness. How could he do this to me? To us? With a note? Why not discuss it face to face, then scuttle out with his case, if he really had to? While the children were in bed. He'd taken the easy way out. Gone to a hotel. Waiting for Stacy to leave her husband too? I didn't know. All I was sure of was that he was a *coward. Fucking coward.*

Every word of the note had stabbed me to the heart, but I was still desperate to read it again. I knew it was masochism but I needed to look at those words until I'd properly understood them. I'd get the kids settled, then stew over it and, crucially, start thinking about what to do next. I always had a plan. I *had to* have a plan. 'Who's for hot chocolate?' Both looked up briefly, nodded, dipped their heads again to their own far weightier concerns.

Honestly, let them wait until they were pushing 40 and had built a fortress, and then got home to find a note on the kitchen table. A cannonball breech in their walls. Then they'd know what misery was. What desperation was. The milky smell turned my stomach, as I let the carton gush into one of my lovely Le Creuset non-stick pans. Reminded me of that Vermeer, a jolly maid, round-cheeked, the endless blue-white stream flowing on through eternity like her mindless fecundity. I was now a nightmare version of that.

'Mum, the milk!' Giles, sharp, anxious. I put the empty container down. Shaky laugh. Took the brimming pan over to the sink, poured some away, sloshing everywhere. Wiped down the surfaces with metres of kitchen towel. 'Silly Mummy.'

I had my own way of making hot chocolate – the best, of

course. Take the powder, add a drop, make a paste, then whisk into the milk heating on the hob. I busied myself, hands moving slowly, methodically, while my mind raced on a different track, two hundred miles an hour. The note smouldered away in my bag. Useless to speculate on his reasons, without reading it again, and I couldn't do that until I'd got the kids sorted. But nor could I stop the ideas flailing through my mind, an out-of-control kaleidoscope.

Another woman. Another life. *Stacy.* And the fact that we were about to be chucked out onto the street. But there was a bigger question still.

How did he think he was going to get away with this?

Chapter 52

Now

Becca

Becca looked up from her laptop and rubbed her eyes. She knew, to her cost, how much her blink-rate slowed up when she was working, meaning blurred vision and sticky, itchy lids – to add to her other attractions, as her mother would no doubt point out. But this stuff she was finding on Mrs Louise Bridges. Well, it was an eye-opener, if you liked. No wonder she'd been sat here for hours, glued to her chair in her tiny square kitchen.

How had the woman got away with this for so long?

She stretched her arms above her head and willed herself to move, shuffled her feet to get a bit of circulation going. Another coffee? Or maybe tea? What time even was it? She leaned forward, squinted at the right-hand corner of her Mac and whistled. 2 a.m. This was crazy. But now she'd started, she really didn't want to stop. This stuff she was onto, well, it was dynamite. She got up stiffly and pottered the tiny distance to the kettle and back, wondering if she should at least change into her pyjamas. Instead, she snapped open the button of her jeans. There. She sloshed water on a herbal teabag – camomile or some such. It had been lurking at the back of her cupboard for aeons. As the steam rose, it smelt unappetisingly of stale grass clippings, reminding her suddenly of the lawns of Louise Bridges' precious Woodwarde Road. She hurried back to the table.

This was detective work. This was what she should be doing, not filling in endless forms about lost dogs. Here, with her cursor gliding from pane to pane, she was doing her best work in months. She was finally laying bare Louise Bridges' life.

It wasn't hard, if you knew where to look. Johno's files had been a perfect entry point. Her own sleight-of-hand ability to bypass barriers and access police records really helped. Already, she'd put together a surprisingly clear picture of Louise's antecedents. And, she didn't mind admitting, she was pretty stunned.

She'd made a lot of assumptions about the woman. What was that dreadful cliché? 'Never assume, it makes an ass out of U and me.' But in this case, yes. She'd been fooled, utterly.

Louise Bridges was not what she appeared to be. She wasn't even who she said she was.

Chapter 53

Then

Money. You needed money to make a new life. The records I'd seen showed we weren't just on our uppers, we barely had a shoestring left. Sure, the company was dragging itself along from day to day. But there was nothing left to prop it up with. Unless Patrick was hiding something? I considered it briefly. Could he have had a cunning plan all along? Stashed something away, for this rainy day that was rapidly developing into a monsoon?

Everything I knew about Patrick said no. He was basically decent. That might be an odd thing to say about someone who'd systematically cheated on me for years, but somehow I knew that all his little subterfuges had actually been designed, at some strange level of his psyche, to protect me. He'd never had any intention of leaving me – until he'd decided he'd fallen in love with *Stacy* – so all the years of deceit had been mainly to spare my feelings, save my face. And possibly to inject a bit of a thrill into his mundane couplings.

Don't get me wrong, I wasn't grateful for the deception and I didn't forgive him for all he'd put me through. Infidelity on an industrial scale meant, yes, he was a habitual liar. But actually, he wasn't very good at it. I still caught him every single time. So much practice, yet still so rubbish. Didn't that prove, in a very

229

strange way, that it went against the grain, deep down? That he was honest at heart?

He'd kept a lot from me. Rocky times at work. The re-mortgage. And all the women. But I remained convinced he hadn't been squirreling money away to make an escape. He was simply evading reality, in denial about the truly catastrophic mess he'd made, and the only alternative to telling me the truth was running off with someone who didn't know the full measure of the mess that she was getting into. Patrick might think he'd fallen for her; that he'd finally found someone worth leaving me for. But how would Stacy feel about poverty? She probably thought Patrick was loaded, that the company was making money hand over fist. It was always the image that I'd cultivated. That, at least, made me give a wry smile. That could be my revenge on dear Stacy.

There was a hiss from the stove. The hot chocolate! I turned back, just in time to catch the Hiroshima cloud as it boiled over. I shoved the pan onto an unlit burner. There were plenty of them, it was a huge range cooker. Another bone of contention. Why did I need one so big, when all I did was reheat Waitrose's lazy bugger range? *Why not?* was always my answer. No point trying to explain.

Patrick came from a past where there'd always been enough. Fridge full, mother upright and cooking when he got home from school. Holidays, sun, skiing, cities, swimming pools. Years of peace, the fat of the land. He didn't understand it. Or me. Couldn't.

No one who's got home to find the two-bar fire cut off in winter because the electric's run out, who's known the distinctive reek of an empty fridge, wonders why it's nice to have one of those big American jobs you could curl up and live in, if things got bad. Or why, when there's only a microwave, you might dream of searing, grilling, boiling, even if you never get round to doing it when you can. In fact, not doing it makes it all the better. I could have a hog roast, any day of the week. I love that. Possibilities.

But the letter, the letter. Taking all that away from me. Reducing it to cold embers. If Patrick had his way, this cooker would be gone. We'd be living separately. In his fantasy, he no doubt saw himself living somewhere swanky, with the new me, *Stacy*, and she would have a fabulous cooker all of her own. I could be back to a microwave, for all he seemed to care, reheating stuff for his kids every night. But the reality was that none of us would have much more than a cardboard box, the way he was going. And that was not going to happen. Not to my children.

My mind was churning faster than the hot chocolate I was whipping up. I plonked down the two frothy mugs, biscuits on a plate, stroked Em's hair as she shied like a pony trying to get rid of a fly, and hovered my hand near Giles's shoulder, reluctant to ruin his concentration while he glanced at his homework diary instead of his phone.

'This hot chocolate's *hot*,' Em complained.

'Clue's in the name,' I said, over my shoulder. 'Blow on it. It'll cool.'

His letter was cool, if you like. I fished it from my bag, darted back to the loo, bolted the door, sat there on the seat. There was a white orchid trembling on the grey marble, a stack of towels so pristine they looked new. They were folded with the edges tucked away, so all you saw was the plumpness of the Egyptian cotton pile. I stroked them. I loved that little loo. It was one of the most perfect rooms in my perfect house. But it brought me no comfort now.

My fingers were trembling as I smoothed out the note again. Prayed I'd somehow read it wrong. But it was all still there, every last calm, cruel word.

Part of me was amazed I cared so much. Once, mine had been a passion as vast as empires, but he'd begun to wear away at it long ago, sloughing off a layer with every infidelity. Eventually, he'd become the grit in my shoe. A one-man laundry and mess-making machine, who moved through the house like a tornado, dropping shoes and papers and gadgets and chargers and car keys in his wake, and never able to find anything or pick anything up for himself.

So he wasn't the demi-god I'd put on a pedestal years ago, the man I'd breathlessly tracked as I'd worked on reception. But he was still my husband and once the obsession had burned out, as these things do, against all the odds the love beneath it had remained.

It was this love that had made me keep turning away from the flings, kept me from ringing a lawyer, kept me trying with the weekends away and the endless facemasks and negligees. And it was this heart full of love that was breaking now.

He had gone. Despite all the tricks he had played on me over the years, despite the thick skin I'd tried to develop, I was destroyed by his departure. I took a shaky breath. Another. Realised I was on the verge of hyperventilating, underarms and forehead clammy. God, he was making me look a mess. I steeled myself to read the letter again.

It was just a scrawl, dashed off quickly so he could move on to his new life as fast as possible. That was all I'd been worth.

He could have made the effort. I tutted at my own stupid self. Would it have made any difference if he'd written it with a quill pen, on papyrus? Got a monk to illuminate the initial letter, surround it with curlicues and tiny birds and beasts? Had it etched in stone, or set in gold?

It was the words themselves that counted. And, though these were as cold as ice, each one burned right through me.

Chapter 54

Now

Becca

It was amazing what you could find out if you knew where to look, Becca thought, brows steepling, eyes staring. She'd been up for hours, her shoulders were stiff and sore. She had the beginnings of a headache and she knew she needed to sleep. 'Keep to a regular timetable, plenty of rest and exercise,' they'd told her, when things had got bad. Easier said than done. She felt her eyelid twitch slightly and put a hand over it, stilling the movement, and concentrated again on her screen.

Official certificates were often the starting point, helping the whole of a life to lay itself bare before you. They were normally straightforward, a linear path from birth to marriage to death to Becca's scrutiny. But this time, with Louise, things had been very different indeed.

Her wedding certificate had been Becca's first port of call, and immediately, the lies had leapt out off the page.

To be fair, they weren't lies, exactly. They were revisions. Louise hadn't been born with either the first name or last name on that wedding certificate. Obviously, her surname had changed on marriage, to Bridges. Before that, she'd been down as Louise Beecham.

But Louise Beecham, it turned out, was not the name she'd

started out with. It was not even the first name she'd adopted by deed poll, but the second. The first she'd taken up at the age of 16, the earliest point at which a person can change their name without parental consent in the UK. At that juncture, she'd stopped being one Leanne Butcher, and morphed into the much posher-sounding Louise Bullmer. Within a year, she'd adjusted that even further upscale to Beecham. There she'd left it, though Becca now knew you could change your name once a month if you felt like it. There were no restrictions, as long as you could afford the nominal sum it took to cover the paperwork, and the worry lines no doubt caused by changing your details on every bill, bank account and official document every single time.

Leanne Butcher. It didn't suit Louise, not at all. Becca thought about the yards of silky hair, the endless legs, the snooty look. She could see why the woman had done it. There was so much in a name. Mind you, Leanne *Bridges* sounded fine to her ears. But then, at the age of 16, Louise couldn't have known she'd one day be married to a man with a solidly spiffy-sounding surname.

Nominative determinism, that was a thing, right? People ended up suiting their own names. So Butcher could be significant . . . She could just imagine Burke's face if she ever tried to convince him that this was yet another valid reason to suspect the woman.

Becca brought herself up with a jolt. What about her own surname? Holt, *halt* – she hoped that meant she'd be making plenty of arrests. Starting, she thought with a tiny chuckle, with a certain Leanne Butcher.

Because it wasn't just the name thing, was it? The more she dug into Louise/Leanne's past, the more there was to find.

Chapter 55

Then

It had been easy enough to tell the children that Daddy had been forced to dash off on a business trip. It was a lie that had become well-worn over the years, covering Patrick's liaisons. And of course, sometimes it was even true.

I knew he'd be too much of a coward to tell the children he was leaving himself. There was no danger he'd ring them that night, and I was pretty sure he wouldn't want a little chat with me to sour his mood as he finally got together with his new lady love. Stacy.

I remembered the gorgeousness of that feeling, requited love, from our first date, long ago. The way my bar stool had been poised on top of the world, and only the gentle pressure of his hand kept me tethered to this earth.

I spent the evening allowing Em's favourite show to wash over me. Giles was upstairs, no doubt spending far too long gaming, but for once I'd leave him to it.

I yearned to go upstairs myself, pull the duvet over my head, and never leave my bed again. I felt the same the next morning. But that couldn't happen. Life went on, relentlessly. I had to get the children to school.

This, of course, would involve seeing Stacy at the gates. I steeled myself for it, gritted my teeth, did my best unconcerned stroll. Then saw she wasn't there. Another mum was dropping Violet. I didn't know whether it was tactical or not. Was she with Patrick already, steamy in some hotel bed? Planning her life with him – the life that belonged to my kids by rights? Well, she'd find out soon enough what all his promises were worth.

I'd seen her once since the make-up weekend, on the Monday, and not shown her by so much as an eyelash that I knew her filthy secret. Another mum had taken and fetched Violet on Tuesday. But now here we were on the Wednesday and Patrick had upped the stakes. He was leaving me for her. Yes, I had my reactions under control, but how long would it last? I needed to burst the boil.

I spent the day gearing up to it, making pointlessly sure my armour was unbreachable – my hair, nails and make-up were beyond reproach, not that it mattered one jot. Apparently none of it had ever been about appearances at all.

When I was as perfect as I could be, I got in my car, then marched right up to Stacy's door. I'd timed it perfectly. Close to the school run, but not too close. She'd be in, surely, unless the excitement of getting my man had thrown all her good mother credentials to the wind.

I'd played this scene a million times in my head. What was I hoping to achieve? Nothing concrete. I knew I couldn't change Patrick's mind. He wasn't at home, for me to work my wiles on. His phone was off, his office was telling the same story as me, that he was away on business. Without access to him, I couldn't turn his head the way I'd always done before. And I wasn't expecting Stacy to beg my forgiveness and throw him back at me, either. He wasn't a parcel, an object for us to bicker over. More's the pity. He'd made a decision, and while I didn't respect it, I had a bad feeling that it was irrevocable.

No, I just wanted to see if she really loved him. If she was a worthy victor. If she'd care for him, the way I had all these long years.

The look on her face, when she opened the door to me, was so comical it was almost worth the pain they'd put me through. *Almost.* She was terrified.

Did she imagine there'd be a catfight, here on her doorstep, with the neighbours tittering behind their curtains? She really needed to give me a little more credit.

I made my voice broken, my eyes were filled with tears. It really wasn't hard. 'Can I come in? Just for a moment?'

She backed away, ushered me through. I surprised her by bobbing my head into her sitting room as we passed. Messy, but no sign of upheaval. No case anywhere in the hall or kitchen. What was going on? Then I got it. Patrick was leaving first, to show he'd actually go through with it. She must have had her doubts. Or wait, maybe this was a strategy? To make sure Stacy didn't get any of the blame, that her husband didn't kick off because she was scarpering with another man. That would give her a clearer shot at full custody of Violet. Oho. Now I saw her game. I took a seat at her kitchen table as she automatically filled the kettle.

I broke the uneasy silence. 'Something terrible's happened,' I said, peeping at her through lowered lids.

She turned ashen. 'Oh!'

'I think Patrick's got another woman.' I saw her hesitate as she got down two mugs. I let the pause go on, didn't say a word more. Her hand, which had stopped in mid-air, moved again when she realised I wasn't going to add the clincher. When she turned back, her face had been correctly arranged but her movements were suddenly faster, less full of fear. She thought I had no idea.

'God, Louise. That's awful.'

She didn't ask the obvious question. *Who?*

Well, she knew the answer, didn't she?

I batted it all back and forth, tried to dig. *Had she seen the signs? Any suspicions?* I let slip my view that whoever it was must be a gold digger, after all Patrick's millions. Not a blip. So even true love hadn't convinced my husband that honesty was the best policy. She didn't know a thing about the perilous state of the company. She evaded my questions like a boxer ducking blows. *Top marks, Stacy.* I could see the thoughts going round her head. *Just look astonished, amazed, make sympathetic noises but actually say as little as possible.*

I was beginning to get annoyed. There was a box of matches in the mess on the table, the sort they keep in a glass dish at the reception desk at posh hotels. I picked it up, looked at the name. Five-star, only a few minutes' drive from here. Why would anyone with a house on the doorstep bother going there? *Why on earth.* But Patrick always loved a mini-break, as I knew all too well. And I'd just seen the bill for this one on his credit card statement.

I eyed Stacy carefully, slipped a match out of the box, admired its deep pink tip. She'd got up again, couldn't seem to sit still. Almost dropped her empty mug in the sink. She'd swigged it back, no doubt hoping to encourage me to do the same. But I was enjoying sipping mine slowly. Now she was faffing about over by one of the work surfaces, piling up papers. A picture came free of the stack she was trying to make, wafted to the ground. I reached down and plucked it out of the air, before it got ruined on the stained floor.

'That's the project Violet's been working on. With your Em. They've got their presentation next week,' she blathered.

I put back the match, slid the box closed, looked at my watch. The school run. 'We'd better shoot off, pick them up,' I sniffed, dabbing my eyes again.

'No, Violet's going back with Belinda today. I . . . I've got an appointment,' she explained. Couldn't miss it. *Of course not, bitch.* The door clicked shut behind me. I could just imagine her slumping to the ground, thanking God I'd left. She didn't know the half of it.

On the drive to school, knowing Stacy wouldn't be picking up Violet herself, I relaxed and went back over the scene in my head. What had I learned?

That my *best friend* really was a prize performer.

And that she had no idea about Patrick's financial mess.

And that she definitely didn't deserve to share my husband's future.

Still, the meeting had helped me. It had been cathartic. I now knew that I could face her from now on without crumbling, without flying at her, without screaming, without letting anything slip. And this would give me time, the time my family badly needed, to regroup. To sort everything out, as we women always do.

I tried even harder than usual, that afternoon, to come up with the perfect impersonation of a normal mum when the kids came out, nervous they'd see through it, today of all days. But they didn't notice a thing. The silent car journey suited them perfectly, headphones plugged in to rival soundtracks, no interest to spare for their mum. In a flash we were back at home. Em dragged her brand-new designer must-have school bag along the hall tiles in a way guaranteed to wear it out and set my teeth on edge in one easy motion, Giles bumbled along, head in his phone, earbuds still in.

It was good that they were both so distracted, it gave me time to think. About all the mistakes I'd made, the signs I'd misread, and the way I was going to put it all right. So that my lovely kids would never find out how badly their dear dad had fucked up.

Chapter 56

Now

Louise

The clunk of the Volvo door has a sombre finality about it today as I slam it shut, bleep it locked, get my key in the front door. Em and Giles are standing, heads down, pretending to be on their phones, but I know that their hearts aren't really in these constant updates from their friends.

What is there to say about the journey home, anyway? Why be in contact twenty-four-seven? This world they've made for themselves is exhausting. But I know they are only going through the motions, not really participating. It makes it easier not to talk to each other, though. And not to talk to me.

We are, all three of us, in our own separate bubbles, now. The rest of my life feels strangely unmapped. We are an uneasy bunch, on this mild autumnal day. There are a few leaves swirling on the drive, I notice, as I rake my gaze left and right as usual, just checking. What for? Reporters, maybe. Police? Never again, I hope.

The kids, they follow like little lambs, not looking up, but not worrying either. Surely this is a success? Something I can congratulate myself on. We are still in our house, we are safe, they are not anxious. Yes, they are sad, and their grieving is a great big thick grey veil across our lives, suffocating the fun, smothering the joy. I'm not sure how long I will let it lie over us, though.

Don't get me wrong, I miss him too. As soon as he was gone, I felt his loss. Much more keenly than I'd ever thought might be possible.

I mourn him. Not surprising, when you consider how much of my life I've spent dancing round Patrick. First, trying to get his attention. Then trying to keep it. But of course, the Patrick that I really yearn for was the man I first met, on that first day, in that bright, shiny building, all those years ago. The Patrick I had imagined. Cocky, yes. Glib, yes. Confident, always. A charmer.

But a liar?

I suppose if I'd read between the lines, I'd have realised that it's hard to be all of the above without being a liar too. If you rely on charm to pull you through, why would you stop at that little boundary called the truth? If a word or two more will close the deal, you can bet a charmer will tiptoe over the line. And once you've been there a few times, well then, it's your territory, isn't it? Part of your bag of tricks.

There had been a time when I'd thought Patrick saved his spiel just for the others. That I was as close to him as anyone could get; that we were soulmates and that he would be incapable of betraying me. But all it really took, I saw now, was for me to want something a tiny bit different from him. To persuade me to his point of view, he'd do what he always did, and bend the truth as nimbly as one of those entertainers I used to book for the kids' parties, who'd make hearts and crowns and swords out of balloons, quick as a flash. Patrick would take what I wanted to hear, scrunch it about a bit, and present it back to me with a flourish. Truth? No. Convincing? Up to a point, yes.

It was always enough to keep me here, anyway. Here, where I belong, in our lovely house, with my children.

But now, what are we left with? What do I have? I sling my bag down on the kitchen island. Expensive leather meeting polished marble, a conjunction which used to give me so much pleasure. The bag is ludicrously pricey; I'd set my heart on it for almost a month before I took the plunge and splurged on it. Had been expecting Patrick to raise an eyebrow, at least. Even he knew how much this brand cost. But no, nothing. He'd been too deep in the mire by then. What was a bag, against all he'd squandered?

I sigh, a little more gustily than I'd intended. Both Em and Giles look up. They have their own weight of sorrows, regrets and what-ifs and if-onlys that they drag around with them from morning to night. But they are looking at me to see if they can lighten my load, check whether I need a hug.

What have I done to deserve such children? *Nothing*, my head shrieks. *Nothing*, my heart bleeds. They are my solace.

I loved Patrick so much, for so long. Not in a healthy way, but as an obsession, even to the edge of doom. It was always bound to end in tears.

Chapter 57

Now

Becca

Becca let the words flash across her face, the laptop the only point of light in the kitchen. The social workers' reports all spoke of Louise's mother, Monica, as deadwood. An alcoholic. An occasional prostitute. A known drug user. And she was accident-prone, as well. Broken arms, front teeth, ankle one time. It didn't take a genius to see she'd been used as a punchbag, but whether by one particular man or a succession of them – or even, Becca thought, by her daughter – was less clear.

But Becca looked more closely and shook her head. However much she'd like to pin the blame, all of it, on Louise, she surely hadn't been old enough to inflict these injuries. They'd started before she was born, and continued haphazardly, until Louise must have been in her teens. And there was nothing in Louise's own file that suggested that she was interested in random violence. She *so* wasn't a random person.

Finding that Monica had gone through with her pregnancy, kept the child and then somehow brought her up – or at least fed her enough to keep her alive while the child grew without intervention – was surprising reading. No father on record, of course.

Here, Becca felt a pang. Her dad might be long gone, but the memory of his kindly smile, the loving concern, his certainty that

Becca was the most wonderful girl in the world, had done much to help her sail past her mother's regrets. What must it have been like, growing up without that support? Without someone there who'd always take your side?

Poor Louise, she caught herself thinking for a second – then brushed that off angrily. What was she thinking? This woman was a killer. There was no excuse for that. And maybe she was tight with her mother instead? In a way that Becca herself had sadly never been.

Though, looking through the pages, each seeming to be in a different social worker's hand, it was hard to read a story of maternal devotion or daughterly duty in these sparse lines. 'Leanne seen today. Clothes not clean. Fridge empty.' 'Leanne seen today. Bruises on shin. She refused examination. Fell in playground.' 'Monica seen today. Very sleepy. House not clean. Refused leaflet on alcohol abuse.'

There had been brushes with the authorities on a regular basis, and occasional attempts to take the girl off the mother's lacklustre hands. But something had always prevented it. It wasn't the mother pleading not to be parted from her child, that was for sure. But nor was she going the other way, and demanding Louise be put into care. Whether that was because she reaped some small advantage from having the girl around, in the shape of benefits, extra leverage from the council on accommodation, or whether she was too lethargic to try and get shot of her, was hard to ascertain.

Reading through the case conferences, Becca tutted. It seemed to be the usual. A hand-wringing stance from the powers that be, veiling a central reluctance or inability to act. The situation wasn't quite bad enough for the social workers to be sure they wouldn't be making things worse. Becca sympathised, but at the same time, despaired. She was hardly Louise's biggest fan, but even she could see the evidence was stacking up here.

Scrolling through the file, Becca noticed that, from the age of

10 onwards, Louise herself played a greater part in the interactions with social workers. 'Surprisingly articulate', 'achieving at school', 'wishes to stay with her mother,' the case file noted. It sounded as though Louise's own ability to thrive, despite the stony soil in which she'd grown, had in some ways acted against her, lulled the social workers into feeling things couldn't be so bad if the child was bright. There was so little time, Becca knew, to spend with any one family. So many were at risk, and if there was a home where the child seemed to be doing, not well exactly, but *all right*, as opposed to being even more obviously maltreated, then the authorities were happy to take the easiest and cheapest course, and let sleeping dogs lie.

'Doing all right', of course, was open to interpretation. Bruises, hunger, filth and a drunk – at best – for a mum. It didn't sound good. But would a care home have been better? The stories about such places were rife, and rank. Becca shook her head. Much though she didn't want to, she felt the ghost of the girl Louise had been pulling at her hem. An unwashed girl in a smelly flat. Who now looked like she bathed her tresses daily in bleach and lived in a show home so clean it squeaked.

Becca looked up from her reading, feeling grubby herself. The first fingers of dawn were creeping across the dark kitchen window, the glass beaded with condensation. Thank God she wasn't on duty today. She'd had a hundred things earmarked to sort out – light bulb for the bedside lamp that hadn't worked for six months, ordering something online for her mother's birthday. And ringing her mother, of course, and trying not to take every significant pause and hurried mention of next door's adorable new granddaughter as further proof that she was squandering the family's one remaining set of functioning ovaries.

She ambled to the cupboard, shook a last lonely KitKat free of its multipack shroud and flicked on the kettle again, chucked her untouched herbal tea down the sink, busied herself making coffee. No point now in pretending she wasn't awake. And chocolate for breakfast? She deserved it, after the night she'd had. She wanted to sluice away everything she'd read, lose that feeling of pity in bright normality, the rich, peaty aroma as the boiling water hit the coffee grounds in the cafetière, the search for her favourite mug.

She paused, looking blankly out of the window, watching the blackness giving over to grey and the light lending shape to trees and wheelie bins, yet not taking any of the familiar streetscape in. She couldn't deny it. Despite herself, she did feel a shiver of sympathy for Louise.

Thanks to the files she'd spent the night poring over, she could picture her life all too well. Grim estate, mother a waste of space, unexplained injuries . . . on both of them. Though all she had was snatched photos, and now this stuff she'd unearthed, still the stench of that little girl's life rose up. The piss in the lifts, graffiti and worse in the stairwells, the dingy flat itself, the dirt and chaos of a life of addiction. Monica Butcher's focus, always on her next drink, next fix, and not on the little girl, skulking in the shadows. The mustiness of an unwashed body. Children didn't sweat much. To start to get whiffy, they had to wear the same clothes for a very long time.

Becca cursed her tendency to empathise. But she'd paid enough calls on the estates round here to know, all too well, the sights and smells of deprivation. It seemed the place Louise had come from was different only in that it might have been worse.

None of it was sounding good. And it was very hard to tie all this in with the overlay of glossy perfection that was now Louise Bridges' life. Or had been, until her husband had turned up dead as mutton.

She'd got the woman wrong, she had to admit it. She'd thought Louise was one of those blessed creatures who lorded it over kids like her at school, and went on to gilded lives, but no. *Leanne* had been far from that. She must have been lower in the pecking order even than chubby young Becca.

246

Schoolkids always knew the ones with the troubled backgrounds. Sometimes it was easy to tell, though when you got to the teenage years, grease and zits were suddenly everywhere, dodgy homes or not. In fact, the more adolescent they got, the more difficult it was to spot problems. A gangly, monosyllabic lump was pretty similar, whether from a palace or a pigsty. But even when it wasn't easy for an adult to spot the difference, children, with that finely honed herd instinct, would still ostracise the runts, the weaklings, the weirdos, those marked as other.

Taking a sip of her coffee, wishing she'd made it even stronger, Becca realised she was now even feeling a streak of admiration for the Bridges woman. To have created all that, her perfect life, her apparently solid marriage, her two-point-four kids and her 4X4 car, from the shedload of misery that was in her file? It was no mean feat.

Damn, what was it about the woman? Burke had openly had his tongue lolling out for her. Johno was eager to shut the investigation down and move swiftly on. Anyone looking at her felt either envy or lust. And now even Becca, who'd conceived that intense dislike from the very moment she'd clapped eyes on Louise, when she'd finally deigned to appear in the doorway of her home, was being forced to reassess the woman.

Had her first visceral reaction to Louise just been that childhood rejection of the outsider, a bit of damaged goods? Everyone else thought it was jealousy, pure and simple. The contrast between the two of them was so glaring. And so, as Becca had thought, unfair. She'd been blaming genetics, background, upbringing. Anything but herself and her addiction to sugary crap, a sedentary lifestyle, an easy acceptance that she'd never be skinny. She put down the KitKat, or the mangled centimetre that remained. Looked into the dregs of her syrupy-sweet coffee, then she hefted herself out of her chair and swilled it out at the sink. She poured in the remainder of the cafetière and nuked it in the microwave for a minute, until she could hear it fizzing.

No more sugar for her. Well, not in this cup of coffee, anyway, she thought more honestly.

It looked as though she'd been wrong. About a lot of things. But she was still willing to bet her initial instinct about Louise Bridges was on the money. Something was off. Something smelt wrong.

Well, something *was* off. Louise's whole life was built on lies. She wasn't what she seemed at all.

But hang on, did that mean Becca simply resented the fact that the woman had risen above her pitiful beginnings? If so, what did that make her? Surely she couldn't begrudge Louise a better life than the one her junkie mother had thrown at her?

Becca yanked the coffee out of the microwave, drank too quickly and winced as she scalded her mouth. No, it wasn't the way that Louise had risen like a phoenix above the ashes of her upbringing. She didn't have a problem with that, 'course not.

It was the fact that Louise Butcher was exactly what it had said on the original tin, the one she'd tried to chuck away so long ago. Becca must never let herself forget it.

The woman was a killer.

Chapter 58

Now

Louise

The horrible truth, the most horrible of all the truths, might well be that we were as bad as each other, Patrick and I. I'd had the honesty knocked out of me at an early age: *say a word about this, and you'll get it. Tell anyone what I did to you, and you'll be dead, see?* And Patrick? Maybe it was his father's defection that showed him how to lie.

Sometimes it was my mother doing that breathy rasping whisper thing that goes with threats, sometimes one of my 'uncles'. Looking back on it, I'm not sure she could have carried out all her evil promises. She was a feeble thing by the end. Shorter than I was, by that point, and endlessly weakened by the fags, the booze, the junk. They do say don't do drugs. Anyone looking at my mother would say, fair enough, and give up pronto. Aversion therapy didn't need to look any further for its poster girl.

I could have taken her, probably from the age of 12 onwards. But you don't know that as a child, do you? You live in terror. The threats grow to fill the space around you. Even if that space is a box room running with condensation, with walls you could touch from your bed, the threats are bigger than you, that's for sure. And they could crush you just like that. Sometimes the anticipation of violence and pain is worse than the physical reality itself. That's something an experienced torturer knows. And any old child abuser, of course.

I freeze, as I do when remembering that stuff. It's as insidious as the black mould that coated our flat, memory is. It creeps in under my perfect door, swirls around this bright and beautiful kitchen. On days like today, when we are already sad, I feel even more at its mercy than usual. But I don't want the flashbacks to start. The kids are already living in past times, thinking about their dad. I have to be here, in the present, doing positive stuff. I start to bang pans around.

'I'm making a lasagne, kids. How about that?' My tone is so bright that I almost want to don sunglasses. It feels like shouting obscenities in a church. But I want to break the mood – for their sake, more than my own.

'Not hungry,' Giles mumbles. I suppose I should be grateful he's spoken at all.

'But, Mum, I keep telling you! I'm *vegan*,' Em moans. Aha! Ironically, this is something we can get our teeth into. A familiar wrangle, trotted out every few months, that I traditionally have no truck with. I leap on it and in moments Em and I are bickering gently, Giles looking on. He's not quite smiling, but I'm glad to see the over-bright sheen has gone from his eyes. Not that I don't want him to cry for his dad, you understand. But I don't want him to keep on crying, forever.

'You can go vegan on your own time, when you're 18. Until then, it's my rules.'

'And your rules are death and murder, are they?' says Em, her cheeks flushed, looking more engaged than she has for weeks now, since that fateful ring on the bell.

'The mince is dead anyway. I didn't personally chop it into bits,' I say, as she mimes gagging.

I don't add that if I had to, then yes, I would kill that cow for her. Bare hands, if necessary. And the rest of the herd, too.

Chapter 59

Now

Becca

Becca couldn't help it. She breezed back into the open-plan office with a bit of a swagger, not even the body armour, truncheon, radio and cuffs getting in her way today. In fact, they sailed in her wake, like tiny tugboats around a cruise ship. She didn't sidle, she walked four-square and tall – well, as tall as she could at 5ft 4in. Plonked herself back at her desk with a satisfied sigh. A few heads lifted from the never-ending paperwork, clocked her ear-to-ear grin. Like meerkats, faces popped up over parti-tions. She was causing a bit of a buzz, and for once it was for the right reasons. One of her colleagues wandered over from Traffic. Bored stiff by the RTAs and the DUIs, yet unlike Becca, seemingly happy for such mundanities to roll onto her plate forever. Becca felt smug. She'd put all that behind her now. Well, she hoped.

'So what was that with the Sarge, then?' Abigail asked her, wedging her much-too-small arse on one of Becca's own drifting mounds of forms, sadly neglected in the past weeks.

Becca looked up at her from her creaky chair, shifted slightly so that it turned from side to side. She waited a beat. How much did Abigail already know? How much had the rest of the room gleaned? News travelled fast. Ordinary offices were porous enough, a police station was a sieve with information cascading through like water from a tap.

'That'd be telling, wouldn't it?' Becca's eyes met Abigail's. The other woman stretched hers wide, all innocent incomprehension at Becca keeping the news to herself. Then she shot off the desk and got herself upright in two seconds flat. Becca looked behind her. The Sarge and the Chief Super were coming her way. She stood to attention too.

'Rebecca? Got another moment?' the Sarge said, head sideways. Becca nodded so briskly her neck hurt, and Abigail melted away.

Chugging along in the wake of the top brass, Becca wondered, not for the first time, if she'd got herself in too deep.

Once the office door had shut, Becca stood with her back to the glass windows. She knew her colleagues would be gawping, abandoning all pretence of filing their own reports. She took a moment to breathe. Her mother's voice was in her ear, on auto-nag: *stand up straight. Bet you wish you'd washed your hair this morning, don't you?* She silently begged it to cease and desist, realised the Super was talking, and tried to focus.

'. . . the sort of detective work we like. Not that we'd want anyone to go off grid, strike out on their own . . . but I understand you ran everything past Sergeant Hindlip, here?'

'At every stage,' said Becca quickly. Thank God she'd given him the heads-up this morning. At the Super's side, the Sarge inclined his fat neck imperceptibly. She'd said the right thing.

'Showing initiative. That's what we want, isn't it, Sarge? Within reason.' The Super's meaty paw came down on the desk. All very matey.

The Sarge changed colour slightly. 'Within reason is the word, Guv,' said Hindlip ponderously.

No, that's two words, thought Becca, but her underarms started to prickle and she felt an irresistible tide of colour sweeping upwards from her tight collar. *That shade of red has never suited you.* Hindlip was studiously avoiding looking at her. That wasn't a good sign.

'Just take us through it, PC Holt. What was it that first alerted you to the possibility of, ah, something unusual here?'

'If you wouldn't mind waiting a moment, until PC Burke could join us? He was in on this from the first,' said Becca in a rush. Burke would get half the credit, yes, but she'd double her Brownie points with him, and with that lot outside. Whatever happened to her career next, she knew that in the police, it was important to keep your mates with you. You couldn't do much here without cooperation.

The Sarge and the Super looked at one another. 'Of course, of course,' the Super said smoothly. 'But PC Burke is elsewhere this morning, I understand.'

'That's right,' said her boss, his face getting more thunderous by the moment. He'd been up for the credit, a moment ago, but Becca sensed he was tired of having his strings pulled. 'The sooner we get this over with, the better. Just start at the beginning, PC Holt.'

Becca thought back to the unbearable shine of that kitchen, Louise's hair, her life. No, she couldn't go there. Best skate over the intuition, concentrate on the concrete.

'Sir, while I was at the Bridges' house and we were informing Mrs Bridges of the death of her husband, I noticed her shoving papers in a cupboard. One of the papers had a logo from a well-known life insurer. I thought this was interesting and I flagged it up to PC Burke.'

Becca faltered. From now on, her efforts were moving inexorably off the grid. But both men were waiting for more. She continued, more slowly.

'I was intrigued at Mrs Bridges' subdued reaction to the death of her husband and I thought that this, together with the evidence of life insurance documentation, pointed at a line of enquiry. I ran this past PC Burke . . .'

'Yes, PC Holt?'

'Um, well . . .' Becca thought quickly. The last thing she wanted was to get Burke into trouble. She remembered the swish of the windscreen wipers, his equally fast dismissal of her suspicions.

'He, um, encouraged me to look into it further, but in my own time . . .'

'What exactly do you mean by that, Holt?' The Super was looking like there was a bad smell under his nose. She stumbled over her words, trying to fill in the gaps, allay any suspicion that she'd gone rogue.

'PC Burke knew of my interest in IT systems and encouraged me to make some discreet, very discreet, enquiries . . .'

'You acted with his full knowledge?'

'Yes, of course, Sir. And as soon as I found something, I was then able to flag that up to the Sarge. Using the insurance documentation . . .'

The Super and the Sarge both did a bit of a double take. '. . . and then expanding my investigation . . .'

'Just a minute.' The Super held up that meaty hand. 'Let me understand you. Are you saying you actually took this paper?'

Becca could only stand and blink. He tried again. 'You took this paper from the woman's house? Without her knowledge?'

Becca stumbled on her words and dried up. She nodded imperceptibly.

'You realise that's inadmissible evidence? That you had no business removing anything from the home of a member of the public like that without just cause, a warrant . . . I don't know how many lines you've crossed there, Holt.'

Suddenly the mesh of lies and half-truths draped around Louise was developing holes, holes big enough for her to wriggle through to freedom.

'But it wasn't just the insurance angle I was following up,' Becca spluttered. 'I started investigating Louise Bridges' past, I felt it warranted much deeper investigation, in view of the suspicious death of her husband . . .' The men exchanged shifty looks. Was she coming over as obsessive? She needed to slow down,

254

be measured . . . It seemed they'd liked the hesitant, stumbling ingenue. They weren't quite so keen on the maverick cop, out on her own. She backtracked.

'It was just routine policework, a little bit of digging . . .' She didn't want to do down her own sterling efforts, the hours of peering she'd put into the darkest corners of the internet. But she didn't want to get their backs up. There must be a raft of regulations she'd flouted, she couldn't afford to set herself adrift on it.

'But the death wasn't suspicious, was it, Holt? The office fire. Faulty wiring. Looked into by a detective . . . all fine and above board. Yes, the place was insured, but that is no crime. If it was, half of us would be going down,' said the Super, his irony as heavy as the stomach his belt was holding back.

Becca glanced at her Sarge, for reassurance, but his face was thunderous. Dragged into all this by a PC taking the law into her own hands . . . Becca could just see the anger rising. She'd be for it, if she didn't pull something out of the bag. 'Well, I admit it may not all have been, erm, strictly orthodox, but you'll like this bit, Sarge, Sir,' she said, shaking in her chunky shoes now.

And hoping against hope she was right.

Chapter 60

Now

Louise

I love this. Just being at home. The scents, the sounds. I've got a new diffuser on the go, so we are currently wafting through a very expensive glade of French bay trees. My aversion to Jo Malone, thanks to Patrick and our rekindling weekend, has cost us dearly in every sense. I can't bear scented candles. Always blamed it on Patrick and his so-called aversion to fire, and the kids believe it to this day. Maybe he came to believe it himself.

The sounds are more imperceptible. Teenagers gently munching. Well, Em's not a teen yet, but she's ahead of herself in so many ways. Where does she get it from? No mystery. I smile, shake more crisps into the big bowl on the table. Not that they'll be getting unlimited carbs before supper, oh no. But a few won't hurt anyone. Even me. I take one, nibble it carefully round the edges.

Both kids are content to stay down here, in my lovely open-plan house. I know, in this, that I'm doing well. Other mums moan they never see their kids anymore. When they get home, they disperse, make for their own little burrows – whichever bit is furthest away from a parent. Mine are happy down here. With me.

I know what you're thinking. But it was the case, even when

Patrick was around. They've always enjoyed just hanging out. Except when Giles has a new game. That's when we lose him, but only until the novelty wears off. Then he's back.

Don't get me wrong, they're secretive. If I pass behind their slumped forms on the sofa, there is a flicking of screens as they leap from whatever they've been viewing to something they consider anodyne enough for a mother's eyes. But I know it's nothing terrible. How can it be? I know what terrible is – and their world doesn't contain it.

I glide away from the kitchen counter – it's sparkling, of course. I've just spritzed it with my favourite spray, only available online, and buffed it with a soft cloth. I love it when those shiny bits catch the overhead lights that dangle low. All those little fossils, squashed in swamps so long ago, and I can't help thinking that they didn't die in vain. Here they are, their ancient misery converted to such beauty. I like the circularity of it. The reminder that things that come from mud can be transformed in the end.

I move over to the sofa, slowly so they have plenty of time to finish the endless WhatsApp threads, pause their games, stop watching YouTube crap. Em is sprawled on the chaise longue, her toes now hanging off the end. When we bought it a couple of years ago, Patrick and I, she was just a little thing, could curl up there with the cat nearby, plenty of room for both to co-exist peacefully. The thought gives me a little stab.

We were hand in hand in the showroom, in the middle of a good phase, no shadowy other-woman lurking on his phone then, and the firm seemed fine – but what did I know. Oh yes, good memories. But mostly, I think, it's high time we got a new sofa.

Oh yes, and we've always had a cat. Ever since Mephisto. This one is Hagrid, which dates him to the kids' full flush of Harry Potter mania. A big black boy, as ever. I don't love him as much as Mephs. Nothing could replace that furball in my heart. I think it was the shock of realising that I could be attached to a fellow creature. I'd had a lifetime, by then, of contempt for my mother, for her men, for everyone who came into our orbit.

But when I saved Mephisto from my mother's place, it was as though I opened my heart a chink. It showed me that love was possible. It wasn't so very long after that I saw Patrick for the first time. Would I have been capable of that degree of love, obsession, call it what you will, if Mephs hadn't wormed his way under my defences first? Then once they were both in my heart, I was able to think about kids too. I owed that cat a lot.

Hagrid isn't my favourite creature in the house, not by a long way, but he isn't in my bad books either. And I know how important it is for kids to have something to love. Who could know better than I?

I meet Hagrid's yellow eyes with grudging respect, and he purrs dutifully at the sight of me now, casting a quick look to make sure his bowl is filled with horrible dried food. It is, he approves, and rolls onto his back. I rub my hand along his fur. I can cope with this kind of transactional love – and with the unconditional love I feel for Em, her toe poking through a hole in her slipper sock, and Giles, crouched now over his Switch console. I reach over and pluck it from his hands. He moans, but it's a token protest. 'Homework first. And you, young lady. Those socks are a disgrace.'

'Don't throw them away, Mum. It's just a hole. They're so cosy.' Her little face is pinched with anxiety. I love the fact that this is her main worry, and that I can allay it with a word. 'OK. But you're getting new ones for Christmas. And then they're out.'

Books open at the table, pens spread across the sparkling surface. Glasses of water half-drunk, heads bent and studious. I feel a glow. I feel genuine happiness. Patrick? Yes, he's gone. But we're complete. We're whole, and will only get better as the years roll by. This is my place, my home, my domain. My world.

Chapter 61

Now

Becca

Becca stood uncomfortably in front of her betters, dying to snap the top button on her trousers, to sit down, have a cup of tea, munch a doughnut, anything. But this was more important. She had to walk them through the mound of evidence pointing to Louise Bridges' guilt. In slow motion, if that was what it took.

First, the insurance documents. A red flag. The search for the amount. The surprisingly large number of zeros that popped up after Patrick Bridges' name. Then her deepening searches.

Louise's names, very fruitful, very intriguing. Her employment history, much more straightforward. Showing an upward trajectory, but one that had been permanently interrupted by marriage and children. Not unusual, but, to Becca's eyes, a bit odd, a bit old-school. That was a lot of faith to put in one person. And spending all that time with kids?

At this stage, both men grew pink and restive. Didn't take a detective, hoho, to realise their own wives had taken similar paths.

At first, it had seemed that Louise's confidence had been fully justified, where the wife of a policeman might feel some regret. Patrick Bridges, like Louise herself, was a blessed, golden creature. Not as attractive, certainly, but the odd snapshot on a company report showed a man who was handsome enough. It was his Midas touch with business that was so interesting. He'd been doing well, in the firm where he'd met his paramour. But once he struck out on his own, well, things took off with a bang.

Becca was still hazy about management consultancy. She'd Googled it and investigated what she could, and come up with not much that she could wrap her head around. It was a bit of a mystery, as far as she could see. But whatever it involved, Bridges had certainly had it mastered. He was brilliant at it. Firms fell over themselves to sign him up. Whatever it was that he did, he did it very well.

Until, that is, the economy started to falter. That's when a lot of companies started to find they could do without the frills and folderols – and suddenly Patrick's accounts, lodged at Companies House and under Becca's interested gaze, started to blush red, like a debutante who'd heard a dirty joke.

The Sarge and the Super sat there, hands tucked over their tummies, Tweedledum and Tweedledee. It was a long time since they'd personally worried away at lines of enquiry like these, got a tangle to unravel so satisfactorily. Nowadays, their job was to join other suits, fending off the cruel truths about modern policing by writing slogans on whiteboards. And they didn't want to hear this tale, either. But Becca was determined that they should, whatever the cost.

Now it was back to Louise, her past. The social workers' reports, when they'd got near enough to this elusive child to have any findings. You could only catch a glimpse of her, now and then, in the forest of missed appointments, beginnings of medical treatment which were rapidly abandoned, attempts to delve that were effortlessly evaded by either the mother or, increasingly as she grew up, Louise herself. Or Leanne, as she'd then been.

Hiding must have been second nature to her, by the time she'd emerged from the crucible of that childhood. But leaving it, and her mother, behind, had been one of the few events in Louise/Leanne's life that was properly documented.

Becca shifted on her feet, a little nervous now she'd come to the crux of the matter.

'Well, spit it out,' the Sarge said, shooting a covert glance at his watch and then at his superior officer. If the Super was happy to sit there, listening, then who was the Sarge to jump up and say he had more pressing things to do with his time? Becca enjoyed seeing his inner struggle. He settled himself again, flicked her a half-smile to soften the words.

'Right you are, Sarge.' She inclined her head. 'We're getting to the interesting bit, here.'

Again, there was a murmur from the Sarge. 'About time.'

'Well, the next bit covers why Louise left the flat. The one she shared with her mum, on the estate,' said Becca, surer of her ground now.

'Yes, yes?'

'Well, the reason she left is . . . the place burned down.'

'A blaze, eh? Well, they happen, estates like that. Look at Grenfell. What was it? Faulty electrics?'

'It started in the kitchen. Hard to say how, the damage was so extensive. Table was the epicentre. Plenty of vodka bottles around, would have gone up with a kaboom. Little bit surprising that there was so much, for a junkie's place. It wasn't investigated very thoroughly at the time. There was a feeling that, you know, what can you expect? And it wasn't like she was even a nice junkie. Neighbours hated her, social services, reading between the lines, found her almost impossible. The kid was hard going too.'

'What's your point, Holt?'

'Just that this . . . incident may have taught Louise, or Leanne, whatever you want to call her, that she was invincible.'

The Sarge sat up straight, started to splutter. 'What on earth do you mean? This is sounding perilously like yet more evidence of your bias against this woman.'

'Well, since you mention it, Sarge, yes. I do have something against people who get away with murder.'

261

Both men looked at her impatiently. Then she decided, finally, to put them out of their misery. As she imagined Louise Bridges had done with her mother, that day long ago. 'You see, only one of them got out of that fire alive.'

'Monica Butcher was burned to death.'

Chapter 62

Now

Louise

Patrick's mum is making me see a psychologist. Paying for it, too. I resisted as long as I could, but I suppose I should be grateful to her. That twaddle is expensive. Eighty, ninety pounds a session, at the outside. And you don't even get a full hour. Fifty short minutes. Barely time to get going. I already knew this, having arranged sessions for the kids. Never thought I'd be sitting here myself.

Does it work? I'm the last person to ask. But I've agreed to go. You might say that tells its own story. Well, it does – but maybe not be the one you thought you'd be listening to.

Jill was sweetly worried; my response to Patrick's death has been so profound, so prolonged. My wretchedness has been palpable. My tears have flowed long and hard, like the bathroom taps on that weekend break. Oh, not when the children were around. But when I've seen her on my own. There's such pain in her own eyes, her soft skin lined now by age as well as the cigarettes and booze. It gets me every time. And she still wears those cashmere sweaters, like the one that brushed my arm that very first day long ago in the garden, when Patrick was still everything to me and I yearned for her acceptance. It's an irony that she put all her doubts on one side and welcomed me into the family and then, such a short time later, Patrick started to move away from me.

I still long more than anything to be wrapped in her arms, as though she could make all this go away. It's kind of her to spare me a thought in her grief. Losing a son is so much worse than the fate that's befallen me. She seems to be dealing with it better, though. Her sorrowing eyes are now dry, and she can almost always talk about Patrick without faltering. I try and avoid thinking about him as much as possible, except when I'm here, in his childhood home.

She thinks she's being frightfully modern, embracing psychobabble. And she's transparently worried about the effect my blubbing will have on the kids. She doesn't know that I hold it together much better when I'm with them. I have to, I know I am the responsible adult. Well, when wasn't I? But now it's official.

People want to put a label on things, and she's no different. They need to be able to classify people. *He's a player. She's a shopaholic.* It just makes it easier. Makes it quicker to spot the anomaly in your midst. And then you can deal with it, make sure it never happens again. Patrick's mum just wants me fixed and categorised and tidied up and sorted – and I completely get it. She thinks I'm not coping.

We disagree on that. I think I'm doing fine, under the circumstances. But as ever, I like to keep everyone happy. I don't mind going through the motions. Don't get me wrong, I love the sessions. The fun thing is that, as usual, I know the answers, even as the counsellor is blundering through the fog, trying to work his way towards a diagnosis. But I don't want to make things too easy, spoil the journey. Like dealing with any expert, if you face them up with the truth from the start, they're apt to ignore it, mansplain it back to you, or try to make another theory fit, just to prove themselves right and you wrong. It can be tiresome.

Instead, I'm leading the lovely psychotherapist Trevor Goodwin by the hand. We are tip-toeing together through the recesses of my mind. I'm trying not to scare him by having too many nasty bogeymen jump out all at once. No, they are forming a queue, each one adding its own grain to my unique make-up. Sometimes we both get terribly upset, have to stop. He proffers tissues, I sob a little.

Sometimes, I admit, I get carried away. For it is a horrible tale. And when we get to some bits, well, it's pitiful. But as usual, I do have to be a bit careful. It's a fine line, between a convincing performance and a farce.

He's confided to me that he thinks I may, just possibly, have had an abusive childhood. I affect astonishment. *You could be right, Trevor.* Then he goes a bit further, suggests diffidently it's possible I may have some narcissistic traits. Now I draw back, frankly offended. Aren't we all more fascinated by ourselves than by others? And anyway, I've always been a lot more interested in my children than anything else, myself, my marriage, Patrick . . .

I'm not denying that I have an ego. And I suffer from that self-consciousness that afflicts all of us, from time to time. For instance, when we walk into a room and aren't quite sure of our reception. Or my constant dread, that I have somehow misread a bit of social code I didn't even know existed, and managed to get a crucial element of my outfit or conversation wrong.

But I've done a bit of DIY work on this subject, over the years. You remember the self-help section I kicked under the bed, long ago, when Pete first came round? You thought it was just those *Women Who Love Men Who Don't Love Them* books that were so popular back then, didn't you? When women were told they came from Venus and men were allowed to hope they were from Mars. Nope. I had enough hardcore psychology textbooks there to keep most uni libraries going for decades. There's not much I don't know about the murky messes of the mind – or the way people like to analyse it, anyway.

I've always known I was unusual. Surviving life on the estate, getting out from under, leaving Mum behind – even taking Mephisto with me. These were all singular acts. Then, when I started having the flashbacks, the panic attacks, I knew I had to

265

sort myself out. They weren't surprising, when you put them in the context of all I'd seen and done. It would have been more astonishing if I'd been entirely unscathed.

Post-traumatic stress disorder was my first diagnosis. Living in terror will do more than make a kid wet the bed, it will warp every part of their personality, train them in modes of vigilance and avoidance that would exhaust the rest of you.

My childhood was a blur of hiding, placating, attempting to broker deals – not only with my mother, so that she would stop hitting me, consider feeding me, and possibly even protect me, but also with the nasty men who hung around her like flies on dung. But, by the time I was in my teens, the story was changing. My mother was ageing rapidly, in dog years almost, as junkies will. Meanwhile, I was blossoming.

That was our problem. Mum didn't enjoy our role reversal, and nor did I. She, however, was prepared to use it – and me – to her advantage, happy enough to pimp me out for her next wrap or rock. I'd put up with a lot, by this stage. I was well versed in the art of hiding in plain sight. I could become invisible, in my own head at least, and have a little *que sera, sera moment*, to distance myself from uncomfortable reality. But enough was enough.

Never say nothing comes of nothing. There is a set of skills that become honed with abuse. I was preternaturally able to tune in to other people's moods. My survival, thus far, had depended on my ability to judge just how drunk Mum was, or how desperate. If she'd got beyond a certain point in booze, she might well be aggressive, but the blows wouldn't connect. If she was itching for a deal, then she was at her meanest, and my best bet was to make myself scarce. If the door wasn't locked.

Look, none of this was fun. But it did teach me to read people. And, by the time I got back from school that day when I was 16, I could tell as soon as I opened the door that there was trouble brewing.

There had been certain aspects to having a child that suited my

266

mother. Mostly, she was just a weak person, but a weak person in charge of someone powerless can become as strong as a minotaur. She did to me what others did to her. Why not give me up for adoption, you may ask? But what would she have done when I was gone? Who would she have to torment then? She would have been alone. It's hard to imagine that she thought it would be worse, but apparently she did.

Until the age of 16, a compensation for my wearying company and all my assorted needs was that the state paid her to take care of me. A pittance, yes. But to a pauper, a pittance is a fortune. My mother needed that money.

Then, at 16, my child benefit stopped.

My birthday wasn't marked, of course. The family was long gone, the social workers by now sporadic as I'd done such a good job of surviving. The only post that day was a manila envelope from the government telling my mother that I was no longer a source of income.

I hadn't expected a cake, presents, even a card. If anyone had asked me about my hopes for the day, I would have been stumped, but would have probably settled for another day of skulking around the corners of my mother's life, an animal who's learned how to avoid those random kicks. I hadn't been expecting the worst present of all; her rage. I knew it well, of course, it was almost an old friend. But today it was as though the true, terrifying breadth and depth of it had been contained in a box, all these years, and tied up with a blood-red ribbon, waiting for just this occasion. Once unpacked, it was a thing to behold. Almost a separate person, it transformed her from enfeebled junkie into a stormtrooper. As strong as a raging fire.

The actual fire was an accident.

My mother, anger now burned out, was already slumped unconscious on the sofa. She had been railing long and hard against me stamping out her income stream – all my fault of course, how dare I get older – but she wasn't yet so poor or so ugly that she couldn't find a bit of smack around the walkways and stairwells of our home sweet home. The drug had wafted her from our malodorous flat onto the stretching sands of Xanadu, where she was languidly searching for her own Kubla Khan.

I sat in the kitchen, stony-faced, with the cupcake I'd bought myself from the corner shop. I put it on the table, fished out a pink-and-white striped candle from the box in my fourth-hand school blazer. I jammed it down into the rubbery sponge. From my other pocket, I took the box of matches.

I swear, it was just unfortunate. Before I lit it, I turned the cake this way and that, and the white stripe seemed to spiral up the candle. The effect was so pretty, it took up all my focus. I allowed the smeared walls, the greasy clotted counter-top, the mess of bottles, the dripping tap, smell of mildew, even the drugged snores of my mother, to fade into a pleasant blur around me. She wasn't the only one who could tune out reality when it suited her.

There had been cheaper matchboxes at the corner shop, its usual policy being never mind the quality, look at the price. But I'd chosen this fancy one, the crisp white swan swimming across the green, the box as bright and yellow as my cake. The gritty sandpaper at the side was rough against my fingers as I fumbled to strike. The box had a touch of style about it. A birthday present to myself.

The candle flame leapt pleasingly upwards, unfurling as I had, from unpromising beginnings to new maturity. Sixteen years – of this. The match flickered too, still alight. I didn't want to blow either out, not yet. I let my eyes close. *It's your birthday. Make a wish.* Ouch, I can still feel that smart as the fire reached my fingers, burned them. A reflex, I dropped the match. Watched it fall, almost in slow motion, into the puddle of vodka. The sheet of blue shot up with a boom, a warm wind that rapidly turned scorching, forced me back, out of the kitchen, out of the flat.

I just had time to get my backpack. And the cat.

Chapter 63

Now

Becca

The Super and the Sarge both looked at Becca as though she were a bad smell. 'Oh, come, now, Holt. You're suggesting this Leanne Butcher, this teenager was responsible? That is a massive leap to take. And it hardly left her in an enviable position, surely? Alone in the world. I imagine the father wasn't in evidence? One shouldn't make assumptions, but . . .'

Becca knew she was losing their interest, coming over as a crackpot. What had the diagnosis been before? 'Obsessive delusions.' And this time she had clambered all over police procedure as well. But she'd come so far now. She had no choice but to crash on.

'Exactly right, Sir. No sign of the father. Lots of wannabes auditioning for the role.' The Sarge raised his eyebrows. 'Or, that is to say, her mum had a lot of sleazy boyfriends.' Becca looked down at the battered folder. 'I don't think any of them stuck around long enough to make much of an impression on Leanne's upbringing.'

'Poor kid,' the Sarge said. Becca decided sourly he was thinking of his own pampered brood. They'd probably seen little enough of their dad when they were small, she reckoned. *Daddy's working late again. Don't bother Daddy, he's had a tough day at the office.*

269

But at least he'd been around, nominally at least. And making sure they had all the extras. Her own dad had, she knew, been pretty average, but had managed to make her feel loved. Compared to Louise, she had to admit she'd been lucky.

'In this case, probably a blessing. I doubt any of these men were thinking of taking Louise to extra netball practice, helping with her homework, if you know what I mean.'

'Sounds like she didn't need much help with schoolwork, though. Smart enough girl.'

'Oh yes, Sir,' Becca said. 'And they thought that was one of the reasons why the fire got out of control so quickly. Her books. They kept themselves to themselves, the pair of them. But according to one neighbour who'd managed to get her nose inside the door, there were books floor to ceiling in Louise's room. Wouldn't have taken much to send that lot up in flames.'

'And she would have known that full well, I suppose you mean, Holt?'

'Yes, Super. But it's more than that. The fire that killed Patrick Bridges has a similar MO.'

The Super crossed his arms more firmly and looked at Becca, hard. 'Most fires have a similar MO. Light a match, and off you go.'

'Yes, Sir. But with respect, Sir, there's more to it here. They were both suspicious fires. Why was all that vodka in Butcher's flat? And with Patrick Bridges, a faulty electrical item, in this case a portable heater? I'd question its place in a set-up like Bridges' office. Swanky, newly done up, all the mod cons – why did he need a crappy little heater? It seems off to me.'

The Super paused, rubbed his chin, looked at the Sarge. 'I don't know, Holt. You're not suggesting this 16-year-old bulk-bought vodka in order to burn her own home down, are you? That sounds insane. As far as the heater goes, I quite like a bit of extra warmth on the toes. Was this positioned under his desk?'

'It was, Sir,' said Holt unwillingly.

'Well, then.' He sat back, looked to the Sarge, who nodded along happily.

'Yes, but, Sir—'

'There's no similarity between a heater and a lot of vodka. No, it sounds like these two fires were very different. And we don't have anything placing Louise Bridges at the office, do we?'

'Well, no, Sir, but—'

'Holt, it's very laudable that you've taken on all this, um, extra research, but we have to be wary of officers going off at their own tangents. You have your own assignments to do, jobs which you've been given by superior officers, tasks which we expect you to complete. We simply don't have time for this kind of, for want of a better word, witch-hunt. Do you understand?'

'But, Sir—'

'No, Holt. Just listen.'

'Yes, Sir, I am—'

'So why are you still talking, then?'

'But, Sir, think back. It was a heatwave. One of those, what do you call them? Indian summers. Roasting, during the days. Why would he have needed a heater?'

'Because it got cold in the evenings, Holt. Right, now, that's enough. You've overstepped the mark on this by a considerable margin. First, by taking paperwork, which would taint any evidence trail, we don't even need the CPS to tell us that.'

He paused for a moment. Becca hoped he might be thinking better of it, considering everything she'd said, seeing the germ of truth there . . . but it turned out he was just gathering strength to knock down the rest of her painstaking arguments.

'Secondly, frankly, everything you've got on this woman suggests she escaped a horrible life and managed to better herself, then her husband had a tragic accident. Nothing off in the pathologist's report. Nothing odd according to the fire chief. The man used an electric heater on a cold evening, even if that followed a hot day. Then a malfunction, whatever, and there we have it.'

271

All three of them looked at each other. Becca, leaning forward a little, her eyebrows arching to the ceiling, begging for leeway, for that chink which meant belief was going to creep through the cracks, chase uncertainty away. The Super had retreated into his suit, mind made up. The Sarge, undecided, swivelled between the two, head moving like a Wimbledon spectator. The silence lengthened. Becca squirmed, sweating through her polyester uniform blouse. She wished she could pretend this didn't matter to her. But it really, really did. She thought again of Louise Bridges. Whatever her background, the woman was a cold-blooded murderer. Why couldn't they see it?

She looked again at the Super. He blew through his lips, glanced at the Sarge, then finally stared at her, very hard. Her heart sank. It was all over. Back to her desk, to a lifetime of paperwork and listening to Tom Burke pontificate. The only bright spot would be the occasional caution she'd mete out to hapless members of the public with faulty brake-lights or foul-mouthed children, who'd hate her and the police force with a vengeance from that day forward. Her shoulders sank as she exhaled and accepted her fate. Maybe her mum was right, it was time to apply for something else. Something with a uniform that didn't make her look, all too appropriately, like a pig in a blanket.

The Sarge burst into speech. 'Maybe it is a little odd, after all . . .?'

Becca's head shot up. Was there hope? Could there be?

It was all the Super needed. His brows came down, his lips pursed upwards. 'No, Holt. You've over-reached yourself. All right, I understand your enthusiasm,' he said, talking resolutely over her protest, 'but this has gone far enough. We don't want anyone saying we've launched a personal crusade against this unfortunate woman for, ahem, any reason,' he finished, staring hard at Becca. Immediately, she knew all the buttons on her shirt were straining, while her thighs pressed at the seams of her trousers. She'd never felt so flabby.

'Quite right, Guv,' said the Sarge, nodding sagely. Sucking up frantically. Becca could see it all too clearly. He didn't want to be on the wrong side of this decision. That was her fate, and hers alone.

'All right, then. Off you go, to your proper duties, mind,' the Super said, not unkindly. But as Becca showed herself out, both the men were chuckling behind her back. She didn't need to be a genius to know who the butt of the joke was.

Chapter 64

Now

Louise

I blame that old film, *The Silence of the Lambs*. That was when everyone decided psychopaths were sexy. Male ones, of course. There's something about that arrogance and control that makes Mr Darcy morph into Mr Darkly, and still come out the most eligible bachelor for miles around. A man calling the shots like that? It plays straight into those fantasies of domination that we women hide so coyly. Enough to make you go all shivery. We have a sneaking sympathy for the big bad wolf. Feel his silky fur. *My, what sad eyes you have.* We can be the one to tame him. Then, surprise, surprise, he eats us all up.

I don't think anyone feels the same way about women psychopaths, but luckily the trick-cyclist community has convinced itself that the female of the species is a) very, very rare and b) a lot less deadly than the male.

I'm just a deprived child, so that's all OK. A bit of PTSD, but what could you expect? Otherwise, as sane as anyone. As sane as the person next to you at the school gates. As sane as you are, yourself.

It's lovely of Jill to worry and to throw money at her concerns. But there's self-interest, too. The loss of her son must be a daily dagger in her heart, however well she masks the pain. And with one parent down, she wants to buttress the walls of our family castle, ensure the survival of her grandchildren – her DNA, after all. Only the best will do for them, and that isn't a mother who weeps so much her eyes resemble uncooked pork sausages. And the panic attacks, the freezing. It isn't surprising, but it isn't convenient either. I don't want to be rigid on the sofa when the time comes to head off on the school run. I only mentioned the insomnia in passing, but that was enough for her to make the first appointment with Trevor. It's good of her. In her day, a grieving widow would have been told to pull herself together, maybe via a few bracing country walks. To give her credit, Jill has moved with the times and is all for talking cures. As long as she doesn't have to indulge in one herself.

I don't have to keep saying Patrick's name to someone else to miss him, though. He's here in everything we do, in the way that Giles looks at me out of the corner of his eye sometimes, in the way that Em ducks questions. But also in the easy charm that beguiles their droves of friends. And their doting mum.

Seeing them swanning through life is my reward for everything I've been through. Even when I start to feel that tightness across my chest that means a wave of panic is coming at me. Now I start the breathing exercises that Trevor has taught me, slow and steady, in and out, and wait for the tsunami to pass. While I feel the whistle of air coming and going, I visualise their glittering futures. And the look on the faces of all those who have held me back and held me down. Sad to say, but Patrick is in that role call.

Usually, I'm splayed on the sofa when this happens, Hagrid the cat beside me. On days like this he reminds me so strongly of Mephisto, my familiar from long ago. Does Hagrid sense my distress and come out of curiosity, or gratitude, as Mephisto used to, in return for being saved from the flames? That moggy and his successors have taught me so much about the deep wells of affection that run through life, to be tapped into when we need them. God knows, I relied on that so much when I had my kids.

They were so defenceless, so vulnerable. Who knows what could have gone wrong, without that love to call on?

But a mum who not only loves her kids, but washes their shirts and puts a home-cooked meal on the table? Nothing much could be wrong there, could it? Yes, I have the tigress instinct, I will do anything to protect my young. But that's natural. Trevor will understand that.

And, like all the best stories, it has the great virtue of being the truth.

Chapter 65

Now

Becca

Becca stomped up the stairs, huffing and puffing. No way she'd pass her fitness test if she had to do it today. But she'd cut down on the crap, she really would . . . starting soon. She was late, her hair was greasy, she knew there was a mountain of files a mile high waiting for her undivided attention. But for once, it was an enticing prospect. She slowed down reluctantly. There was someone up ahead, blocking the way. And he looked familiar.

'Tom!'

Tom Burke stopped bumbling down the stairs, looked up briefly and fixed her with a less-than-friendly smile. 'Well, if it isn't PC Holt, as I live and breathe.'

'Good to see you, Tom.' Becca puffed slightly as she came up level with him. 'How's it all going?'

'Oh, same old,' he said, his pale blue eyes now everywhere but on hers. 'But I don't suppose you'd know, would you? All new and shiny where you're going, isn't it?'

'Don't be like that, Tom,' she said, disappointment making her voice very quiet. 'I just did what I had to do.'

Burke shook his head. 'No idea what you're on about. But then I never did have, did I?' He looked ostentatiously at his watch and went on his way.

Becca took the next couple of steps slowly, but soon turned the next corner and sped up, taking the last flight two at a time. She wasn't sure what Burke's beef was with her. All right, she'd carried on telling him that they needed to dig deeper, then she'd taken her concerns to the Sarge – but she hadn't got what she wanted, had she? Louise Bridges was still out there, large as life and, in Becca's view if no one else's, twice as dangerous.

Through the double doors she went, past assorted bent heads, glad last week's curious glances had now abated. She soon made it over to the sanctity of her new desk. Yes, it was a mess. Yes, the pile of folders seemed to have grown overnight. And there was yesterday's smeary bakery bag, telling its own tale of dark impulses fought and lost. But, as Becca took her seat and stuck her coffee cup next to her terminal, she smiled.

Through the window, three rows of desks away, she could just about see the car pound where her former colleagues were trudging out to their marked cars, ready for another day annoying the good people of the city. Burke would be among them, with a new acolyte by his side. Becca hoped they'd be more appreciative of his little homilies than she had been. Salt of the earth, was Burke. But too much salt was bad for your blood pressure. Definitely best avoided.

Being on the beat had never suited her, he should know that. He just begrudged her luck, if you could call it that. A space had come up in Computer Forensics, and before she knew it, the Super had paved her way in. If she didn't know better, she'd say it was a little pat on the back for shutting up about the Bridges case. Now she had an even bigger caseload than before. She sighed, pulling the first folder towards her. She'd never have time to go off-piste again. *Be careful what you wish for*, her mother's voice shrilled in her ear.

Louise didn't have a mum, didn't have a voice in her ear. For a second, Becca shocked herself by thinking how nice that would be. She switched on her computer and settled down to sift through

278

her work, not even looking up to see if there were crumbs left in the bag until almost an hour had passed.

When, finally, her bladder told her it was time to get to her feet, she strolled back through the maze of desks, passing the windows again. Sure enough, Burke was down there, back to the wall, scowling sourly, puffing on his cigarette. As she slowed to watch, he took a final drag, ground it out with his heel and left his smoking partner to it. It was Johno.

Still puffing away, from this angle Johno was all beer belly. All right, she was hardly Miss World, but she wondered yet again why she'd ever felt anything for him. And that chin! Why had she never noticed the way it jutted before?

But wait a minute. She'd seen that chin recently. And on someone it suited even less. Who was it? Who could it be?

Far below, Johno greeted another smoker, gesticulated with his fag, laughed. Then it came to her, like dawn breaking, like a flower opening up on a time-lapse film. The kid who sometimes hung out with Louise Bridges' daughter. She'd seen her climb out of the back of that massive car, trot into the huge house, laugh the same way, her jaw like a signpost. All friends together. So cosy. *She* had the chin. Johno's chin. She was Johno's daughter.

Johno, who had not exactly obstructed her, but had not helped her investigation one jot either, despite his promises. In fact, she sometimes suspected that he had got in first, talked to the Super before she had about the Bridges case, persuaded him everything was all above board and tickety-boo.

This was something that nagged at Becca. Johno wouldn't have wanted Patrick out of the way for any reason, would he? No, surely not. Not if their daughters were best mates. She dismissed the idea. Maybe the Super was right. She'd given Louise and her chums far too much headspace. She shouldn't dwell on it anymore, particularly not on what a fabulous job the woman was making of widowhood.

Becca suppressed the pangs of envy and annoyance as she

thought of her, wafting in and out of her big car, ferrying the children back and forth between the plush school and the gorgeous house. She was willing to bet it wouldn't be long before Louise caught the eye of someone new, another hotshot to replace her late, unlamented husband. And then the story would start up again. This time, though, Becca would be waiting.

Her mouth set in a line of grim determination. Though she now knew that the woman's glossy exterior hid so much, she was also certain that not all underdogs deserved her sympathy. Becca needed to toughen herself up, take a leaf out of Louise's own book. She wasn't in the force to make friends, or further her mother's faint hopes of grandchildren. She was here to do a job.

But first, she'd just pop down and get a sandwich. And maybe one of those milkshakes. A snack for later, too? Why ever not. She levered herself up and swung through the door again, banging her hip against the frame, but rubbing it briskly and shrugging off the pain. The diet could start tomorrow.

Chapter 66

Now

Louise

Welcome to my home. You've caught the odd glimpse, but you haven't really had a chance to poke around. Not that there's much for anyone to find. I've had quite a decluttering session after recent events, as you can imagine.

That girl, the policewoman. At first glance, once I'd taken in the grim message she was bringing, I actually felt sorry for her. I didn't try and shoot the messenger, deflect all my pain into anger. No, I spared her a pitying look, winced at the inept way she broke the news, felt she was almost a kindred spirit in her unlovable outsider status. All right, I wasn't ever going to be her best friend, but I did treat her kindly, I thought. Then she paid me back by swiping that paperwork.

I would never usually leave anything like that in plain sight. You know me, I make the most obsessive-compulsive among us look like some insane hoarder off a TV show. But I'd only just opened the letter confirming our policy renewal. It had arrived in the post that morning, but I'd been running around as usual; pilates, the supermarket, the school run. I'd just been casting an eye over the figures, checking it was all ship-shape, while I supervised Giles's maths, sorted out the supper. Thank God I'd decided to cough up, despite our financial woes.

Well, thanks to her sneaky little impulses, here I am, still free to run a loving hand across my marble worktop. Turns out the police aren't meant to steal stuff. Naughty, naughty girl. Oh, Becca, Becca. I underestimated you. And it never pays to underestimate a woman, as I know all too well.

She tried her best to get to the bottom of my story from the start, like a deep-sea diver intent on dragging all my secrets up to the light. I'd say damn her, but she did me a colossal favour. Besides, having looked into her eyes, I know she spends quite enough time hating herself.

Spending Patrick's last pennies on a top-notch brief, just in case, was the best investment I ever made. Jill wasn't so forthcoming with her own dosh then, was she? Not when there was any sort of question mark in the air. Fair enough, I wouldn't spring for a lawyer for Giles's wife, if there was the least whisper of suspicion. But when my solicitor got it noted down at the inquest that Patrick had always kept a little heater at the office and, according to his team, used it frequently to warm his fussy toes, it was game over. The insurance policy was old. Yes, it was huge, but then so had Patrick's fortune been, at the time we took it out. Nothing odd about it, said the coroner. Accidental death.

Oh, Patrick. Why couldn't you just have come to me sooner? Asked me to sort things out? You know I would have done it. But by the time I'd stumbled on your latest mess, it was all much too late. And once I knew for certain who you were making the mess with . . . I'll be honest. It would have been a lot harder to help you. But I like to think I would still have done it.

But how could you, Patrick? Beggaring your children, spaffing good money up the wall? Stacy, for God's sake. And then, the candle on the top of a miserable cake, your note announcing you were leaving us, abandoning me and the children?

It would have been too much for anyone, I like to think. Most women would have crumbled, being both dumped and fleeced in one fell swoop. But I was made of sterner stuff. For me, poverty was no novelty, though they'd have had to drag me kicking and screaming from my lovely kitchen. I could have clawed my way up again. It would have been no prettier than the first time, but I could have done it. *But not your children and mine, Patrick.* How could you think of putting them on the street? I couldn't allow it. They are never going to know fear and hunger and want. And that's thanks to me, not to you.

I often find myself talking to you, Patrick, as we sit here in the evenings. The kids' heads are bent over their books – I love Em's fine blonde locks. She was an ash-blonde toddler, her hair like her own little in-built halo in the old photos. Now she's growing, it's darkening inexorably. But never mind, there'll be money to spare for the most subtle of highlights. And Giles. Like father, like son – he loves all his expensive tech. And that doesn't come cheap.

I really didn't like doing it, but I had to. I hope you know that, Patrick. You were my children's father, after all. It was a tough decision. In the end, I made it on purely economic grounds, and I like to think you'd have respected that.

I'm not sure you ever expected me to stop turning a blind eye. But Stacy? No. When you picked *her* to run off into the sunset with, after pinching the kids' money too, well, you just went too far.

Oh! What a tangled web we weave. Did Stacy seriously think I wouldn't notice she was fucking my husband? Did she? I see her weak, self-pitying face in my head and I want to throw something, I want her to . . . disappear, forever.

But there's nothing to throw here, except my mug of tea, and the only things it would hit are my children and my cat. I breathe in and breathe out slowly, in the approved style. My heart stops banging in my chest, my body slows its distress signals. Stacy has to stay. Her continued existence is my penance now.

The closest betrayals are always the ones that hurt the most. And how Patrick could go from me to her, I'll never understand. The most insulting thing of all was that she thought she was keeping it all from me, the thrill of her little fling. She thought I was stupid.

That really gets the anger welling up. But in this case, it helped me hugely. It told me, yet again, what I knew but hadn't faced up to for years. Because, angry as I was with Stacy for opening her legs, I knew she wasn't entirely to blame. She'd been ignored, put down and belittled for years by her own vile husband. And like me before her she fell, faster than a suicide from a skyscraper, for Patrick's delicious charm.

I didn't have any sympathy to spare for her husband. He'd chosen to marry her. No one was holding a gun to his head. Apart, possibly, from his bookies. The result of his years of neglect was that she dropped her pants quicker than a desperate high-street store. And only Patrick was bold enough, bullish enough, to want to plunge into that rancid pot. He'd had enough easy lays over the years. He'd had that little intern from the firm on the go as it was. But my best friend? And leaving me for her? That was really taking the piss.

I'd like to say that I cottoned on as soon as Stacy started exhibiting the usual signs – the unbecoming bright red flush every time Patrick was mentioned, secretiveness with her phone, a sudden unavailability for the coffees and chats we'd always enjoyed, even an odd way of looking at me which suggested, damn her, pity. But the truth didn't come out until Patrick and I were on our 'special' weekend.

I tried to park my hurt, though there was enough of it to fill a multi-storey; instead, I looked at the situation calmly. It didn't take too long to realise she did have one thing going for her, apart from this 'love' that Patrick was now apparently feeling. Her bank balance. Jeff had been whistling their money down the tubes ever since I'd known them, betting on which raindrop would slide down a window first. She – or her family – had bailed him out, time and time again. Deep pockets. This must be one of the things Patrick was after. The thought that, if she could be detached from Jeff, she would have a financial cushion to add to all her fleshy ones. A wodge of cash to save his business.

But Patrick would have been barking up the wrong tree. She had money, but not nearly in the quantities he needed. Maybe she'd exaggerated her fortune to him, boasted a bit more than she should about the family coffers. Made herself seem like more of a catch. Well, he would have found out soon enough.

Stacy had another asset, as far as I was concerned, though. And this one was important. Her husband was in the police. Yes, Jeff Johnson was weaker than water. Yes, he was a gambler and a spendthrift. But yes, he was also one of the nation's constabulary, sworn to keep us all safe in our beds at night, God help us.

There were regulations, I knew, saying that policemen had to declare financial difficulties, as these made them targets for bribery. But, no surprise, Jeff was as tricksy and unreliable about this as he was about everything else. He never breathed a word to anyone in authority about his gambling, his debts. He was definitely corruptible.

Stacy loved Patrick madly by this stage – almost as madly as I had. I knew he'd have fucked her on his desk, he always enjoyed that. Maybe once, maybe many times. This was one of his favourite fantasies – a scenario he'd developed with me and then, I beg your pardon, used with most of his bits on the side ever since. The boss surprised by his secretary, who has the hots for him, takes off her knickers and spreads herself all over his workspace. What's a man to do?

I ask you, is nothing sacred? Apparently not for Patrick. I found out he was using our fantasy with the others, years ago. I'd popped in to surprise him one evening, I'd booked a babysitter, got dressed up, the works. Then I saw him at it through the window in his office door. I didn't say anything, just took myself off home again, sent the surprised sitter away with a chunk of cash.

You can imagine how I'd felt. But the point isn't to rub my own nose in all that again; it's simply to say that I knew Stacy would have come across Patrick's workplace by now, if I can put it that way.

Well, all's fair in love and war, Patrick. Stacy was my Exocet missile, unknowingly delivering the payload to bring you down.

What Patrick's staff told the police was true, he always liked warm tootsies at his desk. And though it was a hot autumn, as soon as the sun set, the temperature dropped like a stone. So I suggested an outing to John Lewis. My visit to Stacy's house had completely allayed her fears. She and Patrick had no idea that I'd guessed her dirty secret. She might not have wanted to spend time with me anymore, now she'd won first prize, my husband, but she didn't want to do anything suspicious, out of character. We'd been going on little shopping trips together forever, this was just another in the same old vein. So I towed her casually to the small electricals department. *My gosh,* I said. *That's the exact same heater Patrick used to have in his office. My, how he loved it!* Two seconds later, she'd snapped it up, saying she needed one desperately.

Now I just had to swap hers for the one I'd prepared earlier. I'd done a bit of judicious tinkering, thanks to a few tomes on electrical wiring I happened to have about the place. It was ready in the boot of my car, in my biggest gym bag.

While Stacy nipped in to see a teacher that day after school, I borrowed her car keys to get a textbook Em had left on the back seat. It took two seconds to make the substitution. If this hadn't worked, I'd had a million other plans up my sleeve, but it was all smooth as silk. I took it as a sign.

Next I had to pray that Patrick would use the heater, before he had time to fritter away any more money. But I was lucky there, and in that stroke of fortune I've been able to tell myself again that there is such a thing as divine providence. Someone up there wanted to see my children keep their home.

It was the day after I swapped the heaters that I got that little visit from Becca Holt and her PC chum. I was surprised enough to fool one of them. I'd thought it might take days, even weeks. I was hoping it wouldn't take months. I really wasn't counting on little more than twenty-four hours.

Ah, Stacy. Those heaters cost a fortune. I would say an arm and a leg, but in Patrick's case, it was a lot more.

Stacy had obligingly dropped off his death sentence, and no doubt got her reward on his desk. I'd already dumped my wiring manuals – not the juiciest reading I've ever enjoyed, but necessary – into a recycling bin far away. Now it was just a question of ensuring that Stacy's Jeff did his part.

Jeff. What a funny little man. His tongue always hung out when he looked at me. A cut-price version of Patrick, But, unlike Stacy, I wouldn't do that to a friend. There were ways of getting him to do his bit, without making it obvious that strings were being pulled. The main factor, working in my favour, was Stacy's overwhelming guilt. Because she was the one who'd brought the heater in, she thought she was responsible for Patrick's death.

Well, that suited me down to the ground. Of course, she sat in my kitchen and wept puddles on my surfaces. She still hadn't admitted her evil deeds to me, the adultery or the unfortunate gift, so she was risking a lot, showing me the raw depth of her sorrow. I found it hard to offer any sympathy to the woman who'd been my husband's last whore. But I rose to the occasion. We had a hug. More than one. It was like embracing a soggy tissue. I was only surprised she didn't come apart in my arms.

The acting was getting me down at this point. The whole necessity of continuing to see Stacy, of pretending nothing was wrong, of having her at the funeral, well, it was the pits. But I needed her onside, so I could suggest to her how great it would be if Jeff took the case. I didn't have to point out to her the distinct advantage of Jeff brushing any lumpy-looking facts under the most convenient bit of carpet. As far as she was concerned, the faster the file was closed, boxed up and wheeled off to a storage facility in the back end of nowhere, the better.

I don't know whether Jeff was in on the secret of her affair. I suspect not. But he owed his wife, for all the thousands he'd blown himself. And if she said he'd be doing it for me, maybe he thought he was chivalrously helping his wife's best friend. Or maybe he hoped it would give him an in with the widow. Whatever his motivation, he actually did his job for a change.

So here I am, safe in my kitchen, with my children close to my side, my mother-in-law rooting for my recovery, and quite a tidy sum tucked into the bank, thanks to the good old insurance company.

You may be sitting there, judging me, saying to yourself, *crime isn't supposed to pay.*

But wouldn't the worst crime have been doing nothing as my children were made homeless?

Epilogue

Now

Louise

Don't say a quick mercy killing hasn't crossed your own mind, when your husband starts snoring on the sofa or talks over you yet again or drops his dirty pants on the floor with the blithe expectation that you'll pick them up. And those are the small provocations. If he was screwing your best friend and ripping you off as well, just ask yourself what you would do. If you thought you could get away with it, that is.

Accidental death, that was the verdict. My mother's was misadventure, due to the drugs in her bloodstream and the amount of booze lying about the place. I've had a misadventurous, accident-prone life, if you like. But these things find me, not the other way around. I've never meant to harm anyone – unless they came between me and what I know is right.

Em looks up from her homework, demands an orange juice. I hand her water instead. Giles is really concentrating on his maths for a change. I have no doubts anymore that I am a good mother, and on my way to being a good person.

Yes, I'm a work in progress, always feeling my way between good and evil. It's as much of a seesaw as you'll see at any children's playground. You'd never guess it, though, would you? From the outside, I know I now look like the real deal.

Does that make you feel insecure all of a sudden? A cold breeze in your warm, safe world? Maybe you hope I live far away, and would never tangle with you and yours. Possibly you'll tell yourself I'm one of a kind. Do you really think I am? Or will you meet my double at the school gates this afternoon? Could there be unquenchable rage behind every wide, wide smile? Don't we all have lies we need, at all costs, to hide? Or are you weak as water, destined to flow as others want you to, as long as you live?

I know Patrick's old flame Jane thought I was just another ordinary girl, not fit to lick his boots. A good solid push between the shoulder-blades showed her. Now I'll leave it up to you to decide whether I'm really unique or not. My misadventures are over. Maybe yours are just about to begin.

Love, Louise.

*

Want more?

To be the first to hear about new releases, competitions, 99p eBooks and promotions, sign up to our monthly email newsletter.

Acknowledgements

Thank you first of all to Abigail Fenton, Head of Digital at HQ, who has put up with my obsession with Louise Bridges for so long and has done so much to make this book possible. I couldn't have done it without you and I'm incredibly grateful. Thanks, too, to Belinda Toor, Dushi Horti and the rest of the amazing team at HQ Digital, including Anna Sikorska who designed the brilliant cover. Kitchen tiles have never looked so scary!

I feel as though everyone I know has been on a journey with me and Louise, not least my friends Clare Pillman and Lucy Woollatt. Thanks as always to my wonderful Dulwich book group and to my mother, Anita Freeman, for her support.

I found Judith Herman's book *Trauma and Recovery* and *The Mask of Sanity* by Dr Hervey Cleckley useful when researching the book.

And thank you to mothers at school gates everywhere, for inspiring this story.

A Letter from A.M. Castle

Thanks so much for choosing to read *The Perfect Widow*. I hope you enjoyed the story.

As soon as Louise Bridges popped into my head, I knew I had to write about her. I love the idea of secrets hiding in plain sight, and Louise has plenty of those. And I always wonder how far people will go to protect the life they love.

If you've enjoyed *The Perfect Widow*, please leave a review. I love hearing what readers think of my stories. You can also get in touch via my website, Facebook page or on Twitter.

www.alicecastleauthor.com
www.facebook.com/alicecastleauthor/
www.twitter.com/AliceMCastle

Bye for now,
Alice

Dear Reader,

We hope you enjoyed reading this book. If you did, we'd be so appreciative if you left a review. It really helps us and the author to bring more books like this to you.

Here at HQ Digital we are dedicated to publishing fiction that will keep you turning the pages into the early hours. Don't want to miss a thing? To find out more about our books, promotions, discover exclusive content and enter competitions you can keep in touch in the following ways:

JOIN OUR COMMUNITY:

Sign up to our new email newsletter: po.st/HQSignUp
Read our new blog www.hqstories.co.uk
🐦 https://twitter.com/HQDigitalUK
f www.facebook.com/HQStories

BUDDING WRITER?

We're also looking for authors to join the HQ Digital family!
Please submit your manuscript to:
HQDigital@harpercollins.co.uk
Thanks for reading, from the HQ Digital team